BAD KARMA II
Final Revenge

RICHARD CHARTRAND

◆ FriesenPress

One Printers Way
Altona, MB R0G 0B0
Canada

www.friesenpress.com

Copyright © 2025 by Richard Chartrand
First Edition — 2025

All rights reserved.

This is a book of fiction. Any names, characters, businesses, events or incidents, are fictitious. Any resemblance to actual persons, living or dead, or actual events is purely coincidental.

No part of this publication may be reproduced in any form, or by any means, electronic or mechanical, including photocopying, recording, or any information browsing, storage, or retrieval system, without permission in writing from FriesenPress.

ISBN
978-1-03-833536-4 (Hardcover)
978-1-03-833535-7 (Paperback)
978-1-03-833537-1 (eBook)

1. FICTION, THRILLERS, CRIME

Distributed to the trade by The Ingram Book Company

BAD KARMA II
Final Revenge

CHAPTER 1

ESCAPE TO ST. LOUIS (PART I)

US Marine veteran, Malcolm Jennings, and his gang were on the run from the US Border Control, the Detroit police, and the Michigan State Police. The night before, Malcolm's team had robbed and assassinated Carl Tillman, former CEO of Grenadiers Military Resources, in his country mansion in Kitchener, Canada. Malcolm had pressed the barrel of his pistol against Tillman's temple and pulled the trigger without flinching. He blamed Tillman for the death of his younger brother, Eddie, a contract soldier who had been tortured and hung under a bridge over the Euphrates River in Falluja, after being denied backup support. A cost-saving measure, Tillman had said.

Tillman had hidden funds in overseas accounts, and Malcolm had kneecapped the executive to obtain the passwords. Malcolm's wife Gerta, a cyber expert, had transferred $30 million to a secret account of her own.

But Malcolm's revenge had gone badly after that. The Reliant Detective Agency, hired by Tillman for extra protection, had stumbled on the raid in progress. The operation had turned into a bloodbath. A firefight had ensued, and one of Malcolm's team had been killed. Reliant had lost one of their agents, and Malcolm's teammate, Larry, also a Marine veteran, had executed a visiting reporter. Tillman's wife had perished from friendly fire.

After spending the night in a safehouse, the team had made a run for the Detroit border that morning. Their Jeep and two cargo vans had slipped successfully past Ontario Provincial Police roadblocks but hit a snag at the crossing. Team member Steve's fake documents had not passed police scrutiny. He and his passenger, Malcolm's daughter, Danielle, had had to abandon their cargo van and escape on foot through Detroit side streets, but Malcolm had picked up the escapees in his Jeep.

Now Malcolm's black Jeep Wrangler was headed toward St. Louis. Gerta occupied the passenger seat. Danielle and Larry sat in the rear. Danielle, with two years of military training under her belt, had insisted on joining her parents on the revenge project.

Malcolm turned to Larry, "I'm sorry the team voted to cancel our last target. I know how important it was to you to avenge your mother. You sure you're okay with this? It was the reason you joined my revenge project in the first place."

Larry had been quiet, staring out the window. He pursed his lips, then answered without turning to face Malcolm, "Yeah. I guess. I understand why the team decided to call it quits. After the mess we left behind in Kitchener, we can't return to Chicago, to our homes, to the electrical shop. Another execution would just be too risky."

"I can tell you're pissed off, and I don't blame you," Malcolm said. He looked at Larry in the rearview mirror. "Let me know what's on your mind, Larry. We go back a long way, you and I, Iraq, Afghanistan . . ."

Larry didn't answer.

Malcolm added, "Let's talk about it some more tomorrow once we've settled into our new hideout. Okay?"

Larry nodded and continued staring at the hilly brown fields along the country road.

Gerta had been listening to the local police communications on her scanner. She removed her earbuds and turned to Malcolm. "It's happened," she said. "Word has reached the Indiana State Patrol. They're on the lookout for a black Jeep Wrangler and a white Chevy cargo van. But they're looking for Ontario plates, the ones we crossed the border with this morning. They don't know we switched to Missouri plates."

Malcolm considered this for a moment, then said, "The FBI's been quick at marshaling a multi-state operation, faster than I thought they would. Are they setting up roadblocks?"

"Only on the major thruways from what I can tell."

"Are they saying anything about covering the country roads?"

"Not that I've heard."

Malcolm bit his lip, then said, "We have the last wave of the pandemic to thank for reducing the available police officers. We've got a fair chance of reaching St. Louis."

Gerta placed a hand on Malcolm's arm. "I've always admired your optimism."

She put her earbuds back on and stared at the road ahead. After a moment, she raised her head and said, alarm in her tone, "They've dispatched a helicopter from Indianapolis." She turned to Malcolm, "That has me worried."

Danielle leaned forward from the backseat and placed a hand on her mother's shoulder. "Mom, do you know which area the helicopter will be covering?"

"No, honey, not yet."

"I'm worried for Tom and Steve," Danielle said.

Tom and Steve were traveling along Indiana side roads in the Chevy cargo van, their destination a warehouse in an industrial district in old St. Louis, with instructions to park the van inside the building and wait for Malcolm to pick them up.

Tom, a twenty-two-year-old farm boy, had been recruited as wheelman for the raid on Tillman's mansion, but he was no greenhorn. He was the prime suspect in the murder of a man in Kitchener who had raped the woman who had been Tom's surrogate mother since his own mother had died during the pandemic.

Tom turned to Steve, "I was surprised when you voted to call it quits. I thought of you as an adrenaline junkie, immune to fear."

Steve smiled. "I did join up for the adventure, the camaraderie . . . and the money. My conditions to join Malcolm were, one, I don't assassinate anyone, and two, I can leave with my share at any time." Steve fixed his gaze on Tom. "But I swore to fight when needed, and I did." Tom nodded. Steve added, "But I need a new adventure now."

"Like what?" Tom asked.

"Casablanca, my latest dream destination," Steve said as he investigated the distance. "Rick's Café, jazz, orange glamour cocktails."

Tom smiled. Steve punched him softly on the shoulder. "And what's lover boy planning to do with his sweetheart?"

Tom blushed. "Danielle and I want to move to Vancouver. We'll buy a hobby farm, grow weed, and keep a few animals, more like pets though."

"That's cool." Steve returned to scanning the road and the horizon for police cruisers or helicopters. His gaze moved to the hills and the brown fields surrounding the van. He reminisced about joining Malcolm's revenge project some three months before. Their first target had been Jamie Stonely, CEO of Stonely Holdings in New York. Stonely had engineered and benefited from the bankruptcy of the company where Malcolm's late father had worked, leaving the employees without a pension or health benefits. Killing Stonely had gone without a hitch.

As they drove down the main street of the town of Noblesville, hunger gnawed at Steve. "How about we grab a sandwich and a coffee someplace? I'm hungry," he said.

"Good idea," Tom answered.

They spotted a diner and Tom slowed down. But as Tom was about to turn into the diner's parking lot, they spotted a white Indiana State Police cruiser parked in front. Two state troopers were leaving the diner and walking toward their vehicle. The officers were laughing at some joke.

"Better not stop here," Steve said.

Tom accelerated gently and drove on. Steve watched the troopers through his window. One of them was staring at the van. Then she turned to her companion, reached a hand to the two-way radio on her lapel and spoke into it, still looking at their van.

"I don't like the way those troopers are staring at us," Steve said. "Better floor it and take the first side road you see. We need to hide somewhere. There's no way we can outrun their Dodge Charger with a V8 under its hood."

Malcolm's Jeep was following country roads east of Indianapolis. Danielle leaned over from the back seat, touched her mother on the shoulder, and said, "Mom, I think I can hear a helicopter in the distance. It's faint still."

Malcolm lowered his window. "I can't hear it."

Gerta and Larry had lowered their windows. "I can't hear it either," they both said.

"Can we look for a place to hide just in case?" Danielle said. The other three looked at each other and shrugged their shoulders. "In Detroit, Steve had us hide under a tree canopy and the helicopter didn't spot us."

"Okay. Let's play it safe," Gerta said as she searched the road and the fields ahead. "I see a thick copse of trees on the left, up ahead."

As they approached the woody area, the *wop wop* of a helicopter became audible to everyone. Malcolm turned sharply onto an earthen path that led to an old, dilapidated barn crowded by overgrown black maple trees. A gate blocked the entrance. Larry rushed out, opened the gate, and ran back to the Jeep. Malcolm sped ahead and parked under a large canopy of leafy branches. A cloud of black crows rose up toward the sky.

The helicopter whirled louder as it passed overhead. Everyone held their breath. The loud thrum peaked, then faded gradually, and slowly died. Gerta turned to her teammates. "That was close. Thanks Danielle. Your young ears saved the day." Danielle blushed.

Just then Gerta's phone rang. It was Steve. His voice crackled. "Gerta. We've got a police cruiser on our ass!"

CHAPTER 2

ESCAPE TO ST. LOUIS (PART II)

Tom turned down the first side road and floored the van. He kept a close eye on his side mirrors. Steve was doing likewise. Distant, flashing, red and blue roof lights appeared in the mirrors.

"Uh oh. They're coming after us," Tom said. A blaring siren soon filled the air.

"I'm calling Gerta," Steve said. "We'll need the team's help to get out of this."

After calling Gerta and putting their teammates on standby, Steve turned to Tom. "I can take care of one patrol car. Let's hope that's the only one that shows up." He climbed in the back of the van, rummaged through the weapons bag, and found what he was looking for. He turned to Tom, "Park and let me know how far the police cruiser stops behind us."

Tom coasted to a stop and watched the police cruiser stop behind him. "They're about twenty feet behind us."

Tom pushed a rear door open and walked toward the patrol cruiser. The trooper in the passenger side opened her door, climbed out, and unholstered her Glock. She raised the pistol in a two-handed grip and shouted, "Return to your vehicle, sir!"

Steve kept walking. The trooper brandished her pistol at Steve's chest and shouted again. "Stop now. I mean it!"

By then Steve was a short throw from the front grille of the cruiser. He looked off to the side and shouted, "Now boys!" The trooper turned to look in that direction. Steve quickly pulled a frag grenade from his jacket pocket, armed it, threw it into the windshield wiper well, and shouted, "Frag Out!" He ducked down and rolled flat underneath the car's front end.

The trooper stared at the grenade, exclaimed, "Fuck!" and ran for the ditch. She dove into the grass as the grenade exploded.

Metal and glass flew in all directions. The cruiser bottomed onto its suspension and rebounded some two feet in the air before settling back into place. Ears buzzing, Steve stood up. He peered through the smoke at the wide gap where the car's windshield had been. The hood had ripped and flattened against the engine. The trooper in the driver's seat lay halfway out of the car, unconscious, his legs still in the front footwell. The car door lay unhinged, covering part of his body. Tiny pieces of glass littered the ruined vehicle and the surrounding roadway.

Steve turned to the trooper in the ditch. She raised herself on all fours, turned, and stared at Steve, her face white with shock. Steve ran back to the van, closed the rear door, raced to the passenger door, and climbed in. "Go, man, go!" he shouted. Tom floored the accelerator.

As they barreled down the country road, Steve called Gerta and updated her.

"You need to switch vehicles, fast," Gerta said. "There's a Cabela's store in Noblesville, about fifteen minutes away. They'll have a large parking lot with a lot of cars. There's a key fob cloner in one of the duffle bags. You should find some spare Missouri plates in there as well. Steal an older model if you can. They're less likely to alarm on you."

"Thanks," Steve said. "Wish us luck."

Tom drove into Cabela's parking lot and parked at the end of a row of cars in the far corner. Steve, with the cloner in his jacket, walked through the cars in the direction of the store entrance. He reached the front door without spotting a good candidate. He walked back through the parking lot, watching for any vans arriving at the store. Some ten minutes had passed when he noticed a blue Chevy Express cargo van driving in. Steve ambled slowly along the row of cars to where the van was parked, and as the driver climbed out and brandished his key fob to lock the doors of his vehicle, Steve cloned it. He continued walking until the driver entered the store, then returned to the cargo van, unlocked it with his cloned key fob, climbed aboard, and drove over to where Tom was waiting. He waved Tom to follow him to the far end of the parking lot, where the men transferred their bags and equipment into the Chevy. Steve found the spare magnetized Missouri plates and slapped them over those of the stolen vehicle.

Five hours later, Tom approached St. Louis through Collinsville Road. The clock on the dash read 8 p.m. Highway lights sparkled in the mid-September night sky. The van's GPS directed Tom to the Stan Musial Veterans Memorial Bridge. The van rode between long suspension cables hanging from the bridge overhead supports. Tom gazed at the myriad lights illuminating the riverfront industrial neighborhood. The Mississippi river flowed lazily below. A musky smell filled the van.

Tom exited I-70 at Branch St., drove up to North Broadway and turned right. He stopped in front of number 2835, and Steve called Malcolm. "We're at the warehouse."

"Good. Use one of the keys Gerta gave you and park the van inside, then have a look around. This'll be our workshop for the next while. I'll pick you guys up in about an hour's time."

"Okay," Steve said. The line went dead.

Steve took the keys from Tom and ran out. He slipped into the warehouse, opened one of the roll-up doors, and waved Tom inside.

When his Jeep reached the outskirts of St. Louis, Malcolm let out a deep breath. "We finally made it," he sighed. He looked into his rearview mirror and read relief on the faces of his companions too. "Where is that house again?" he asked Gerta. She had rented it, along with a warehouse and a small office, as part of Plan B.

"Pershing Place," she answered. "It's a century home with six bedrooms and four bathrooms on a street with other older houses, so there's always a lot of renovation work on the street. Our cargo van won't look out of place."

"It has a garage?"

"Yes. A three-car that backs onto Carriage Lane. We can reach the house through the backyard. The yard's surrounded by tall hedges."

Danielle had been following the conversation from the back seat. "Tom and I will get our own bedroom?"

Malcolm and Gerta looked at each other and smiled. "I don't see why not," Gerta said.

Malcolm entered the city by the Poplar Street Bridge. A full moon lit the evening sky. They all stared in awe at the moonbeams reflected on the Gateway Arch.

Malcolm followed the elevated I-64 thruway. The cityscape stretched before them. He took the Forrest Park exit and followed the wide boulevard as it led westward. The outlines of Saint Louis University buildings appeared through the darkness. Malcolm turned right on South Taylor Avenue. Gerta peered out her window, looking for something, found it, and pointed into the distance. "There's the Cathedral Basilica of St. Louis," she said. Her teammates turned their heads to peer at the large, dark structure illuminated faintly against the cityscape.

Malcolm turned left on Pershing Place. Stately old residences bordered the narrow tree-lined boulevard.

"Ours is number 4640. It'll be on the right," Gerta said.

Malcolm spotted the number and parked the Jeep. The house stood some fifty feet from the street. All four climbed out and followed the concrete path to the front porch. Lights came on automatically and illuminated a white square-shaped portico. The house stood three stories high. Cream-colored stucco covered the walls. Three dormers and decorative white molding adorned the roofline.

"This place is charming!" Danielle said.

"Wait till you see the inside," Gerta said. "It came fully furnished."

The team stared at the shiny red front door. A lockbox hung from the door handle. Gerta punched the combination, retrieved the key, and opened the door.

They walked in and stopped in the entrance foyer. A study stood on the left, and the living room on the right. They followed a wide hallway and reached an open-concept kitchen and dining room area. The kitchen island, the counter, the appliances, and the furniture sparkled.

"Wow!" Danielle exclaimed. She turned to her mother. "How long will we be staying here?"

"A week, ten days? Until I've printed our new IDs."

Malcolm placed a hand on Gerta's arm. "I'll leave you guys to inspect the place while I go fetch the guys at the warehouse."

Gerta nodded. "When you come back, park in the garage on Carriage Lane. The patio doors in the kitchen open onto the backyard. We'll be watching out for you."

Malcolm leaned over, planted a kiss on Gerta's cheek, and left.

He stopped on the porch to look over the neighborhood. The moon sat low in the sky. He noticed a silhouette in the window next door. A dark, backlit figure was staring at him.

CHAPTER 3

THE HIDEOUTS

The warehouse, a large one-story, flat-roofed building with red clay tile walls, sat on the corner of North Broadway and Wright St. in the old industrial part of St. Louis. An entrance door and three roll-up doors opened onto North Broadway.

Malcolm drove slowly in front of the warehouse and noticed Steve watching the street from a window. One roll-up door opened, and Tom waved Malcolm inside.

Malcolm climbed out of his vehicle and hugged Steve and Tom. "Have you guys had a chance to look around the place?" he asked.

"We sure have. It'll be a great place to tinker and while away the hours until Gerta has printed our new papers," Steve said with a smile.

Then he led Malcolm on a tour of the place. Paint-encrusted, steel-framed windows lined the upper section of the walls. Open web steel joists supported the roof. Fluorescent fixtures hung from chains attached to the joists. Metal work benches and shelving ran along one wall. A monorail with a hoist lined up with the far roll-up doors. One roll-up door opened onto a backlot.

The men walked to the office area. They entered a lunchroom with a kitchen counter, tables, chairs, a stove, fridge, and microwave oven. A door led into a front office with a metal desk, chairs, and a filing cabinet. A hallway led to two washrooms and three spacious storage rooms.

The men returned to the shop and stood in a circle. Malcolm took one more panoramic view, then said, "It's a good place for prepping and relabeling our vehicles."

As part of Plan B, Gerta had registered a numbered company with a St. Louis address, prepared Missouri vehicle registrations and insurance papers, and obtained Missouri license plates.

Malcolm looked at his men and said, "You guys follow me in the van. It has Gerta's portable printer, laminator, and some supplies." Steve and Tom climbed into their van and followed Malcolm to Pershing Place.

Malcolm and Tom parked their vehicles inside the garage and followed a flagstone path that curved around a large oak tree and led to the back porch. They climbed the steps and approached the white French doors. They could see Gerta, Danielle, and Larry sitting at a large kitchen island. Malcolm tapped on the door. Danielle ran over to let them in, and everyone hugged.

Danielle grabbed Tom's hands in hers. "You won't believe how grand this house is! Come, I'll show you around." She led him away to explore the house.

Malcolm placed his hands on Gerta's arms and looked into her eyes. "What do *you* make of our temporary home?"

Gerta smiled. "It's even nicer than on the real estate website. You'll *love* the master bedroom with its en suite bathroom. There's even a walk-in shower." She pointed at the kitchen island. "Look at the size of this! We can hold our planning meetings in here. How convenient is that?"

"Have you assigned quarters for everyone?"

"Yes. Danielle chose a bedroom with an en suite for herself and Tom." Gerta looked up at Malcolm. He nodded and smiled. She continued. "Larry and Steve will have individual bedrooms, but they'll have to share a bathroom."

Malcolm kissed Gerta. "Well done." He stepped back. "I've inspected the warehouse. It's pretty much like the ad, a large shop with an office and lunchroom. And two washrooms." Gerta smiled at that.

Gerta turned to Larry and Steve, who were sitting at the kitchen island. "We need to empty your bank accounts before the FBI seizes them. I'll set up my computer in the den. I had high-speed Internet connected before our arrival. If you guys bring me your account details, I'll be ready in ten minutes."

Larry and Steve ran upstairs and returned with their banking information. They looked anxiously over Gerta's shoulder as she transferred the funds. "I'm transferring everything into one account for now," she said, "but once I've created a new identity for each of you, you'll have your own separate accounts."

"You're not planning to leave the country without telling us, are you?" Steve asked, faking an anxious look. Everyone chuckled. Gerta continued, "Give some thought to what your new surnames will be. I can get started on your new identities tomorrow." She looked up at Malcolm. "But I can't print them until we get my equipment over from Chicago."

"There's plenty of room in the warehouse for the equipment," Malcolm said.

"No, no. The printers and laminators need a clean environment. I've rented an office in town for them."

"Moving the printing equipment here better be our first item of business at tomorrow's planning meeting," Malcolm said. He looked at the group. "Say 1000 hours?" Everyone nodded.

After Gerta finalized the bank account transfers, she rejoined the group at the kitchen island. Tom and Danielle had returned from their tour of the house. Gerta opened the fridge. "We need to go out for groceries."

Malcolm turned to his teammates. "Give me a list of anything you need from the grocery store. Gerta and I will go shop for them first thing tomorrow morning. We'll be back by 900 hours." He looked at Tom, "I'm putting you in charge of breakfast."

"Glad to do it. Bring lots of eggs, bacon, breakfast sausages, tomatoes, ketchup, light rye bread, plain bagels, dark roast coffee, and ten percent cream,"

Malcolm raised his eyebrows. "Will do."

"And get beer and red wine, too," Steve said. "In large quantities, please."

"There's beer and wine in the cooler in the Jeep," Gerta said. Malcolm slid the key fob over to Steve, who grabbed it and left through the French doors. He returned with the cooler and placed some beers and bottles of wine on the island. "The Lord provides," he said. Larry nudged him in the ribs.

Everyone chose a drink except for Tom. He had joined AA. He abstained from alcohol but smoked medical marijuana to help with his mood swings and anger. "I've got some high-grade weed left over I can share," he said, but there were no takers.

Gerta took Malcolm aside. "How's your supply of Percocet?"

Malcolm took the pain killers for his hip that had taken a bullet in Afghanistan. He walked with a slight limp. "I'm running low," he said.

"I'll fake another prescription for you. We can fill it tomorrow morning."

"Thanks, Dr. Mueller."

Gerta gave him a friendly jab in the ribs. "I'll use a local doctor's name, not mine smarty pants. But you'll need photo ID, and it can't be the one you used at the border. I have enough supplies on hand to make a driver's license and credit card for you to use. But first I want to visit the Basilica and say a few prayers for our safety." She looked up at Malcolm, "We've been playing God, and our luck may not last."

Malcolm took her hands in his. "Our rough justice has been tame compared to the slaughters by the God of the Old Testament."

Gerta bit her lip and nodded, "I won't be gone long."

"You can't go alone."

Larry, who had overheard, stepped forward. "I'll go with Gerta. I need quiet time to think through a tough decision I need to make."

Malcolm placed a hand on Larry's shoulder. "Let me know if I can help." Larry and Gerta left.

Malcolm joined the others around the kitchen island. Steve was enjoying a beer while Tom and Danielle smoked joints. Soon everyone was cracking jokes and laughing. An atmosphere of well-being and companionship descended on the troupe. The hard planning could wait until morning.

CHAPTER 4

INSPECTOR WEBER

Inspector Walter Weber of the Region of Waterloo Police Services in Canada, studied the preliminary forensic report on the murders of Carl Tillman, a visiting reporter, and a private detective. The report baffled him. None of the fingerprints lifted from the crime scene matched those of the Jennings crew. How could that be? At least four of the Jennings gang were Marine veterans, their fingerprints—and DNA profiles—would be on file in the FBI data banks.

The Waterloo police and the Reliant Detective Agency had joined forces to provide protection for Tillman after he had received an untraceable email concerning four contract soldiers in his employ who had been killed in Iraq. The email urged him to make restitution to the soldiers' families or face "the ultimate retribution." Tillman had no intention of making restitution, but lacking confidence in his private security team and the local police to protect him, he had hired Reliant, based in Ann Arbor, Michigan, to identify and hunt down the vigilantes before they reached him.

Weber's team and Reliant had stumbled on the raid in progress at the Tillman residence, but in the firefight that ensued, the vigilantes had escaped.

Weber mulled the fingerprint mystery over, then decided to call Captain James Morris at Reliant. Although the agency's contract had ended with the death of Tillman, the men had agreed to exchange any information that could help capture the Jennings gang. Weber had already sent Morris a copy of the forensic report.

"Morris here."

"Captain Morris, this is Walter Weber from the Waterloo Regional Police Services. How are you?"

"I'm good, Inspector. How about you?"

"I'm very puzzled. That's the reason for my call. Have you had time to read the forensic report I sent you?"

"Yes, and I've had my team look at it. Thank you for keeping us in the loop."

Morris's team consisted of Louise Jackson, a cyber expert, and Ashley Hurd, a sharpshooter. Another team member, Pierre Chamberlain, had been killed during the firefight at the Tillman residence. All had been recruited from the Marines Intelligence Corps.

"I can't figure out why none of the fingerprints collected at the crime scene match those of the Jennings crew on file," Weber said. "How is that possible?"

"The FBI fingerprint data banks have obviously been compromised. Agent Jackson believes Gerta Jennings must have done it. Both women did contract programming for NSA and the FBI back in the day. Gerta must have programmed a backdoor at the time and returned later to substitute fake prints and DNA profiles for her teammates. That's how they've avoided discovery until now. We've alerted the FBI, and they're looking into it. Meanwhile, they've confirmed that the prints gathered at both crime scenes—Tillman's and Stonely's—match. We now know for sure that the Jennings gang committed both murders."

"Thanks for clearing that up," Weber said.

"Agent Jackson has obtained a copy of the report from Border Control. I'll send you a copy, but would you like a verbal summary now?"

"Yes, please."

"Four members of the Jennings gang crossed the US border in Detroit around noon yesterday. They carried false papers, but we know who they were from scans of their passport photos and the camera footage. One van slipped through unchallenged. The other ran the border rather than submit to a secondary inspection. The two occupants abandoned the van on a side street, set it on fire, and escaped on foot. Border Control dispatched their chopper but couldn't locate the fugitives."

"Was the entire crew in the two vans?"

"No. Malcolm Jennings and Larry Schmidt crossed the border in Port Huron in a Jeep a half hour earlier."

"Are they heading back to Chicago?"

"We don't know. Border Control has roadblocks on all the main arteries out of Detroit, and they have a chopper flying overhead, but they've lost the gang's trail." Morris paused for a moment, then added, "The FBI has taken over the investigation. We've learned since that they have triangulated burner phone communications they believe belong to the Jennings. The timing and the trajectory match. The communications died at the Pilot Travel Center in Monroe, Michigan. Staff at a local Denny's identified several members of the gang from photographs. We don't know more at this time."

"Clever criminals," Weber said. "My chief has initiated the extradition paperwork for the gang. Once they've served their sentence for the Stonely assassination in the US, we want them back here to stand trial for multiple murders." He was silent for a moment, then added, "My condolences for the loss of Agent Chamberlain. How's his family handling this?"

"Thank you for asking, Inspector. Chief Harrington has informed Agent Chamberlain's family. He was single with no children, a small consolation. As a Marine veteran, he'll receive full military honors at his funeral."

"I'll ask permission to attend. I hope to see you then."

"I look forward to it, Inspector. Let's keep in touch." Morris ended the call.

Weber reached into the growing pile of reports on his desk and retrieved the transcript of the conversation between Tom Cole and his father from the day before. Tom had called on a burner phone from Monroe, Michigan, to reassure his father that he was fine but had given no indication where the Jennings gang was going next.

Weber rose and walked to Constable Kidnie's workstation. "Constable, can you join me for a visit to Robert Cole?"

Kidnie rose. "Any news on his son, the kid who killed that bastard who raped Sharon Doyle?"

Weber shook his head. "No. That's what I want to talk to him about." He considered, then said, "We haven't proven the kid guilty yet."

CHAPTER 5

ROBERT COLE

Robert Cole was cleaning up his Airbnb. The gang had stayed over for two nights. Even with his new commercial grade washer and dryer, it had taken six full loads to wash and dry the bedding and towels.

With a mug of coffee in hand, he retired to the front porch and sat on his rocking chair. Mac, the cat, followed him, climbed on his lap, curled up, and was soon purring.

Robert scratched Mac's neck as he looked at his orchard. The apples had ripened earlier this year. The leaves on the tall oak and the large maple trees had already burst into golden, rusty, reddish hues.

Robert was lonely without Tom around. His son's phone call had been brief and cryptic. Robert despaired at Tom having joined the Jennings gang. This could only end badly. And if Tom really had murdered Duke Ferguson—and Robert suspected he had—his son would be facing up to twenty years in jail. Surveillance cameras had placed Tom at the hospital when Duke Ferguson was murdered by an opioid injection. Duke had been recuperating from being mauled by Robert's sow after the idiot had attempted to steal her piglets for a pig roast.

Robert didn't blame Tom for killing Duke if that were the case. He himself had considered doing it but had been deterred by the idea of jail time. He knew he was being callous, that every life is sacred, even that of a brutal rapist like Duke.

As Robert was mulling over what he could do to help Tom, a police cruiser turned into his driveway. Inspector Weber stepped out from the passenger side and walked over to the porch. Constable Kidnie disembarked but stayed by the cruiser. He stood there, contemplating the orchard, the barn, and the fields.

"Good morning, Mr. Cole," Weber said. He climbed the steps and extended his hand.

"Good morning, Inspector." Robert shook the proffered hand and gestured to the rocker beside him. "What brings you here on this fine day?"

"I came to talk to you about Tom."

Weber sat down slowly and stared at the beautiful surroundings. Mac inspected the visitor, stretched his body across the chairs, and climbed on Weber's lap. Weber petted Mac's coat softly without taking his eyes off the scenery.

"I'll help if I can," Robert said. He waited for Weber to ask questions, but none came. Finally, he volunteered, "Tom called yesterday. I asked him to call you for advice, as you'd suggested. I asked him to return home, but it's up to him now."

"He hasn't called me, not yet," Weber paused for a moment, then asked, "Has Tom contacted you since? He called you from Monroe, Michigan, by the way."

Robert furrowed his brow. "No, nothing since."

Weber already knew that. The police were tapping Robert's phone and monitoring his email. "He's running with the Jennings gang. We know they carried out the massacre at Tillman's residence." Weber let a moment pass, then continued, "But there's no evidence placing Tom at the residence. If he were to come forward and cooperate with us, his lawyer could negotiate a reduced sentence for him." Weber looked at Robert for a reaction.

"What about Duke's murder? That's the one that has me worried most," Robert said.

"We haven't found his fingerprints in Duke's hospital room, but the technicians are looking for DNA evidence. If there is some, they'll find it."

"You speak as if he's guilty," Robert said.

"I believe he is. And you do too, judging from the worry on your face."

Robert looked into the distance and did not comment.

"Since Ms. Doyle was like a surrogate mother to Tom, a jury would sympathize with him and show leniency." Weber paused, then added, "Please mention that to him next time you two connect."

Robert reflected on the inspector's suggestion. "Shouldn't we wait for proof of his guilt—if there is any?"

Weber sat back in the chair and rocked slowly. He continued gently petting Mac. "The FBI are chasing the Jennings gang in full force. The arrest is likely to turn into a bloodbath. Tell Tom I can bring him back safely before it's too late."

CHAPTER 6

THE RELIANT DETECTIVE AGENCY

Chief Chuck Harrington, manager of the Criminal Investigation Division at Reliant had read the reports from each member of Captain Morris's team. The documents now lay in a fan-like shape on the surface of his desk. They contained detailed descriptions of the raid on the Tillman residence in Kitchener, Canada, and the gang's escape.

The lawyers handling the Tillman estate had immediately terminated the protection contract, and Harrington had prepared a final invoice before closing the file.

The invoice was substantial. The firefight had been vicious. The armored Suburban his team had driven was a write-off. The gang's bullets had punctured the outer shell of the body panels, cracked the windshields and windows, penetrated the instrument panel, and shredded the two front tires. Replacement would cost $200,000. The invoice total was a few dollars shy of $400,000.

The contract with Tillman had been the first to be carried out under the post-pandemic emergency law granting private contractors the same powers as police services. The killing of Tillman was a blow to the agency's bottom line, but Harrington had been hoping for more such contracts. And *when one door closes, another opens*, Alexander Graham Bell had written, Harrington mused. Only a few moments earlier, Michael Tyler, CEO of Retail Conglomerate in New York City, had called to request a quote to investigate a death threat he had received and arrest the perpetrators.

As Harrington placed his follow-up call to Tyler, he braced himself. He expected tough questions about Reliant's failure to protect Tillman.

Tyler skipped the salutations when he picked up the phone, "What the hell happened up there in Witchener or whatever that bumfuck town is called?" he barked. "It doesn't make me feel all warm and fuzzy," he added without waiting for an answer, "to learn your team's sharpshooter killed Tillman's wife."

Harrington couldn't deny that Reliant's sharpshooter, Ashley Hurd, had accidentally shot Mrs. Tillman during the firefight. He took a deep breath and channeled his management training—never give excuses, give explanations, and stay calm.

"That is true," he said. "Mrs. Tillman was killed by friendly fire. In our favor, I will stress that we predicted the attack on Tillman before the FBI did, and we were also first to link the Jennings outfit to the assassination of Jamie Stonely in New York City three months ago. We stand behind our record."

"If those same criminals are responsible for the threatening email I received, that just makes me even more friggin' nervous."

"You are right to worry, Mr. Tyler. We believe the Jennings gang are behind that email too. It is similar to those sent to Stonely and Tillman, similar wording, same origin—the Chicago area. Our AI program reports a ninety-nine percent probability they're all from the same author, someone with above average IQ and technical abilities, most likely female. Gerta Jennings fits that profile."

Tyler remained silent for a moment, then said, "So what will it cost to capture those killers *before* they get to me?"

"We charge ten thousand dollars per day, plus expenses plus ten percent. We suggest an initial budget of two hundred thousand dollars. We will then locate the Jennings gang and either arrest them ourselves or assist the FBI to do so."

"Christ. That's a lot of money."

"We will assign a team of four agents, each one recruited from Marine Intelligence Corps. One will be a cyber expert equipped with hardware and software equal or superior to that of the FBI. We will provide you with daily updates."

After another silence, Tyler said, "But there's no guarantee you'll catch the bastards, is there? I've got two senators pointing a blowtorch at the FBI director's ass. Maybe I should wait till the Bureau boys catch these murderers, as my taxes already pay them to do, and save myself a ton of money."

Harrington reminded himself that $200,000 was peanuts in the security budget of large corporations. Inspiration came to him. "Unlike the FBI, Mr. Tyler, we offer discretion. Any information we discover during the investigation remains strictly confidential between you and Reliant. We'll make that part of the contract."

On hearing this, Tyler went silent again. After a moment, he said, "If I give you the go-ahead, what's your next step?"

"Our team will search Internet transactions and telephone communications for any trace of the culprits. We can access all government-operated highway and street cameras and run facial recognition software on all of them."

"That's a lot of communications to sift through."

"True, but the gang will need new passports, driver's licenses, credit cards, cellphones, business name, lodging. All these transactions leave traces. We'll pick up their trail."

"Hmm . . . okay. I like your optimism. I'm approving your budget, but with two conditions."

"What conditions are those?"

"For one, you will review my private security team's preparedness to fend off those criminals should they attack my home."

"Excellent suggestion. I'll have Captain Morris contact your security chief. And your second condition?"

"I don't want that cross-eyed sniper woman assigned to your team. I won't feel safe with her walking around my property with a loaded weapon."

Harrington mulled this over before answering. "I'm sorry, but I cannot accept that condition. Agent Hurd is an integral part of our team. To hold her responsible for a death by friendly fire would be unfair, and it would undermine the morale of the entire team."

"Are you saying you'll turn down a lucrative contract to protect the job of one employee?"

Harrington weighed his words carefully. "Agent Hurd is a skilled markswoman with over ten years of excellent service. She's an integral part of our contract offer."

"I don't believe this." Tyler cursed under his breath, then said, "All right, but she'd better not fuck up on my dime. And send those daily updates to my personal email address. For anything sensitive, call me directly on a secure line."

"Thanks for your approval, Mr. Tyler. I'll have a contract proposal in your hands today. If you have any questions, please —"

But Tyler had hung up.

Harrington placed an internal call to Captain Morris and ordered him to assemble the team in the conference room immediately. When he entered the conference room a few minutes later, Harrington surveyed each face carefully. Ashley Hurd's was reserved and composed. She was keeping to herself. *She blames herself for the death of Carl Tillman's wife*, he thought. *It will be a tough mishap to live down.*

The team sat, solemn. Agent Pierre Chamberlain's usual chair sat empty. A grief counselor had met with every member of the team and had flagged Ashley for a psychological review and regular counseling sessions. Harrington had tasked Captain Morris with keeping a close eye on her morale.

Paul Collins, a new recruit, also from Marine Intelligence, was sitting at the conference table, alert, looking eager to serve.

The chief addressed his group, "Good afternoon, everyone. I bring good news. CEO Michael Tyler of Retail Conglomerate in New York City has approved our budget." Everyone clapped. He turned to Captain Morris, "Popeye, how do you propose to tackle this project?"

Popeye coughed to clear his throat and fixed Louise with a careful look. "All the work will fan out from Louise."

Louise nodded and picked up the ball. "The gang will need to build new identities. My search engines will sift through all daily transactions with the government departments and major institutions they will need to deal with. The starting point is September 16, when they returned to the US." She turned to her teammates. "I'll distribute the printouts that the search engines generate. Ashley, you'll sift through vehicle licensing, business licensing, office, warehouse, and lodging rentals. Paul, you'll check new passports, social security numbers, bank accounts, credit cards, cell phones, cable, and Wi-Fi installations. I will sift through emails and phone communications. We'll post all promising leads on our project website and look for correlations."

Popeye raised a hand. "I'll play pinch hitter and help anyone who's swamped."

Harrington nodded, pursed his lips, then said, "Thank you, Louise. Good plan." He paused, then added, "The FBI have posted the photos of the Jennings gang on their Most Wanted Fugitives webpage. This will produce a lot of leads. Can we access those?"

"I believe I can," Louise said. "I'll post all relevant FBI reports I can get my hands on."

Harrington placed his hands on the conference table. "Let's get to work."

CHAPTER 7

THE FBI'S CHICAGO FIELD OFFICE

Special Agent in Charge Arlene Hale relished her recent promotion at the FBI's Chicago field office. Floor to ceiling windows, a fantastic view of the city skyline, new furniture, and a new computer. She leaned back in her high-back executive chair and breathed deeply, inviting calm and composure. Her silky gray pantsuit and white shirt spoke of authority. Now she would put that authority to the test. She had summoned Special Agent Aiden O'Keefe to her office for a dressing down.

O'Keefe entered Hale's office and stood, wide-eyed, surveying the room. Hale savored the look of envy on his face. O'Keefe's workstation—drab, gray steel desk, squeaky filing cabinet, threadbare carpet, and wobbly chairs—did not measure up.

Hale had beaten O'Keefe for the promotion, and word had reached her that he was claiming reverse discrimination. He was male and not from any visible minority.

"Agent O'Keefe. Please sit down." Hale pointed to the visitor's chair facing her desk. After O'Keefe sat, she leaned forward and said, "I want to share with you a big mistake I may have made."

"A big mistake?" O'Keefe said, eyebrows raised.

"Yes. After the Jennings gang ran the border in Detroit two days ago after murdering that Canadian CEO, the Director assigned the investigation to me because the criminals lived in Chicago. I turned around and put you in charge. I believe that may have been a mistake."

O'Keefe fixed Hale with a cool stare. "I, too, must confess to a grave mistake."

"Oh? And what would that be?"

"Accepting that assignment."

Hale rubbed her chin with one hand, nodded, and stared at O'Keefe with narrowed eyebrows. "How is this smart-alecky attitude working out for you?" she asked and watched O'Keefe restrain himself. She felt sure she could read his mind and what he was thinking. *About as well as sarcasm is working out for you.*

Hale pursed her lips. "The Director is asking me why we had to learn the identity of those criminals from that private detective agency, Prince Valiant or some such name. And the same agency pointed out that this same gang may also have murdered CEO Jamie Stonely in New York City three months ago." Hale paused, then asked, "What progress are you making in arresting this Jennings gang?"

Agent O'Keefe squirmed in his seat. He leaned forward. "They've slipped through Border Control's roadblocks, but we've captured their cellphone communications and by triangulation have reconstructed their trail up to Monroe, Michigan. They must have ditched their burner phones there, because they have since disappeared from the air waves."

"We've no idea where they are?" Hale asked.

"The Indiana State Patrol stopped one of their vans. In Noblesville. They've identified Steve Adams as a passenger. It was a lucky arrest because the van had new Missouri plates."

"Did they make an arrest?"

O'Keefe paused and squirmed again. "No. Adams and the van's driver got away. But not before blowing up a patrol cruiser with a grenade and killing one trooper."

"Jesus!" Hale swore. She bit her lip, then said, "Surely we know where they went from there. With the highway cameras."

"Our license plate scanning program is useless," O'Keefe replied. "They keep changing plates. We're having to scan manually, looking for a black Jeep Wrangler and a white Chevy cargo van, but it's a slow process. And they may have switched cars by now."

"Damn," Hale swore again. "Have the photographs of the fugitives on our Most Wanted website produced any good leads?"

O'Keefe's face turned red, and he said, sheepishly, "We only posted the photos yesterday."

"And it took so goddamn long because . . . ?"

"We're badly understaffed since the last wave of the pandemic."

Hale let out a deep breath, then said, "Our phone lines will clog up with reports of sightings from Anchorage to Key West. Do we have the personnel to handle all those calls?"

O'Keefe stopped himself from pleading understaffing again. Instead he said, "Our field offices have enlisted the help of state and local police departments to follow up on all promising leads."

"Is there *any* positive news I can report to the Director?" Hale asked.

"With warrants in hand, we've searched the Jennings' electrical shop and private residences in Chicago."

"Did we find any evidence we can use?"

"Fingerprints. They match those found at the Tillman and Stonely crime scenes. The DNA results will come later, but there is no doubt the Jennings gang committed both murders." O'Keefe hesitated before adding, "But we've discovered a problem."

Hale stared at O'Keefe with raised eyebrows, urging him to explain himself.

"The Jennings crew's fingerprints and DNA samples are on file, as Marine veterans, but they don't match those at the crime scenes."

Hale frowned. "How is that possible?"

"Someone tampered with the files. Our IT boys are looking into it."

"Damn. We look like incompetents." Hale stared at O'Keefe and prepared herself for more bad news. "Anything else?"

O'Keefe swallowed, then said, "We've frozen all their bank accounts."

"Good," Hale said. "Reliant said the gang has robbed millions from the victims' oversees accounts."

O'Keefe bit his lip before saying, "The accounts were empty when we got to them."

Hare leaned back in her chair, swiveled, and looked out the window. "I'm taking a lot of heat from upstairs about this investigation. A heavy political campaign contributor, Michael Tyler, the CEO of Retail Conglomerate in New York City, is worried for his safety and has sicced the two New York State senators on the Director, demanding results." She swiveled back and faced O'Keefe. "We need results soon. For both our sakes."

CHAPTER 8

ONE LAST TARGET

The sun rose at 6:45 a.m. on Pershing Place. Malcolm had risen twenty minutes earlier and performed his daily exercise routine. Keeping his muscles strong and flexible helped keep the hip pain from getting worse. The Percocet did the rest.

He and Gerta were now standing in front of the double sinks in their en suite, preparing for their first day in the hideout. "Is there a grocery store open this early?" Malcolm asked Gerta.

"Yes. Straub's. It opens at seven and it's only minutes away."

"That's convenient. Ready when you are."

After Malcolm and Gerta had finished purchasing the groceries, they stopped at a pharmacy where Malcolm picked up a supply of Percocet. Back at the house, they carried a first load of grocery bags through the balcony's French doors and into the kitchen. Larry and Steve, who had been sitting at the kitchen island, rose and helped bring in the rest.

Tom arrived shortly and started brewing coffee. He retrieved two frying pans from a cabinet and started cooking breakfast.

Danielle returned from a run in the neighborhood, showered, and joined the group. After greeting everyone with a cheery good morning, she placed cutlery and condiments on the kitchen island. Tom handed over platefuls of pancakes, sausages, and bacon, and she served everyone.

The crew engaged in small talk as they ate. Danielle kept everyone's mug topped up with strong coffee.

"How did everyone sleep?" Gerta asked. "Was there enough bedding in the closets and dressers?" Everyone nodded. "If you give me a list of the toiletries you need, I'll send Danielle and Tom on a shopping trip." Everyone nodded again.

Malcolm rapped on the table to get everyone's attention. "Planning time. Our most pressing task is getting Gerta's printing equipment from Chicago." He turned to Gerta. "Have you contacted Uncle Karl?"

Karl Wagner had immigrated to Chicago from Germany with Gerta's late father, Alfred Mueller, years ago, and the two men had been close friends until Alfred's death. When Alfred's employer, a security document printer, had terminated him with no pension or benefits for refusing to get vaccinated during the first wave of the pandemic, he had retaliated by masterminding the theft of security printing equipment and software from the firm. Uncle Karl, who owned a rigging and moving company, had moved the stolen equipment to a secret location in the Chicago suburbs. Alfred had handpicked some of the equipment for Gerta's use, and Karl had sold the rest on the black market. The two friends had shared the proceeds.

"Uncle Karl has agreed to recover the printing equipment for us," Gerta said.

"Did he give you a price?"

"He'll do it at cost plus twenty percent. I gave him the go-ahead and told him it's urgent. He'll confirm the timing."

"Great."

Gerta wasn't finished. "I told him we're on the run. He asked about the equipment in our electrical shop."

"Did you warn him that the shop will be under police surveillance?"

"Yes, but he's interested anyway, especially if we're leaving everything behind."

"Karl's got more balls than I do. He's welcome to the equipment," Malcolm said.

"And we have a small safe hidden in the shop," Gerta said. "I've been slowly transferring Stonely's overseas money into it. That was before our raid on Tillman and the police surveillance."

"How much?" Malcolm asked.

"There'll be close to a half million by now."

Malcolm rubbed his chin. "If Karl decides to recover the equipment, I'll go and get the safe while he's at it."

"I've already sent him a list of the equipment in the shop," Gerta said. She pointed at copies on the kitchen island.

Malcolm picked up one of the printouts. "How much is all this equipment worth?"

"The book value is close to a million," Gerta said. "Uncle Karl could get close to half that on the resale market."

Larry and Steve had been listening intently to the conversation. Larry spoke first. "I'd like to recover the weapons and ammunition from the cache." The team had a stash of weapons and ammunition hidden behind a false wall in the shop.

Malcolm gave Larry an inquiring look.

Larry straightened and said, "I'm going after Tyler myself. I'll need those weapons."

The rest only stared at him with raised eyebrows.

"I'm not letting the bastard off the hook. He has to pay for the pain he put my mom through." Larry's single mother had been terminated without severance after having rebuffed Tyler's sexual advances. The CEO's corporate lawyers had easily defeated her lawsuit for wrongful dismissal. Her legal fees had eaten her house and her life savings.

Everyone looked at each other. Gerta looked up at Malcolm and placed a hand on his arm. Malcolm nodded back and turned to Larry. "You can count on me and Gerta to help you."

"Thank you. I could sure use your help."

Steve who had remained seated, deep in thought, raised his head and said, "Okay, Larry. If Malcolm and Gerta are on board, count me in too."

Tom and Danielle stared at each other with questioning looks. Danielle put a hand on Tom's arm, looked up at him, and nodded. Tom turned to Larry. "You can count on me and Danielle as well. Whatever we can do."

Larry looked everyone in the eyes, one by one. "Thank you guys. I will take you up on this."

They all turned to Malcolm. "That's settled then," he said. "We have one last job to do."

The team bumped fists.

Malcolm approached Larry. "Do you have a list of everything in the cache?"

"Yes, I do. It's upstairs." Larry ran up to his bedroom and returned with the list. He placed it on the kitchen island in front of Malcolm.

Malcolm went through the list and read the categories aloud. "Assault rifles, pistols, Kevlar vests, night vision goggles, ammunition, grenades, C-4 blocks." He raised his head and looked at Larry. "It's everything we need, but we could buy these on the black market."

"If Karl is going in for the equipment, and you for the safe, let's get the weapons as well," Larry said.

Steve raised his hand. "I've a crate of grenades in that cache. Those babies are hard to come by." The Marines had dishonorably discharged Steve after he was caught removing a crate of grenades from Stores. The warrant officer would only allot two grenades per combat mission, nowhere near enough for Steve.

Malcolm turned to Gerta. "Tell Uncle Karl, I can meet him in Chicago as early as tomorrow, and we can look the situation over and plan how to recover the equipment and the weapons." Gerta nodded.

After making her call to Uncle Karl, Gerta approached Malcolm. "He'll meet with you tomorrow. Can you be at his shop by noon?" Malcolm nodded.

Gerta addressed the group, "I need a new name from each of you for your new identities. I suggest you keep your first names. Pick a surname that makes sense to you, and that's easy for us to remember."

They all stared back at her, wide-eyed.

"Come on, gang. It's not that hard. Don't pick a fancy one. That will only attract attention." The troop sat down and went to work.

She turned to Malcolm. "You and I need to change our first names too, though. They're not common enough. The FBI's search engines could locate us. And if Reliant is still on the case, Louise Jackson will never quit until she's found us."

"Right," Malcolm said.

Gerta addressed the group, "Let's meet in an hour's time and review your choices." Her request was met with nervous stares.

Gerta turned to Steve and Tom. "Could you guys bring my printer and laminator from the van?" The men left through the rear porch and soon returned with the equipment.

"Put those in the study," Gerta said, "and follow me back to the van. There's more supplies I need." Gerta and her helpers returned to the garage.

After an hour, the team convened around the kitchen island. Gerta opened the meeting. "Starting with our captain, Malcolm, what new name have you adopted?"

"I'm choosing Arthur Downing."

Danielle looked at her father and spoke. "King Arthur of the kitchen table. It'll be easy for me to remember, and it has a nice ring to it."

Everyone smiled. Gerta elbowed Malcolm. "Well, that wasn't so hard, was it? Now for my choice? What would go well with Arthur Downing? Hmm . . . what about Emma? Ms. Emma Downing, if you please. How does that sound, guys?"

Everyone nodded their approval. Malcolm placed a kiss on Gerta's cheek. "A beautiful name. It suits you well."

"And what about you, Larry?" Gerta asked.

"I'm choosing Schuster. My previous name, Schmidt, means blacksmith. Schuster means shoemaker. It's easier work, and I'm getting older." Everyone laughed.

Steve spoke next. "I'm choosing Daniels. Seeing I'm the one who often ends up in the lion's den, it's appropriate, no?" All nodded their heads.

Danielle punched Tom lightly on the arm. "What did you choose for your new surname?"

"I choose Devin."

"What made you choose that name?"

"It's from Old French, meaning divine. My ancestry's French. My father changed our surname to Cole from the French 'Colle' when he moved from Quebec to Kitchener. As for the divine part, well, it's icing on the cake." Tom grinned. Danielle punched his shoulder, then kissed him on the cheek.

"Well, I'll get started on our new identities," Gerta said. "Oh. When asked where you're from, you answer Kansas City. We're electricians working for Downing Electric." Everyone nodded.

Gerta had just opened her laptop when the front doorbell rang.

CHAPTER 9

A NOSY NEIGHBOR

Claire, a slim, gray-haired woman, wearing a gray coat and a red cloche, walked up to her new neighbor's house. Bright red lips covered a wrinkled white face brightened by shiny blue eyes. Her blue dress extended below the hemline of her coat, but that would have to do, Claire thought. She pushed the doorbell. A tall, trim man in his early fifties opened the door.

"Good morning!" Claire said with a big smile. "Welcome to the neighborhood. I'm Claire Chouteau, your next-door neighbor." She offered a small basket of chocolate chip cookies. "Some treats for your family. Freshly baked this morning."

"Good morning, Claire. I'm . . . Arthur Downing." The man said as he accepted the basket. "Thank you, that's very kind."

"I saw you folks move in last night. Where are you from?"

"Kansas City. My wife and daughter are with me. You'll see some workmates milling around. We're electricians. They'll be staying with us until they find a place of their own."

"I live with my husband, Bill." Claire pointed at the house to her right. "He's Bill Brown, but I kept my maiden name. We Chouteaus were one of the founding families of St. Louis, back in 1764." She beamed. "Bill and I moved into that house on our wedding day. We've seen a lot of changes since." She leaned sideways and peeked into the hallway, then straightened and looked up at the man. "If you ever need anything, you just ask."

"That's very kind of you. It was nice meeting you, Claire."

Claire smiled brightly, turned, and left.

She walked to the street and followed the sidewalk back to her house. Cutting across the lawn was not acceptable behavior to Claire.

She entered her house, hung her coat and her red hat, then walked to the living room. She faced her husband, who was dosing in his La-Z-Boy. A western movie played on the TV. Geraldine, their black cat, lay curled up on Bill's lap. She opened one eye to acknowledge Claire, then returned to sleep. *He minds that cat more than he does me,* Claire thought to herself.

Since Bill's retirement, Claire had watched helplessly as her husband turned into a layabout who watched TV and napped throughout the day. How was it possible that a man who had worked tirelessly as a machinist for over forty years could turn into a sloth overnight? She stood, shaking her head.

Bill woke, startled at the sight of Claire watching him. He took a moment to focus, then said, "So you met our new neighbors?"

"Yes, I did." Claire walked to the window and stared at the neighboring house with narrowed eyebrows. "A strange household."

"How so?"

"I met the man of the house. Handsome, friendly, said he was living with a wife and a grown daughter, but he didn't invite me in to meet them." Claire considered for a moment, then said, "The man hesitated before telling me his name. Arthur Downing, he called himself."

"Did they say where they're from?" Bill asked.

"Kansas City, he said. And there's a group of other men bustling around the place. He said they were co-workers, electricians, living at his place for a while. Does that seem normal to you?"

Bill considered for a moment, then said, "I don't know. The men may need time to find suitable lodgings. How many are we talking about?"

"Hard to say. This morning, I saw two men in their late forties bringing in groceries from the garage." Claire pursed her lips, then added, "I hope the wrong sort hasn't moved into our neighborhood."

CHAPTER 10

THE CASE AGAINST TOM

Robert's phone rang. It was Rick, the family's lawyer, on the line.

"Hi Robert. How are you holding up?"

"Worried sick about Tom, to be honest."

"Yes. That must be nerve-racking, Tom running from the police and the FBI."

Robert was silent for a moment, then said, "I'm trying to convince him to return to Canada. Have you lined up a criminal lawyer for him?"

"Yes, I have. Meyer Levin & Brodie have agreed to represent him. They're expensive, but they're the best I can recommend. They're already on the case, reviewing the evidence the police have on Douglas Ferguson's murder. They have Tom on the hospital cameras at the time of the murder. But that's circumstantial."

"I hope they don't find anything else," Robert said.

"I'm afraid they already have. Everett Meyer just called me. He was preparing the grounds for a plea bargain when the crown prosecutor told him forensics recovered hair samples that place Tom in Ferguson's hospital room. Tom's DNA is on file because of that conviction for aggravated assault some time back. This is not good."

CHAPTER 11

RECOVERING THE WEAPONS

(PART I)

Malcolm and Karl Wagner parked a block away from the Jennings's shop on North Elston Ave in Chicago. From their white van, the men watched the dark gray, unmarked police cruiser that was parked across the street from Malcolm's shop. Smoke belched out from the cruiser's tailpipe. Two officers sat on board.

"The FBI will have installed cameras inside and outside the shop," Malcolm said. "They'll be the digital type, so we can block them with a signal jammer." Malcolm took in the surrounding buildings. "But any closed-circuit cameras from local businesses, we can't block."

Karl pursed his lips, then said, "If we move in at night, when police services are running thin, they won't be looking at those recordings until the morning after, and we'll be long gone. If we use unlabelled vans with fake plates, we'll be all right." He put the Ford into drive. "Let's review our escape route."

Karl circled the block. "Let's do the job at midnight. We'll leave through secondary roads, avoid the thruway."

Karl drove to a coffee shop in a distant suburb. The men picked a corner table and ordered coffee. Karl stared out the window. The sun was sitting high in the sky. He pulled out a sheet of paper from his jacket pocket. It was the list of equipment Gerta had sent him. He placed the list on the table, smoothed it flat, and passed it over to Malcolm. "Anything you want to keep?"

Malcolm bent over the list. "The cargo van. I'll have three men with me. We'll throw weapons, ammo, some tools, and a small safe into it, then I'll have Tom drive it back to St. Louis. The rest is yours."

Karl pursed his lips, then said, "You think the weapons will still be there? The FBI will have taken them."

"They're hidden behind a false wall."

Karl looked impressed. "Clever." With a pen, he circled items in groupings numbered 1, 2, and 3. He looked at Malcolm. "That's my loading priority. First, the big-ticket items: the forklift, the scissor lift, and the trencher. As soon as they're loaded, I'm sending the van out. Next, the bucket truck and the trailer. I'll fill the trailer with supplies." Karl stared at the list for a moment, then said, "And last, the generators, switchboards, distribution kiosks, conduit bundles, and cable spools. That should fill my second moving van. Then I call it a night."

"Are you taking the equipment to your shop?"

"No. Too risky. I'm storing them in a warehouse in the suburbs for a month, and then I'm selling them."

The men leaned back in their chairs and sat, pensive, as they sipped their coffee. The server walked over and topped up their cups.

Malcolm spoke first. "That warehouse in the suburbs—won't the police follow your trail to it? There's cameras everywhere."

"A business partner owns the place. He makes sure the local traffic cameras are blocked on the night of a delivery. He knows all the local businesses and has them turn theirs off. For a price. That service is included in the rental of the warehouse. It isn't cheap."

Malcolm nodded his head, then asked, "Can I stop there to switch the plates on my Jeep and cargo van before heading back to St. Louis?"

"I'll ask my partner, but it shouldn't be a problem."

Silence settled over the table as the men reviewed the plan in their minds. Malcolm broke the silence. "You sure this equipment is worth the risk?"

"Contractors are crying for second-hand equipment like that. I stand to clear $200,000, maybe $300,000." Karl rubbed his chin, then said, "But I need to figure out a way around the police surveillance." He looked up at Malcolm. "Any ideas?"

"Gerta can provide you with a signal jammer that'll scramble the police radio."

"Yes, but all the fuckers need to do is drive out of range of the scanner and call for backup. I need to immobilize the cruiser and the officers for two hours. I assume you don't want us to kill them."

Malcolm shook his head. "This job is not worth a human life, not even close."

Karl leaned back in his chair and looked out the window, as if tracking the clouds. "I'll put my best men on the problem."

"When do you want to do this?" Malcolm asked.

"Tomorrow at midnight."

Malcolm nodded.

Karl rose. "Shall we get going?"

Malcolm rose, dropped a five on the table, and walked to the cash register.

Karl called Boris to his office. Boris Dragoslav, a millwright rigger, had immigrated from Serbia to America some twenty years ago. Karl admired the man. In fact, he admired all his tradesmen. Without their skills, his business would fail.

Boris entered the office. He radiated self-assurance but always spoke in a respectful tone to his employer. "You called for me, Mr. Wagner?"

Karl waved for him to approach the desk. "Boris, I need your help with a sensitive job."

Boris beamed. Sensitive was code for discretion and trust. "How can I help, Mr. Wagner?"

Karl opened a map showing the Chicago neighborhood where Malcolm's shop was located and pointed to the location of the shop. He had circled the likely position of the unmarked police cruiser. "I want to recover all the equipment in that shop, but I need to cut the police surveillance. I can jam their radios, but I need to immobilize the cruiser, with the officers inside, for at least two hours."

Boris nodded. He leaned over the map, placed both hands on the desk, then said, "That's a tough one. Have you talked to Bodan about this?" Bodan was the shop's sharpest electronics technician.

Karl called Bodan to join them and explained the situation to him. The tradesmen leaned over and stared silently at the street map and the satellite picture. After a few moments, Bodan and Boris looked up and said, in unison, "I've got an idea!"

CHAPTER 12

RECOVERING THE WEAPONS

(PART II)

It was midnight on North Elston Ave, and the streetlamps beamed a yellow light on the empty sidewalks. The whir of traffic on the nearby Kennedy Expressway filled the night air.

Officers O'Leary and Santini sat in an unmarked police cruiser, parked across the street from the electrical shop. They were chatting away when intense headlights suddenly flooded the inside of their vehicle and the roar from a large diesel engine filled the air. "What the hell fuck *is* this?" O'Leary said to his teammate. The officers turned around in their seats, trying to identify the vehicle coming up behind them, but the glare of its headlights blinded them.

The brakes of the large truck clanked as it shuddered to a stop some three yards behind the cruiser. The truck's engine growled as two outriggers spread out from the vehicle like two giant crab legs.

"It's a friggin' boom truck!" O'Leary yelled. "What are these guys doing?"

As if to answer his question, two men in black balaclavas jumped out of the truck and ran alongside the police car. They each carried a wheel chuck in one hand and what looked like a doormat in the other. They slapped the mats against the sides of the cruiser. The magnetized mats clung to the metal doors. The men then tucked the wheel chucks against the cruiser's front tires.

O'Leary tried opening his door, but it was stuck closed. "Christ! They've blocked the doors!" he cursed. He lowered his window and shouted over the roar of the diesel engine. "What the fuck are you guys doing?"

By now, four masked men surrounded the car, each pulling on a cable that was attached to a twenty-foot shipping container, with an open bottom, suspended overhead. The boom truck's engine roared as a giant hook began to lower the container.

O'Leary floored the accelerator. The cruiser lurched forward, its front wheels climbed over the wheel chucks and the car's front end sat up in the air, engine whining, tires spinning.

"I'm calling for help," Santini said as he pressed the call button on his radio transmitter. The radio screeched, but there was no tone. He turned the radio off, then back on again. Still no tone. "They've jammed our radio."

O'Leary unholstered his pistol, but fumbled the gun, and it fell down the footwell. He reached down with one hand, hunting for the pistol's grip. Sweat flowed from his forehead and his hand was shaking. He finally retrieved his pistol, raised it, pointed it at the chest of the masked man nearest him, and fired. The man fell backward, letting go of his cable. The container struck O'Leary's hand, knocked his gun away, and thudded against the ground.

The cruiser's headlights reflected on the inside surfaces of the container and blinded the two officers. O'Leary nursed his arm as he stared ahead. "What the hell is this?" He stuck one hand outside the window and touched the material. "This is some weird shiny fabric."

Squinty-eyed, the men surveyed the cocoon that now encircled their cruiser. They were trapped. O'Leary turned to Santini. "We're screwed."

Malcolm and Larry ran to open the roll-up doors of their shop and hurried to one of the storage rooms. Malcolm pulled at a hidden latch and slid aside a wall panel mounted on tracks. Weapons covered the entire wall, ammunition boxes rested on the floor, and a small safe sat to one side. Larry drove over with a forklift, picked up the safe, and carried it to the cargo van. Malcolm grabbed an armload of weapons and followed Larry.

Steve and Tom were already pasting blank labels on the van and replacing the license plates. Once that was done, the men rounded up tools from the list Larry had prepared and stacked them in the cargo van. Tom climbed behind the wheel and Steve took the passenger seat. Malcolm signaled for Tom to wait and waved over Karl's electronics technician. Bodan swept the van for trackers. He located one device, removed it, and gave Malcolm the thumbs up. Malcolm walked up to the van's open window. "We'll meet at Uncle Karl's warehouse." Tom drove off.

Karl had supervised the loading of his two transport vans as Bodan checked all the equipment for trackers. Malcolm walked over. "How's your man, the one that got shot?"

Karl bit his lip and shook his head. "His chest is sore, maybe a cracked rib, but he's alive. The Kevlar vest saved his life. The men bitched at having to wear the vests, they're heavy and hot, but I'm glad I insisted."

Malcolm nodded. "Smart thinking." He then nodded toward the container on the street outside. "That was well done, that container."

"I have Boris and Bodan to thank for planning this. Boris is driving the boom truck to the warehouse as we speak." Karl faked a serious tone as he added, "I'm donating the shipping container to Chicago PD." Malcolm chuckled.

Karl put on a reproachful tone and retorted, "Don't laugh. That radio frequency shielding fabric was expensive." Then he got serious again. "Everything looks normal out there. I've had a man spray-paint all the neighborhood cameras he could find." Karl looked around the warehouse. "We'll be out of here before police dispatch realizes something is wrong, and they send the cavalry."

Once the last moving van had been loaded, Karl climbed aboard and waved at Malcolm. "Thanks for the help. See you at the warehouse." The van drove off.

Malcolm and Larry closed the shop doors, climbed into their Jeep and drove off.

A night shift attendant was standing outside the warehouse when Malcolm drove up. "Are you the last of the convoy?" the attendant asked.

"Yes, we are," Malcolm answered. The attendant opened a roll-up door and waved Malcolm inside.

Karl was sitting with his crew. He waved Malcolm over. Karl addressed the assembly. "That was a job well done, gentlemen. I must commend Boris and Bodan for coming up with operation clamshell." Laughter rippled through the crew. Boris and Bodan straightened their shoulders and stood proud. Karl continued. "And I commend the rest of you for meeting our target of one hour to load everything. I will add a bonus to your next paycheck." The men applauded. "And take tomorrow off, with pay." More applause followed. Some men improvised a tap dance, and others threw playful punches at their teammates.

Karl turned to the injured man. "How's your chest, Emil?" Emil straightened and looked up at Karl. "I'll be fine, boss. I thank you for insisting we wear the vests." Karl patted his worker softly on the shoulder,

Malcolm waved Steve and Tom over. "Switch the license plates on your van and you can go." He fixed his eyes on Tom. "Stick to secondary roads, follow the speed limit, and share the driving. It's a long way home."

The Jeep's clock read 8 a.m. when Malcolm drove into the garage on Carriage Lane. He parked beside Tom's van. He and Larry trudged through the backyard and climbed heavily up the steps to the rear balcony that lead into the kitchen. Gerta and Steve sat around the kitchen island. They rose to greet the two arrivals. Gerta hugged and kissed Malcolm. She then served the two men steaming cups of coffee and pastries. "Not too tired, are you?" she asked.

Malcolm spoke first. "It went well. We were out of there in less than two hours. Karl's men were super-efficient. He sends his greetings." He turned to Steve. "How was the drive back?"

"Uneventful."

"Tom and Danielle are upstairs," Gerta said. "Tom's regaling her with his adventures." Gerta bit her lip, then added, "Your daughter is very sore at being left behind. Times have changed, Malcolm. Girls want in on the action." She let a moment pass, then asked, "You remembered to thank Karl for having delivered my printing equipment so quickly? It's all assembled in the printing office. They did a great job."

"Yes, I remembered."

"Good." Gerta savored a sip of coffee before musing, "Karl and his men are a godsend."

"Amen to that!" Malcolm said.

CHAPTER 13

THE FBI DISCOVERS THE HIDEOUT

Minutes after the FBI had posted the photos of the Jennings gang on their Most Wanted Fugitives website, the switchboards at all the field offices lit up. Most callers asked about the reward on offer and when told there wasn't one, they hung up.

One promising tip came from a Claire Chouteau in St. Louis, who claimed to have met Malcolm Jennings the day before, "but the man called himself, Arthur . . . Browning, that's what it was," she had said. But Ms. Chouteau was positive it was the man shown on the FBI's fugitives website, no doubt about it

"Not only have I seen this dangerous criminal," Claire told the agent, "I've talked to the man. He's at 4640 Pershing Place, the house next door!"

"Did you see other people in or around the house?" the agent asked.

"There were three more men, but I couldn't see their faces clearly. They were carrying bags of groceries from the garage to the house. The garage is on Carriage Lane behind the house." Claire paused, then added, "The man said his wife and daughter were living with him."

The agent considered this information for a moment, then said, "We'll have a police officer investigate the situation. Stay indoors, Ms. Chouteau. Lock your doors and remain inside until we give you the all clear."

"Aren't you sending those SWAT teams like we see on TV?"

"We have to confirm the lead first, ma'am. The leads are coming in fast and furious, and we only have two SWAT teams."

After the agent had hung up, Claire stood there, furious. Her heart raced hard against her chest. She clenched her fists, scrunched her eyebrows, and turned to her husband. "I knew from the get-go there was something fishy about those people." Bill and Geraldine stared back, wide-eyed.

Officer Jason Jones sat in his cruiser, biting into his second Boston cream donut, when his police radio crackled. "Jones. This is Captain Ambrose." Jones swallowed too quickly, a piece went the wrong way, and he answered between coughs, "Yes, Captain."

"I need you to drive by 4640 Pershing Place pronto and confirm a sighting of fugitives."

"Fugitives?"

"Yes. Someone claims to have seen the Jennings in that house. I'm sending you the FBI photos of the gang members." The photos popped up on the cruiser's onboard computer screen.

"I see them," Jones said. "What are they wanted for?"

"Multiple murders. If you spot any of them, call it in right away and wait for instructions. Do *not* confront them. These guys are very dangerous."

Jones stuttered nervously, "Shou . . . shouldn't you be sending a detective with a patrol team to check this out?"

"We don't have enough detectives and patrol teams to send to every possible sighting. Just watch from a distance, and if you see one of them, we'll take it from there. Can I trust you to do this, Jones?"

"Yes, Captain." The line went dead.

Jones sat still for a moment, pondering the situation. *How did I end up with a dangerous assignment like this?* He put the donut back in the bag. *And to make matters worse, I'm riding alone today.* Because of reduced personnel since the last wave of the pandemic, the police union had grudgingly accepted the need for patrols with a single officer.

Officers had right of refusal if they felt unsafe, but Jones feared that a refusal would make him look cowardly in the eyes of his superior and his colleagues. Now he regretted having accepted the assignment. Jones studied the photographs carefully. *They look like regular folks*, he told himself.

Reaching Pershing Place, Jones slowed his cruiser to walking speed. The boulevard was empty. He found the address. "What a nice house," he said to himself. "Why would criminals choose a classy home like this as a hideout?"

Jones had been called to another house on this street a couple of months ago after a break-in. He remembered that the garages stood on Carriage Lane behind the homes. He drove past the address, turned right at the first intersection, then right again into the lane. He called up a satellite view on his GPS, located the right garage, and parked a short distance past it. He climbed out of the cruiser, opened the trunk, and retrieved a set of binoculars. Jones then walked along the fence that enclosed the fugitives' backyard. Leafy vines clung to a wire fence and blocked a view of the house.

A patio door creaked open. Pieces of conversation reached him, but he couldn't make out what was being said. He pushed aside some ivy leaves and saw a man walk from the house, follow a path, and reach the garage. Jones couldn't see the face clearly. The man entered the garage. A roll-up door creaked open, and a black Jeep Wrangler backed into the lane. Jones hustled to an empty parking lot across the lane and pretended to examine the pavement for something. The Jeep drove past, but Jones couldn't see the driver through the tinted windows.

He stood still, unsure about what to do next. After a moment, he raised his binoculars and scanned the windows and balconies on the rear of the house. A woman walked out onto the first-floor balcony. She looked to be in her early fifties and wore a white blouse and blue jeans. She leaned against the railing and looked skyward as if soaking in the sun's rays. Her phone rang. She dug the phone out of her jeans pocket and raised it to her ear. After a moment, she raised her head and scanned the parking lot as if looking for someone. She froze and stared in Jones' direction.

Jones lowered his binoculars and brought up the photos of the fugitives on his iPhone. "Mother of God!" he exclaimed to himself. He fumbled the binoculars, and they clanked onto the pavement. He picked them up and raced toward his cruiser.

The call was from Malcolm. "Gerta. I saw a police officer in the parking lot behind our house. The police are on to us. We need to clear out fast."

Gerta scanned the parking lot. "I see him. He's pointing his binoculars straight at me. Now he's racing toward his cruiser."

"Damn. I'm coming back. I'll park in front. You and Danielle assemble the essentials fast and place everything in a pile by the door." Malcolm was quiet for a moment, then said, "I'm calling the men at the warehouse. They'll drive over fast." Malcolm hung up.

Gerta ran back into the house and shouted, "Danielle! We've been discovered. Meet me in the den right away." She raced to the den and began assembling security supplies. *Thank God most of my printing materials are already at the rental office*, she thought. Danielle appeared in the hallway. Gerta pointed at the portable printing and laminating equipment. "Pile them by the door."

Jones squeezed behind the wheel and reached for his radio. Breathing heavily, he said, "This is Officer Jones. I need to speak with Captain Ambrose, quick." The switchboard transferred him.

"Captain Ambrose speaking."

"Captain, this is Jones. I saw her. There's no doubt about it. It's her!"

"Whoa. Slow down, Jones. Who did you see?"

"The fugitive woman. Ah . . . Gerta Jennings. I saw her on a balcony. She's in that house."

"Did you see anybody else?"

"No. Well, yeah. A man left in a black Jeep Wrangler, but I couldn't see who it was because of the tinted windows."

"Good. I'm alerting SWAT right away. Stay on the line." After a few minutes, Ambrose returned. "Did you take down the license plate?"

"Ah. No."

"Check your body cam. It will have caught the plate number."

Jones bent his head forward and looked at his body cam. "Shit! I forgot to turn it on."

Ambrose breathed into the radio, then said, "Check the dash cam in your cruiser. It may have recorded the plates."

Jones looked at the dash cam. "Damn. It turned off when I turned off the cruiser."

After a long pause, Ambrose said in a practiced, calm voice, "All right. Okay. Where are you now, Jones?"

"I'm parked on Carriage Lane behind the fugitives' house."

"All right. Pick a good vantage point and wait until the SWAT teams arrive. Call if the situation changes. Understood?"

"Got it. Oh. What about the front of the house?" Jones asked.

"I'm sending a cruiser to cover the front of the house. You watch the rear and the garage."

"Right, Captain." Jones answered, but the line was already dead.

Jones drove into the parking lot across the lane from the house and looked for the best location to park his cruiser. He picked a shaded area beside a large red brick building. Once parked, he raised his binoculars to the rear of the house.

Malcolm burst through the front door. He looked approvingly at the pile of equipment and supplies in the hallway. "Good. I'll round up our weapons." He turned to Danielle. "Keep an eye on the road." He ran off.

A moment later, Malcolm returned carrying two heavy duffle bags. He stopped by the pile on the floor. "We need to carry everything in one trip." He cracked the front door open and inspected the street. He turned to Danielle and Gerta. "We'll walk casually to the Jeep. No running. I'll open the rear gate. We'll stack everything in the back. Ready?" The women nodded.

The three walked to the Jeep, placed their loads in the cargo area, and climbed aboard. Malcolm drove sedately through side streets and headed northwest.

He turned to Gerta. "Call Larry. Tell him we won't need them. They can return to the warehouse. Have him gather everyone in the lunchroom for a conference call."

"We're not going to the warehouse?" Gerta asked.

"Not just yet. I want to stop at Cabela's and pick up supplies first."

"What if someone recognizes us at Cabela's?" Danielle asked.

"The place will be crowded with customers. We should be all right."

Danielle nodded but did not look reassured.

Gerta's phone rang. It was Larry. "We're all here in the lunchroom, and I have you on speaker phone."

Malcolm spoke first. "We're setting up camp in the warehouse for now to review our plans."

Gerta had opened the FBI website on her iPad, "The FBI uploaded all of our photos on their Most Wanted webpage this morning. A neighbor must have seen us and reported it."

Everyone was silent for a moment. Malcolm spoke first. "Larry, grab a van and meet us at the Cabela's Hazelwood store. Look for our Jeep in the parking lot. You and I will go in and buy sleeping and cooking gear. The rest of you guys stay put for now. Questions, anyone?"

"Did you have time to pick up my guns?" Larry asked. "There was a pistol under my pillow and an M16 with spare magazines in the closet."

"Same here," Steve said. "And I had a bag with grenades on the shelf in my closet."

"I've got all those," Malcolm said.

"Great!" Larry and Steve said in unison.

"I'm on my way. See you shortly," Larry said.

Malcolm ended the call and pointed the Jeep in the direction of Cabela's.

CHAPTER 14

SWAT STORMS THE HIDEOUT

Claire Chouteau had watched from her living room window as the patrol cruiser rolled down Pershing Place at walking speed. "Finally, they've sent the police to arrest that man and his gang," she said, turning to her husband, whose eyes were glued to the TV set.

"Will you turn off that darn contraption?" she shouted. Bill and Geraldine returned the same look of alarm. Claire sighed and returned to looking out the window. The police cruiser had driven past the gang's house. *What the devil*, Claire thought. When she saw the car turn right at the first intersection, Claire rushed to the rear of the house and walked out onto her back porch. She had guessed correctly. The cruiser was approaching along Carriage Lane. It parked a short distance past the criminals' garage. She watched a rotund police officer climb out of the vehicle, open the car's trunk, retrieve a pair of binoculars, and walk along the vine-covered fence of her neighbor's backyard. *My God! They've only sent one officer to arrest all these killers.*

At that moment, a black Jeep emerged from the garage. The officer looked startled. He rushed across the lane into the parking lot. The Jeep proceeded down the lane and out of sight. *Why in heaven didn't the officer stop that car?* The police officer stared at the back of house for some time and then ran to his cruiser. *Finally, he's going to pursue the Jeep.* But no, the officer stayed in his vehicle, not going anywhere

Claire raced back indoors and made for the living room window. And there was that black Jeep. It had returned and parked in front of the fugitives' house. The tall man with the fake name climbed out and walked briskly into his house. "Bill. You've got to see this!" Claire shouted. "Something big is going down." Bill rose with a struggle, sending Geraldine falling to the floor, and lumbered to the window.

"I don't see anything unusual," he said.

"Just you wait. The police will be here soon, and they'll arrest the whole gang of them."

"Really?" Bill stared out the window for a minute, then returned to his recliner. Geraldine climbed back on his lap.

A few minutes later, Claire saw the man and two women, mother and daughter, no doubt, walk out of the house carrying satchels, boxes, and duffel bags. They piled everything into the back of the Jeep, climbed in, and drove off.

"They're getting away!" Claire shouted. She ran to the phone and called the FBI field office.

The same agent she had spoken to before repeated the same instructions—stay in her house and to lock all the doors.

Claire hung up and huffed. "They want us to barricade ourselves inside our own house. Rubbish! If it weren't for me, those idiots wouldn't have known these criminals were hiding in plain sight." Bill and Geraldine stared at her with alarm.

Claire fixed Bill with a fierce stare. "There's a manhunt going on out there, and you plan on sitting here watching those silly westerns?"

"Right." Bill rose again, this time lowering Geraldine softly to the floor. He walked to the front door and set the dead bolt.

"After the horses have bolted," Claire scoffed. She walked to the front closet, slipped on her gray overcoat, placed her red cloche on her head, unlocked the front door, and stormed out. Breaking one of her cardinal rules, she cut across the lawn, climbed the steps of the neighbors' front porch, and knocked loudly on the door. As she expected, no one answered. She peeked through the panel windows. No sign of life. She tried the door handle. It opened. She called out, "Anybody home?" No answer. She entered the foyer.

Claire felt like Alice stepping through the looking glass. She was entering the world of violent criminals like those she had read about: the James brothers, the Daltons, and her all-time favorites, Bonnie and Clyde. Her heart pounded like a drum in her chest.

She turned to her left and walked into the den. It looked as if a tornado had blown through it. Sheets of paper were scattered everywhere. She picked up a sheet of plastic film. Rainbow colors appeared as she moved the sheet around. *Holographic film? To make fake IDs?*

She crossed the hallway and stepped into the living room. It was pristine. *They've never set foot in here.*

Claire continued down the hall to the kitchen. Unwashed mugs and saucers lay on the kitchen island. She turned toward the dining area. A shiny mahogany table and chairs stood undisturbed, as if in a showroom. *They must have planned their next heist while sitting around that kitchen island*, she decided, conjuring up a scene in her mind with the criminals bent over the island, dividing their loot.

She walked to the French doors, which opened onto a deck that looked onto the backyard. She gazed at the curved garden path paved with flat gray stones leading to a rustic wooden garage structure. Trellises, overgrown with vines thick with red leaves, covered the back fence. *How pleasing*, she reflected.

Claire turned and walked to the stairs that led to the second story. She climbed the stairs to a landing that opened onto a sitting area with two white rattan chairs arranged around a white coffee table. A large ficus planter filled one corner, and another set of French doors opened onto a balcony overlooking the backyard.

Claire followed the hallway that led to the bedrooms. She peeked inside the master bedroom, then entered and made for the en suite. *Wow.* She stared with big eyes at the light gray porcelain tiles that covered every surface of the walk-in shower and at the vanity with double sinks and double mirrors. *If only Bill would renovate our old house instead of watching TV,* she fantasized. *Fat chance of that happening.*

Claire returned to the sitting area and looked out the French doors. Her eyes gravitated to the empty parking lot that lay beyond Carriage Lane. *What an eyesore.* Something caught her eye. She squinted and made out a police cruiser parked alongside a large red brick building. At that moment, a black army personnel carrier thundered through the parking lot and skidded to a stop behind the police cruiser. Paratroopers dressed in black, wearing large black helmets with visors, just like in sci-fi movies, jumped out the sides of the personnel carrier. *This must be one of those SWAT teams,* Claire thought.

Four SWAT officers ran across the lane, in crouched postures, and disappeared behind the garage. Two more, one carrying a rifle case and the other, a battering ram, ran toward the back of the red brick building and disappeared. Two or three minutes later, the two officers appeared on the roof of the building. One set up a rifle on a tripod, lay down behind it, and pointed the weapon at the house she was in.

At the St. Louis SWAT offices a little earlier, newly minted marksman, Alfredo Russo, sat across the desk from his supervisor, Captain Antoine Thomas. Alfredo stood at five foot six, on the small side for a SWAT officer, but "a sniper don't need size," Alfredo was quick to point out. "He needs ice-cold blood flowing in his veins and dead nuts accuracy."

The accuracy part Alfredo had mastered to a T, his captain would readily admit, but the cold-blooded temperament was a problem.

Captain Thomas looked at Alfredo with sympathetic eyes, then said, "The army has denied your request to join up." He paused. Alfredo looked crestfallen. He continued, "But that doesn't mean forever." Alfredo lowered his eyes and gritted his teeth. Captain Thomas let out a long breath. "Now don't give me that angry hangdog look. Try to see the army's point of view. You're still unproven. Once you've scored a few kills, they'll look at your request again. And what's the big rush? The Middle East terrorists aren't going anywhere anytime soon."

Alfredo rubbed his hands together and made fists. "Those terrorists killed my brother, Marco. I promised my parents I'd avenge his death." Alfredo narrowed his eyes. "I can't wait to blow off a few of those ragheads."

Captain Thomas shook his head. "There's part of the problem right there. You use language like this in front of the recruiters, you can kiss your chances goodbye. Nobody wants to fight alongside a hot-headed avenger." He reshuffled the papers on his desk. "Give it a year, Alfredo, and apply again. In the meantime, build a reputation as a reliable team player and rack up a few clean kills."

Captain Thomas rose, walked around his desk and fastened fatherly eyes on the young sniper. He placed a large hand on Alfredo's shoulder and tapped it gently. Alfredo nodded, turned, and left the office.

As he approached his locker, a voice reverberated through the building's intercom. *All team members to the briefing room immediately!* Alfredo dressed hurriedly in full combat gear and raced to the briefing room.

A man in a blue jacket with a shoulder tag that read 'FBI' stood at the front of the room. Once everyone had found a seat, the agent flicked a picture on a large video screen. It showed headshots of six people.

The agent adjusted the focus, and when satisfied, he turned to the assembly. "Gentlemen, oh, and ladies." He nodded toward two women in the audience. He coughed into his hand, then continued, "The people on the screen are serial killers, vigilantes. We refer to them as the Jennings gang." He paused, then added, "These criminals have committed seven murders in the last three months. That we know of." He surveyed the audience, then continued. "The leader of the gang, Malcolm Jennings," the agent aimed his pointer at Malcolm's photo, "was last seen at a house in West Central. A St. Louis police officer was dispatched to the address, 4640 Pershing Place, and positively ID'd this woman, Gerta Jennings, the leader's wife." He aimed his pointer at Gerta's picture. "More gang members were seen at the same address by a neighbor." He moved to the photos of Malcolm, Larry, and Steve. "These three men are Marine veterans with combat experience in Iraq and Afghanistan. They carry military grade weapons."

The agent then pointed his laser at Danielle. "This young woman, Danielle Jennings, is the leader's daughter. She has two years of military academy training." He moved the pointer to the photo of Tom. "This young man, Tom Cole, is a recent recruit. He has a criminal record for aggravated assault and is suspected of murder, in Canada, but has no military training."

The agent went back at Gerta's photo. "Gerta Jennings is a cyber expert and the brains of the operation. She produces fake identities for her teammates, which explains how they have evaded capture for three months."

Next, the agent brought up a satellite view of Pershing Place. He moved his pointer to the front of the house. "Team number one will park their personnel carrier here in front of the hideout. Team number two will position their vehicle in a parking lot across the street from the rear of the house." The agent pointed at that location. "Each team will seal off the street and position a sniper on the roof of a building with a clear view of the house." The agent pointed at the proposed roofs. "Questions so far?"

One hand rose. "Do we know how many fugitives are in the house?"

"No. The St. Louis police officer reported seeing Gerta Jennings at the house, but that's all we know. Assume most of the gang is inside." He paused, looked over the audience, then said, "The Reliant Detective Agency of Ann Arbor, Michigan, confronted the Jennings gang in Canada a week ago. A firefight broke out, but the criminals escaped after killing their target, a former CEO, one of Reliant's agents, and a bystander. The detective agency reported that the gang is experienced and heavily armed. Do not expect them to surrender."

Silence spread through the audience, but no questions came. The FBI agent ended the briefing with, "Let's go get them!"

The SWAT members climbed aboard their assigned armored vehicles. Alfredo's team, number two, barreled through the empty parking lot across from the fugitives' hideout in its BearCat and skidded to a halt beside a red brick building. The team jumped out of the personnel carrier, and four officers hustled to the garage at the rear of the hideout. Alfredo, the case with his Remington 700P sniper rifle inside in one hand, ran toward the back of the red brick building. A teammate, carrying a ram, followed close behind. The men turned the corner and faced a loading dock with a row of roll-up doors and a service entrance. They made for the service entrance.

The men were met with the deafening noise of printing presses. A supervisor, dressed in a blue uniform and wearing safety eyeglasses and earmuffs, came forward to check on the visitors, but when he saw the SWAT uniforms and Alfredo's rifle case, he stopped short, stared wide-eyed, then took a step back. Alfredo raised a hand and pointed upward. The supervisor pointed toward a door to his left.

The door gave onto a stairwell. Alfredo and his teammate reached the second floor, looked around, then continued up to the roof. They reached a landing and faced a red roof access door. Alfredo pressed on the panic bar, but the door wouldn't budge. He stepped aside and let his teammate swing the battering ram against the door. It burst open.

Once on the roof, Alfredo chose a spot with a good view of the hideout and its backyard. He set up his rifle on its tripod, smoothed the gravel with his gloved hands, and lay down. His teammate approached. "You're good here?" Alfredo gave him a thumbs up, and the man left.

Alfredo adjusted the focus of his scope and scanned the windows and the French doors at the rear of the house. The reflection from the sun on the glass panes made it hard to see inside the house. A silhouette appeared behind the French doors of the second-floor balcony. It was a woman. Of that he was certain. His radio crackled. "Captain Thomas calling Agent Russo."

Alfredo picked up the radio. "This is Russo. I'm in position. Over."

"Good. Have you acquired a target? Over."

"Yes. A woman is standing behind the French doors of the second-floor balcony. Over."

"Good. Keep sight of the target. A team is moving across the backyard now. They will launch teargas grenades through the windows. You cover them. Over."

"Roger that."

Alfredo prayed. *God make my aim steady and my shot accurate.* He reflected on the opportunity that had presented itself. *If I take out that woman, Gerta, the brains of the operation, that'll be one big feather in my cap.* He focused his scope on the silhouette behind the French doors, slowed his breathing down, and let the adrenaline drain from his body.

Claire watched, mesmerized, from behind the French doors on the second-floor balcony as the SWAT team homed in on the house like a well-coordinated colony of black ants. Two officers emerged from behind the garage. The lead officer held a ballistic shield in front of him while a second man, carrying a rifle with what looked like a tin can stuck onto the end of the barrel, followed in lockstep. The duo advanced through the backyard and approached the house.

Claire suddenly realized the danger she was in. *I've got to signal to the police that I'm alone in the house.* At that moment, a tin can broke through a glass pane on the French doors, flew a mere inch from her head, and rolled onto the floor. A cloud of gray smoke hissed from the container. The acrid gas stung her eyes and burned her throat and lungs. She burst through the French doors in a panic, gasping for fresh air. She never heard the shot.

CHAPTER 15

THE WAREHOUSE

Malcolm drove into Cabela's parking lot and chose a space with a clear view of the exits. He made a mental note of the best escape route: the back exit to Garner Lane, which led to city side streets.

Larry appeared ten minutes later and he parked his white cargo van next to Malcolm's Jeep. Everyone climbed out of their vehicles.

"We'll go inside and buy sleeping gear and supplies." Malcolm told Larry. He turned to Gerta. "Can you get toiletries and groceries for everyone? And then drive directly to the warehouse." Malcolm handed over the key fob.

Gerta grabbed the keys. She furrowed her brow. "We should replace the plates on the Jeep. That police officer may have recorded them. I've got a spare set in the back. I'll find a quiet spot and replace them."

"Good thinking," Malcolm said.

"See you at the warehouse." Gerta climbed behind the wheel and drove off.

Malcolm turned to Danielle. "You stay with the van and keep watch." Danielle nodded, picked the key fob from Larry, and climbed behind the wheel.

The men walked into Cabela's and paused in front of a hand-painted mural, a scene of the Ozark Bluffs. "Reminds me of hunting trips with Kenny and Dad," Malcolm said with sadness in his voice.

The men grabbed shopping carts, and Malcolm turned to Larry, "Buy sleeping gear for three people only and return to the van. I'll go buy camp essentials first, then the rest of the sleeping gear. Meet you at the van." Larry nodded and headed off.

A half hour later, Larry and Malcolm had piled the supplies into the cargo van, and the three teammates drove to the warehouse.

Steve was keeping watch at the office window when he saw Gerta arrive at the wheel of the Jeep. He opened a roll-up door and guided her inside. Malcolm drove up shortly afterwards. Tom walked over and helped carry the gear into the lunchroom.

Gerta surveyed all the rooms. She assigned everyone's sleeping quarters, then focused her attention on the lunchroom. She tried the hot and cold water taps, was satisfied, then moved to the microwave, the stove, and the fridge. All were in working order. She opened the top cupboard doors. Cups, glasses, and dishes filled the shelves. She found cutlery, pots, and pans in the bottom cupboards.

Tom and Danielle grouped four tables and eight chairs into a dual-purpose dining and conference table. While Gerta made coffee, Danielle placed mugs on the table.

"There's nothing like a hot drink to lift morale," Gerta said. Danielle smiled. "I hope to inherit your adaptability, Mom."

"You're fine as you are, sweetheart." Gerta walked over and kissed Danielle on the cheek.

Malcolm entered the lunchroom and walked over to Tom. "You'll take first watch from the front office window." Tom nodded and walked over to his post.

Larry and Steve stood, awaiting orders. Malcolm signaled for them to follow him into the warehouse. He had them position the vehicles to face the roll-up doors. The men unloaded the safe and carried it to a corner of the shop. They placed assault rifles and twenty-round magazines in the rear of each vehicle. Steve added a small bag with grenades in the back of each vehicle.

"You sure like your grenades," Malcolm said.

"They came in handy in Afghanistan," Steve said, smiling at Malcolm. "Remember when our Jeep struck an IED, and the insurgents were firing at us? You were unconscious from a bullet wound, but my grenades kept the bad guys at a distance until reinforcements arrived."

Malcolm nodded. "I'll never forget you saved my life." He gave a playful punch to Steve's shoulder. "And I see you won't either."

Once everything was loaded, the men returned to the lunchroom and sat down around the table. Danielle served the coffee and tea. Gerta placed frozen pizzas in the oven.

The men sat quietly. Steve spoke first. "I never thought we'd be discovered so soon." He looked up at Malcolm.

"Me neither," Malcolm agreed. "We need to rethink our plan."

"Shouldn't we hightail it out of town right now?" Steve asked.

Malcolm mulled this over for a minute. "We're safer here than on the roads right now. The FBI and the police will be monitoring all the exits from the city." He looked at Gerta. "What do you think?"

"All my printing and laminating equipment is here in the rental office. I need them to prepare new IDs for everyone."

"How much time will that take?" Malcolm asked.

Gerta considered, then said, "With Danielle and Tom helping me, four or five days."

"And what about the research and planning for the raid on Larry's target?"

"That I can do on the road."

Malcolm considered this for a moment. Then he addressed the group. "We'll hunker down here until Gerta has completed our new IDs, and then we'll go after our last target in New York City." Steve and Larry looked at each other with raised eyebrows.

"It's bad enough that our pictures are on the FBI's Most Wanted website," Steve said, "but what if our pictures are all over the news too?" All eyes turned to Gerta.

"I'll monitor the news," Gerta said. "But regardless, we need to lay low, and we need disguises." She rose and brought back a box from her bedroom, placed it on the table, and opened it. "I purchased eyeglasses, sunglasses, and hair coloring at the drug store. I suggest we all wear glasses and a hat every time we go out. You guys should start to grow beards, and we gals will dye our hair."

Everyone crowded around the box and examined the eyeglasses and sunglasses.

"All right," Malcolm said. "Let's prepare an escape plan in case the FBI discovers this location." Everyone's expression showed they agreed. Malcolm stood and waved for Larry and Steve to follow him. "Let's get started."

Malcolm led the way across the warehouse and stopped at the roll-up door that opened onto the back lot. The three men stepped outside. A six-foot fence of rusty metal paneling enclosed the backlot. The lot was fifty feet long by sixty wide. The fence on the left adjoined a garden center, the back fence faced the Days Inn hotel parking lot, and the fence on the right bordered Wright Street.

Malcolm led the men to the section by Wright Street. They stared at an abandoned lot directly across the street, which covered the full length of the block. A fence made of metal paneling enclosed it. Malcolm had brought a print of a satellite view of the neighborhood streets. He unfolded the print. The men leaned over and studied it.

"If the police discover this hideout, they'll block all the nearby streets and call in their SWAT unit," Malcolm said. "Our best escape route will be through our back lot, then across Wright Street onto that abandoned lot. From there we make our way to the underpass at I-70 and then scatter through city streets."

Larry peered over the fence at Wright Street. "Even if we make it across Wright Street while dodging bullets, we can't outrun the cops for long. We'll need an escape vehicle positioned on that abandoned lot." He turned to Malcom. "We could use one of our two vans."

Malcolm leaned on the fence. "We'll need to cut openings in the fences to run through." He looked at the print. "Let's walk the route."

The men climbed over the fence, crossed Wright Street, and climbed over the fence around the abandoned lot. They located a good place to park an escape vehicle, then made their way through a parking lot to Branch Street, and over to the underpass at I-70. There, the men stopped and looked around.

"Even if we make it this far, SWAT will have a chopper in the air, and we'll need to switch vehicles, unseen, at some point," Larry said.

Malcolm considered, then said, "I'll put Tom on that and see what he comes up with." Larry and Steve looked at each other with raised eyebrows.

The men retraced their steps back to the warehouse. They returned to the lunchroom. Danielle and Gerta had set hot pizzas on the table. Everyone reached for the hot pizzas and ate eagerly.

Boisterous dog yaps and the clatter of claws resonated from the front office.

"What the devil is that noise?" Malcolm asked. Danielle and Gerta eyed each other, a smile on their faces. Malcom signaled for Steve to relieve Tom on watch duty.

Tom appeared in the open office door with an emaciated, grizzled, tan colored little dog pawing at his legs and running circles around him. "I've made a friend," Tom said. "This guy was begging at the door. I think he's starving."

Danielle walked over, kneeled, and patted the dog's head. "Poor thing." She got up and brought over a slice of pizza. The dog gulped down the food in four swallows. "I'd better wait a while before I feed him more," she said.

Gerta filled a bowl of water and placed it on the floor. The dog lapped furiously at the water, spilling half of it on the floor.

"What are your plans for this visitor?" Malcolm asked.

"To look after him until someone comes looking for him?" Tom gazed down at the dog, bit his lip, then added, "But he looks abandoned." He leaned over and patted the dog. "I'll call him Lucky."

"What breed is he?" Danielle asked.

"He's a mix for sure but mostly Border Terrier, I'd say. I can tell he's got a good temperament, and he's affectionate. He looks four or five years old. Full size now." Lucky stood about fifteen inches high. He looked up at Tom, yapped, and wagged his tail vigorously.

"If you look after him, he can join our team," Malcolm said. Tom smiled and leaned over to rub Lucky's head.

Malcolm waved Tom over. "I need your help with a problem." Tom walked over and sat beside Malcolm as Danielle held and fussed over Lucky.

Malcolm flattened a satellite view of the neighborhood on the table and explained the emergency escape plan, pointing at key locations with his finger.

Tom stared intently at the printout. He pointed a finger at Wright Street and said in a shaky voice. "The police will mow us down if we try to run across that street!"

"Steve and Larry are working on that problem. I need you to find a solution to a different problem." Tom looked on with raised eyebrows. Malcolm continued. "How to switch escape vehicles without being seen by a police chopper overhead."

Tom stared back at Malcolm. "You mean like in an underground garage or some such place?" Malcolm nodded.

"How soon do you need that plan?" Tom asked.

"Tomorrow morning."

Tom mulled this over. "I'll need a laptop to do some research."

"Gerta will lend you one."

Malcolm then signaled Danielle over. "I need your help with something too." She left Lucky in Tom's care and sat down by her father.

"How can I help?"

"Can you buy full-face gas masks and respirators for everyone next time you're out? Home Depot carries them, but don't buy them all at the same store."

"I'm on it, Dad."

Malcolm turned to Larry, "Can you tell us more about this Tyler guy?" All eyes turned to Larry.

"Michael Tyler must be in his mid-fifties by now. He's the CEO of Retail Conglomerate. Their headquarters are on Fifth Ave in Midtown Manhattan. He lives in a mansion in Sands Point, Long Island."

Malcolm turned to Gerta. "Some of that info may need updating. Did you have a chance to look this guy up yet?"

"Yes. The headquarters are still there, and Tyler's still living in Sands Point. A private security firm is guarding the property. His wife and a housekeeper live with him, that's all."

"Has he hidden money overseas?" Steve asked from the open doorway. He looked up at the assembly. "I'm backing Larry's plan no matter what, but a financial bonus would be nice." Larry rose and gave Steve a playful punch on the shoulder.

"As a matter of fact, Mr. Tyler has a shell company in the British Virgin Islands and has transferred over $50 million to it in recent years," Gerta said, "But don't forget, I'm sending twenty percent of everything we make to charities that support the workers harmed by these CEOs."

Steve whistled, then said, with a devilish smile, "Still. There's enough there to shore up my retirement fund nicely."

Malcolm turned to Gerta. "Have you sent Tyler an email urging reparations, as you did with the others?"

"Yes, but his reaction was to hire Reliant to hunt us down. With Louise Jackson on the Reliant team, that has me worried."

"Reliant or not, it's still full steam ahead," Malcolm said, "Gerta and I will put together a plan to corner Tyler and get his passwords." He turned to Larry. "I'll leave it to you to deal with the man once we've cornered him." Larry nodded. Malcolm looked at the assembly. "We all have assignments to work on. Let's get to it." Everyone rose.

Malcolm waved Larry over. "Can you prepare a roster for watch duty? Leave Gerta, Danielle, and Tom out of it. They'll be doing research until late tonight." Larry nodded.

Malcolm walked over to Gerta, took her hands in his, and looked into her eyes. "We've made it his far thanks to you. We owe you big time."

Gerta stretched on her toes and kissed him. "I enjoy doing this work. My father would be proud of me."

CHAPTER 16

THE FBI RECAPS

Special Agent in Charge Arlene Hale had summoned Agent O'Keefe for an update. "Agent O'Keefe, explain to me what happened at the fugitives' hideout in St. Louis. At least two of the Jennings gang were seen at the hideout. We had them cornered like fish in a bowl. What the hell happened?"

O'Keefe fidgeted in place as if sitting on hot coals. He bit his lip, then replied, "The St. Louis police screwed up. They didn't cover the front of the hideout until our SWAT teams arrived. The gang must have escaped out the front door while the St. Louis police cruiser was watching the rear of the house and the garage from Carriage Lane. They should have sent two cruisers."

"Okayyy . . . and what about our SWAT team killing an innocent bystander? How do I explain that to the Director?"

O'Keefe bit his lip again, swallowed, and then said, "The innocent victim was a nosy neighbor who shouldn't have been there to begin with. She was trespassing."

"Wasn't she the person who tipped off the police?"

O'Keefe grimaced uncomfortably. "Yes."

"What happened to the cross-eyed sharpshooter who killed her?"

"He's been issued a letter of reprimand. We're desperately short of sharpshooters, so we didn't fire him."

"And what about the criminals who got away? Do we know where they are?"

O'Keefe fidgeted some more. "Not yet, but we're turning every stone in and around St. Louis. We'll find them."

Hale straightened and pushed back in her seat. She looked out at the cityscape through her floor to ceiling windows, then swiveled to face her subordinate again. "So I'm going to have to tell the Director the gang escaped out the front door while an incompetent St. Louis police officer was watching the *back* door, we killed the neighbor who spotted the criminals for us because she was in the wrong place at the wrong time, and, oh yeah, we only gave the nearsighted sharpshooter a slap on the wrist and plan to keep using him, *and* we're *looking for* the criminals." Hale glared ominously at O'Keefe. "Does that summarize the situation well, Agent O'Keefe?"

O'Keefe swallowed hard but stayed mute, wisely leaving Hale's sarcastic comments unchallenged.

"Find those criminals, Agent O'Keefe, and fast, or we'll all get a lot more than a slap on the wrist."

O'Keefe stood up, red-faced, nodded, and left the office.

CHAPTER 17

THE SECOND DAY AT THE WAREHOUSE

The clock on the lunchroom wall read 7 a.m. as Gerta and Larry each hit the washrooms. Steve was keeping watch in the front office. Tom was sleeping with Lucky stretched out at his feet. Malcolm, his morning exercises and ablutions completed, sat at the kitchen table. Danielle, with freshly dyed and straightened jet-black hair tied back in a high ponytail, was at the counter making a pot of coffee.

When she served a mug of dark roast and a pastry to her dad, he said, "I like your new look, but I'll miss your beautiful blond curls."

"Thanks, Dad. And when I wear large frame black eyeglasses and a baseball cap, I'll look *totally* different."

Larry, in John Lennon eyeglasses and a cap sitting low on his forehead, entered the kitchen, said good morning to father and daughter, and walked over to the front office. He exchanged a few words with Steve, then went out the front door.

Gerta, now a redhead with a stubby ponytail and red-rimmed eyeglasses perched on her nose, walked into the kitchen, paraded in front of Malcolm and said, "How do you like *my* new look?"

"Wow! Sexy." Malcolm stared lovingly at his wife and wolf-whistled.

With a mischievous smile, Gerta kissed him on the cheek, then removed the glasses.

Malcolm addressed both women. "You guys worked late last night. You were still hard at it when I turned in."

Gerta was the first to answer. "Yes, we did. I've begun setting up new identities for everyone, but I'll need Danielle and Tom at the printing office with me. I want to teach them how to run the security document printer and laminator." She turned to Danielle. "I want to teach you how to find and download the building plans your father and Larry will need."

"Danielle is yours," Malcolm said, "but I need Tom for part of today and tomorrow." Gerta nodded.

Malcolm watched Danielle carefully. "How are you coping with all this? Nervous?"

Danielle returned a rueful smile. "Sometimes, sure, but when I see you and Mom staying calm and focused, I'm good." Gerta walked over and stroked Danielle's arm gently.

Tom, wearing amber-tinted Harry Potter glasses, entered the kitchen with Lucky at his heels. "What do you guys think?" he asked, pointing at the glasses.

Danielle tilted her head sideways, pursed her lips, and said, "We'll dye your hair blond. With your tan skin, you'll look really cool." She walked up, hugged, and kissed him. "Ouch! What's with the stubble?" she asked.

"I'm growing a beard to complete my disguise," Tom said as he rubbed his chin. He took a step back and looked at Danielle. "*You* look good."

"Thanks." Danielle smiled and brought Tom a mug of coffee and a pastry, then offered a piece of leftover pizza to Lucky, careful not to get her fingers bitten.

Tom removed his glasses and smiled at Danielle. "That was good work we did last night,"

"Yes. I'm proud of us." Danielle turned to her father. "I think you'll be impressed, Dad."

Malcolm smiled back. "But your report will have to wait till later." He looked at Tom. "I think you're next on watch." Tom picked up his mug and his pastry and walked over to the front office. Lucky followed.

Steve entered the lunchroom and nodded at everyone. "Morning, folks. All quiet on the Western Front," he announced before disappearing into the men's washroom.

Moments later, he reappeared, refreshed but unshaven, wearing amber-tinted aviator sunglasses. He sat at the table, looked up at Malcolm, smiled, then bit into a pastry.

"I notice that all the men are unshaven," Danielle said. "We'll have a band of bespectacled ape men running around the place soon."

Malcolm chuckled, then turned to Steve. "Where did Larry go?"

"He went to talk to the folks at the trailer rental shop up the street. They may have equipment we could use for an escape plan. We came up with some ideas last night."

Malcolm raised his eyebrows.

"I'll let Larry explain it when he comes back," Steve said.

At that moment, the loud rumble of an out-of-tune engine resonated from the street. Tom appeared in the doorway. "It's Larry at the wheel of a rent-a-wreck."

The creaking of a rolling door, followed by even louder engine noise and a cloud of blue fumes, reached the lunchroom. The noise died, and Larry entered the lunchroom.

Larry sat down at the table, nodded at everyone, put his glasses and cap on the table, picked a pastry, and ate with relish. Danielle placed a mug of coffee in front of him. He thanked her with a smile.

Malcolm had been watching Larry patiently. Finally, he said, "So. Let's hear about this escape plan you and Steve put together last night? And what's with the clunker?"

Larry swallowed a piece of pastry, licked his lips, and replied, "I bought that van for scrap value, $200 cash, no plates, no papers. They'd already removed the catalytic converter for the platinum, hence all the noise."

"And may I ask *why* you bought it?"

"I need it to build a turtle."

Everyone stared, silent. Malcolm spoke first. "A turtle?"

"Don't laugh, guys. The turtle was a highly successful military tactic in Roman times." Larry paused for extra drama, then continued. "I'll assemble bulletproof panels in the shape of a turtle's shell and drop the shell over this van. If the police attack, we can drive out the back, cross Wright Street, and reach an escape van parked on the abandoned lot without getting gunned down."

Malcolm furrowed his brow. "Bulletproof panels! And where exactly will you get those?"

"A company in Texas. Armorcore. They manufacture ballistic-rated fiberglass panels that will stop a sniper's bullet."

"Hmm. How heavy are these panels?" Malcolm asked.

"Five hundred pounds each and I'll need four."

"That van won't make it far with that extra weight on it," Malcolm said.

"We only need to get across Wright Street."

"Okay, but how soon can you get the panels? We're leaving in three or four days."

"Armorcore delivers overnight. If I order the panels now, they'll be delivered tomorrow morning and, with Steve's help, I can complete the turtle by tomorrow night."

"We'll need to cut large openings in the fences for that plan to work," Malcolm said.

"We cut out the openings last night and tied the loose sections back in place with zip ties," Steve said.

Malcolm remained silent for a moment, surveying everyone's faces. All looked back with raised eyebrows. He returned his gaze to Larry. "Okay. Place the order. Gerta will give you a safe credit card you can use." Larry nodded.

Malcolm turned to Danielle. "Can you relieve Tom? I need his report." Danielle rose and walked to the front office.

Tom came back at once and sat down at the table, Lucky by his side, smiling with a lolling tongue. Tom flattened a city street map on the table, then looked up at Malcolm. "Danielle and I looked for large covered garages with numerous exits, such as the Stadium, as possible places to switch vehicles without being seen from a copter. The one we like best is the parking complex at the Barnes Jewish Hospital." Tom pointed at a location on the map. "We can drop off our van in one parking garage, walk over to an adjoining garage, and leave in a different vehicle from a different exit."

"I like the idea," Malcolm said, "but there's just one problem." He tapped at the map. "That's a twenty-minute drive away. Is there nothing closer?"

"Not a covered garage of that size with multiple exits," Tom replied, then hesitated before adding, "But I chanced on another alternative."

He flattened three printouts on the table. They showed what looked like sketches of underground caves. "Please keep an open mind. This will sound far-fetched."

They all stared at him expectantly.

"There is a labyrinth of caves and tunnels underneath this city. I looked up a caver group on the Internet and bought these handmade maps." Everyone leaned forward for a better look. "I noticed a lot of interconnections between caves that make it possible to enter at one entrance and resurface at a different place." Everyone looked at each other with raised eyebrows. Tom continued. "There is one entrance less than ten minutes away, on Olive Street." Tom pointed at the location on one of the maps. "And it's possible to enter there and resurface at the old Lemp Brewery way over in the south end of the city." Tom traced the trajectory with his finger, then looked up. "We could park a vehicle there."

"How do you know all this?" Larry asked.

"The caver I bought those maps from claims to have walked the route in an hour and a half." Everyone looked on with scrunched eyebrows.

"How do we find that Olive Street entrance?" Malcolm asked.

"The caver said the entrance is in the basement of an old speakeasy, now a bar. Only a few cavers know about it. It's not open to the public."

"Sounds like we'd have to force our way into that bar," Malcolm said. He looked around the table. "What do you guys think?"

Larry spoke first. "I'm not going down those caves unless one of us has walked the route first." Steve nodded his agreement.

"I was thinking the same thing," Malcolm said. He turned to Tom. "We'll go with the parking garage complex you showed us for now, but keep looking for something closer." Tom nodded and folded up the maps.

Gerta had been working on her laptop at the table during the discussion. She raised her hand to get Malcolm's attention.

"Gerta?" Malcolm said.

"Our hideout on Pershing Place has made the news. Two SWAT teams raided the place minutes after we left. They've posted your photo, mine, and that of an elderly woman, a next-door neighbor, they say. The poor woman was snooping around the hideout, and a SWAT sniper shot her by mistake!"

"Did they publish any other photos?" Malcolm asked.

"No. Only those."

Malcolm walked around to look at the woman's photo. "I know her. It's the woman with the cookies."

"The FBI's public relations man came on the air. He sounded embarrassed, as if he wanted the incident out of the news as quickly as possible," Gerta said.

"We got lucky that time," Malcolm said. He turned and addressed the group. "We have a backup plan for next time, but we need more preparations." He fixed his gaze on Tom. "We're short one van for our escape plan. I want you to go and buy a used cargo van. Disguise yourself as best you can, but if you think you've been recognized, leave right away. You think you can do that?"

Tom swallowed hard. "Yes, I can do that."

"Good. Check local used car dealerships. Choose a van priced at around $15,000. Gerta will give you a credit card, a business name, and a cover story. Leave a deposit and tell them you'll pick up the van tomorrow morning." Tom nodded.

Gerta rose and walked over to Tom. "You'll drop me and Danielle off at the printing office first. I'll prepare your credit card and the cover story at the office. Let's go. We have a lot of work to do."

CHAPTER 18

THE PRINTING OFFICE

Tom, Gerta, Danielle, and Lucky drove to a renovated building on Chippewa Street on the historic South Side. Gerta led the way up to the second floor and stopped at a double door. A label on the doors read 'SL Printing'. She punched in a code that unlocked one door and entered. They walked into a large room containing a floor-mounted printing and laminating machine. Worktables, chairs, filing cabinets, and shelving completed the setup.

Gerta examined the equipment, then whispered, "Thank you, Uncle Karl, for having brought over my equipment and my supplies. You are a godsend."

She surveyed her surroundings. A kitchen counter and cupboards lined the far wall. Two doors opened into washrooms on the left. A door on the right opened into an office with a desk, three chairs, and a filing cabinet. She walked into the office and opened her laptop.

Tom and Danielle pulled two small tables together in the printing room and set up their workstations. Tom then walked over to Gerta. "I'd like to send word to Dad that I'm all right," he said. Gerta gave the matter some thought, then looked up at Tom and said, with sympathy in her voice, "The police will be monitoring all communications to and from your father. They'll figure out we're still in St. Louis." Then she asked, "Is there someone back home you would trust to deliver a letter to your dad? We can courier the letter to them."

Tom searched his mind, then said, "Yes, there is."

"Good. Write the letter and give me your friend's address. I'll take care of the rest."

Gerta reached into her satchel and retrieved a credit card. She handed it to Tom. "There's a limit of $50,000 on it. If you need cash, get some at any ATM. But remember, they have cameras, so shield your face." She handed him a sheet of paper. "Here's a short bio of the electrical contractor you work for. Commit it to memory."

"Thanks." Tom took the card and the paper and returned to his workstation. He composed a letter to his father, then wrote down Uncle Bill's address and gave the documents to Gerta. He returned to his computer and printed the address of three used car dealerships, walked to the kitchen counter, and filled a bowl with water for Lucky. He put on his eyeglasses and baseball cap and announced, "I'm off to buy a cargo van."

"Good luck!" Danielle shouted at his back.

Lucky raced to the closed door, scratched at it, and let out a whimper.

Tom drove to the nearest used car dealership on his list. A salesman latched on to him like a lamprey, and within an hour, Tom had test driven two cargo vans with low mileage and no visible rust. Their engines purred smoothly. Tom negotiated a price of $15,000 for one of them and a promise that the van would be prepped and ready for pickup the next morning. He left a $5,000 deposit using the credit card.

Back in the Jeep, Tom phoned the caver who had sold him the maps. The man gave him the name and number of a contact at the Lemp Brewery Business Park. Tom dialed the number.

"Hello, Fred Fischer here," a gruff voice answered.

"Hello, Mr. Fischer. I'm Tom Devin. I got your name from Billy Becker."

"Billy Becker? Yeah, I know Billy. I let him and his group down the caves on a regular basis. What can I do you for?"

"I'd like to visit the caves."

"Which group are you with?"

"I'll be going down alone."

"Sorry. No can do. I only give access to groups with an experienced guide, and they must book a week in advance. It's a liability thing."

Tom was deflated. The caver had said nothing about this. "Can you make an exception. I'll pay for the favor."

"No. Sorry. You'll have to join an organized tour."

"I can't wait that long. It has to be today. I made a bet with my pals, and I have to show them selfies of me down there."

"A bet? That's a new one," Fischer chuckled. "Sorry, but like I said, no can do."

"Would $1,000 help my case?"

"Christ! That must be some bet you made. What did you say your name was?"

"Tom Devin."

"You're not from around here, are you?"

"No. I just moved here from Kansas City. My boss's opening a new electrical shop in St. Louis."

There was an uncomfortable pause. Then Fischer asked, "How long will you be down there?"

"About three hours."

Fischer considered, then said, "Come at noon and bring $2,000."

"Where will I find you?"

"Park by the door that reads Fermenting Department and wait. I'll find *you*." Fischer hung up.

CHAPTER 19

THE CAVES

Tom stopped at a pet store and bought dry dog food, two stainless steel bowls, and poop bags for Lucky. He then continued to the Lemp Brewery Business Park, located the door marked Fermenting Department and parked. He was fifteen minutes early. When the clock struck noon, a large man in a blue worker's uniform walked out the Fermenting Room doorway, looked around, spotted Tom's Jeep, and walked over. He leaned into Tom's open window.

"Are you Tom Devin?"

Tom nodded.

"I'm Fred Fischer. You got the money?"

Tom handed an envelope over. Fischer counted the bills, nodded, then signaled for Tom to follow him.

Once inside the brewery, Fischer looked Tom over.

"You sure don't look like a caver. Where's your gear?"

"I've no gear," Tom said sheepishly,

Fischer shook his head, then turned. "Follow me," he said and led Tom into a locker room. He opened one of the lockers and grabbed a hard hat fitted with a miner's lamp. He tested the lamp, then handed the hat to Tom. Next, Fischer retrieved a huge flashlight from a shelf and tested that. It didn't light. He slapped it a few times with his hand. It lit, and he handed it to Tom. From another closet, Fischer produced a jacket, work gloves, and rubber boots. "These should fit you," he said. He waited while Tom slipped the jacket on and pulled the boots over his feet.

"You got a map of the caves?" Fischer asked.

"That I have." Tom pulled out the folded printouts from his back pocket and showed them to Fischer.

Fischer nodded, turned, and signaled for Tom to follow him. He led the way to a subbasement, proceeded down a dank hallway, and stopped in front of a dark cedar plank door that dripped with moisture. Fischer pulled out a keychain from his coat pocket and opened the door, which revealed a stairwell.

Tom looked down the illuminated stairwell and swallowed hard.

"You've got three hours," Fischer said. "I'm locking the door behind you. I can't stay here. I'll be back in three hours to let you out." Fischer looked Tom in the eye. "If you're not here then, I'm not going down to search for you. I'm calling 911."

"If I'm running late, I'll call you," Tom said.

"There's no cell coverage down there."

Tom stared back with raised eyebrows, then nodded, turned, and descended the steel steps. Once at the bottom, ceiling-mounted light fixtures revealed a huge cavern. Wet tiles covered the floor. Red bricks lined the walls. Plaster was flaking off the ceiling in places and water dripped from many cracks. Brick-lined floor trenches drained the water away.

Tom knew from his research that this was the Lemp Cave. Tunnels with arched doorways separated the lagering rooms. Rusted rails of a narrow-gauge railway tracked across the floor. Looking up, Tom noticed holes in the ceiling. He had read they were used to drop blocks of ice that kept the cave cool for aging beer.

Tom consulted his map for the way to Cherokee Cave. He proceeded northward and passed by the remains of a theater stage, a ballroom, and a swimming pool. He stepped around debris, rubble, and mud. A large painted mural depicting wild boars filled one wall. Tom had read about the fierce-looking prehistoric pigs, called peccaries. Ancient underground streams had washed the skulls and bones of the pigs down into the caves. He shuddered and pressed on.

Tom followed the tunnel that led to Cherokee Cave. He crossed it. The floor tiles ended here, replaced by wet limestone and mud. The ceiling lights ended too. He turned on his flashlight and the helmet light and stood at the entrance to a man-made tunnel cut into the rock, but it was half full of rubble and clay. Tom had reached the end of the tourist maps available on the Internet.

Tom pulled out the hand-drawn maps he had purchased from the caver. They showed a labyrinth of abandoned tunnels, caverns, and lager rooms that ended at the speakeasy on Olive Street. He summoned his courage and proceeded on hands and knees through the muddy tunnel. After crawling for about fifty yards, he reached a cave where he could stand up again. He thanked Fischer inwardly for lending him caving clothes and footwear.

Tom followed the map through lager rooms linked by tunnels and caves that ran underneath the defunct Pittsburgh Brewery, Stumpf Brewery, and Franklin Ale Brewery. Finally, he reached a heavy wooden plank door, the entrance to the basement of the speakeasy on Olive Street. The door was locked, but Tom breathed a sigh of relief. He had reached his destination.

Tom checked the timer on his cell phone. Two hours had elapsed since he had left the Lemp Brewery. He shivered anxiously as he thought, *I will not make it back in time and Fischer will call 911.*

Tom rushed back, retracing his steps. He recognized most of the landmarks but had to stop often to consult his maps. By the time he finally reached the foot of the stairs to the Lemp Brewery subbasement, he was covered in mud, dripping in sweat, panting, and rubbery-legged. And twenty minutes late.

He rushed up the steps and tried the door. It was locked. His heart sank. He banged on the door as hard as he could. Nothing. He sat down on the top step, despondent and shivering.

Five minutes had passed when Tom heard a key turn in the lock. The door opened. Fischer stood in the doorway.

"What the hell happened to you?" Fischer asked. Tom stood up, looking sheepish. Fischer shook his head. "You got lost, didn't you? You're lucky I didn't call 911. They would have charged you with reckless conduct." Fischer stood aside. "Come on, let's get you and the equipment cleaned up."

Tom followed Fischer to the shower stalls. After adjusting the water temperature to as hot as he could stand, he walked under the showerhead, fully clothed, then stripped down and washed the mud off his body, his clothing, and the equipment.

Fischer handed Tom some cleaning rags to dry himself and the equipment. "I can't let you use the dryers, it would take too long, so wring the clothing as dry as you can." He watched Tom hard at his task, then asked, "Did you get the selfies you wanted?"

"Yes, I did."

"I hope the bet was worth all this trouble." Fischer watched Tom slip into his damp clothing. "Have you got a good heater in your car?"

"I'll be fine. Thanks for your help."

Fischer followed Tom back to the Jeep. Tom climbed in, fired up the engine, and turned the heating to maximum. His teeth were chattering and his whole body shivered. He lowered the window and said to Fischer, "Thanks again. I may call you for another visit."

"Okay. You pay well, I'll give you that."

Tom turned the Jeep around and left. When he reached the printing office, he parked underground, climbed out of the Jeep, grabbed a duffle bag full of work uniforms from the back of the vehicle, and raced upstairs.

As Tom entered the printing office, Lucky, who had been waiting by the door, rose on his hind legs, pawed at Tom's waist, and barked excitedly. Danielle and Gerta walked over to greet Tom. "What happened? You're all wet and shivering," Danielle said.

"I need to change into dry clothes fast. No time to talk." Tom rushed to the washroom with the duffle bag in hand. Danielle followed and helped him strip down and dry himself. She rubbed Tom's arms and back vigorously with dry towels, then helped him slip into a dry uniform. They walked back into the office and sat down. Tom was still shivering, but color had returned to his face. Lucky planted two paws on Tom's lap. Tom rubbed the top of the dog's head.

"You went exploring the caves, didn't you?" Gerta asked with a smile.

"Yes." Tom beamed. "I walked all the way from the Lemp Brewery to the speakeasy on Olive Street and back. It was wet, cold, and muddy, but the worst part was driving here in wet clothes. I nearly froze to death."

"You silly boy," Danielle said. "You could catch pneumonia." She leaned over and placed a kiss on the top of his head. "So those hand-drawn maps were accurate?" Tom nodded.

Gerta arrived with a hot mug of cup-a-soup and handed it to Tom. "Careful. It's hot." She then returned to the kitchen counter. "I'll bring coffee and cookies."

Tom looked invigorated after finishing the chicken noodle soup. He then reached for the coffee and cookies. He gave a cookie to Lucky.

Gerta and Danielle joined him at the table. Gerta asked, "How did it go with the purchase of the van?"

"I put a deposit on a Ford Transit cargo van, white, no logos. $15,000. We can pick it up tomorrow morning."

"You did well," Gerta said. "I've begun entering our new identities into the government data banks. We'll print the documents tomorrow. I'll need you and Danielle to help with that."

Danielle beamed as she announced, "I've built the profile of Michael Tyler. Next, Mom will show me how to find and print the building plans of his home and his office building."

"Wow. You're becoming a cyber wizard's apprentice," Tom said.

Danielle turned to Gerta, smiled, and said, "I'll never be as good as Mom."

Gerta smiled back and said, with sadness in her voice, "What I know will not be useful for much longer. The backdoors and loopholes I've put in place will be discovered soon and plugged up. And I'm finding it harder to break into password-protected files. I'm no longer in the loop. It's a good thing this is our last job."

Danielle walked over, wrapped her arms around her mother's shoulders, and rested a cheek against hers. "You'll always be my hero, Mom."

Gerta wiped tears from her eyes and said, "Let's wrap this up and go home. We can continue our research from the shop." She turned to Danielle. "Do you have shopping to do along the way?"

"Yes. I need to buy the gas masks."

They placed the laptops and the tablet in satchels, slipped the straps over their shoulders, and headed for the door. Lucky barked eagerly and followed them out.

CHAPTER 20

THE THIRD DAY AT THE WAREHOUSE

The sun was shining brightly through the windows of the front office, and the round wall clock read 8 a.m., when Steve relieved Larry on watch duty. The weather forecast called for a high of 75 degrees Fahrenheit on this mid-September day.

Malcolm and his team sat at the kitchen table, drinking coffee and devouring scrambled eggs and sausages that Tom had cooked. Malcolm looked up at Tom. "So you went exploring those caves yesterday?"

Tom described his underground excursion from the Lemp Brewery to the speakeasy on Olive Street.

"We nearly lost him to pneumonia," Danielle said. "He barged into the printing office, looking like he had been mud-wrestling with those prehistoric pigs he talks about." She fixed Tom with reproachful eyes. "He was shaking so badly that Mom had to serve him a mug of hot soup to bring him around." She poked Tom in the ribs, then kissed him on the cheek. Lucky picked up on the excitement and jumped up, his front paws scrabbling against Tom's legs.

Gently, Tom pushed Lucky down and said, "I bought some caving gear on the way home: flashlights, boots, jackets, gloves. If anyone wants to visit the caves, I've got what we need."

"I'm game!" shouted Steve from the front office.

"That will have to wait," Malcolm said. He turned to Tom and Danielle. "You two need to go pick up the van this morning."

Gerta raised a hand. "I'll need Tom later to help me with the printing."

"You can have him all afternoon," Malcolm said.

"Oh, and we'll need labels for the vans, won't we?" Gerta said.

"Good point." Malcolm rubbed his chin, then said, "We need a new name for our fake company."

"I'll come up with something," Gerta said. She turned to Danielle. "Meanwhile our daughter has downloaded building plans of Tyler's office building and his residence."

Malcolm stared at Danielle and bowed. Danielle beamed. Gerta placed a hand on her daughter's arm and said, "And she's preparing profiles of Tyler's two security chiefs."

Malcolm bowed at Danielle again. "Yes, we need leverage over those guys. Money is not always enough."

"I'm off to work," said Gerta and left for the printing office in the Jeep.

Danielle turned to Tom. "I'll drop you off at the dealership and then carry on to the printing shop."

The young people and the dog left in the van.

Minutes later, the roar of a powerful engine boomed from the street. It was followed by the screeching of heavy brakes. Larry ran to the window. "My fiberglass panels are here!" He rushed into the warehouse and opened a roll-up door. Malcolm followed as Larry guided the truck to back into the warehouse. The driver jumped out and handed Larry a waybill to sign. The driver deployed the liftgate, climbed into the van, and brought over a load of fiberglass panels with a pallet jack. He lowered the liftgate to the ground. "You'll need a forklift to maneuver these panels. They're heavy."

Larry pointed at the hoist and monorail overhead. "I'll use slings and clamps." The driver nodded, picked up a signed copy of the waybill, closed the truck gate, climbed aboard, and drove out.

Larry turned to Malcolm. "I'll need some help with assembling the turtle."

"Steve and I will take turns helping you."

Two hours later, Tom returned to the warehouse with the new van and proceeded to load it with weapons and ammunition using a list Larry had prepared. Lucky trailed behind his master, trying to help and mostly getting in the way. Larry walked over, climbed aboard the new van, and disconnected the GPS tracking. Malcolm emptied the contents of the small safe, filled a duffel bag with the bills, and placed it in the van. He turned to Tom. "Make sure you take this bag to Gerta as soon as you get to the printing shop." Tom nodded.

Tom walked to his room and returned with a large sports bag.

"What's in the bag?" Malcolm asked.

"It's caving gear."

Malcolm stared at the duffel bag for a moment, then said, "Put the bag in the escape van, the one we'll park in the abandoned lot." Tom looked up in surprise, then nodded.

After the new van had been loaded, Tom and Lucky climbed in and drove off.

Malcolm closed the roll-up door, then walked over to help Larry assemble the bulletproof panels. He stared at the stack of panels. "Are you sure this van can carry all that weight?"

Larry stared at the panels. "We can't do a trial run if that's what you're thinking. That could destroy the tires and damage the suspension. I'll increase the air pressure in the tires to the rated maximum and ask Gerta to say a prayer." He looked at Malcolm sheepishly.

"And I'll pray we never have to use this contraption," Malcolm said.

CHAPTER 21

RELIANT PICKS UP THE TRAIL

Officer Jones's cruiser idled in the parking lot facing the Donut Drive-In. Cream oozed out the corner of his mouth as he bit into a donut. *This is heaven*, he thought. Savoring the sweetness, he reminisced about the SWAT fiasco on Pershing Place. He had watched in fascination as the SWAT team converged on the house. His heart raced when the teargas canister blasted through the windows and patio doors and smoke belched out through the broken glass. And then that woman had burst out onto the balcony, gasping for air. Inwardly, Jones shamefully admitted to experiencing a high when the woman's head had exploded from the impact of the sniper's bullet.

But the victory dance had been short-lived. It took only a few minutes for the SWAT team to discover that they had killed, not the Jennings gang's cyber expert, but only a nosy neighbor, a Curious George. What a downer. *Life can be so damn unfair*, Jones mused.

His radio crackled. He picked up. "Officer Jones here."

"This is Captain Ambrose. I need you to drive to Dutchtown and check a place out."

"Oh. Why? No, I mean, what am I looking for?"

"Another lead to investigate. The fugitives from Pershing Place may be hiding in an abandoned electrical shop in Dutchtown."

Jones's heart thudded in his chest, and sweat dripped down his neck. "But Captain, I'm alone here. These guys carry assault weapons. I'm not equipped to confront them. You need to send another SWAT."

"Calm down, Jones. You won't have to confront anyone. Just look around and report back There may be no one there. The lead came from a detective agency that's been analyzing Internet chatter on the dark web."

Jones swallowed hard. "Okay, Captain. What's the address?"

"4532 South, Grand Boulevard Drive."

"I'm on it." Jones hesitated, then added, "Can you send backup anyway? As a precaution?"

Ambrose breathed heavily, then said, "One step at a time, Jones. Go take a look first and report back." Ambrose hung up.

Damn, Jones cursed inwardly. He placed his half-eaten Boston cream donut into the bag with the others and headed toward Grand Boulevard South.

He slowed to a crawl as he passed the front entrance of 4532. The place looked deserted. A For Sale sign stood by the front entrance.

The property was on a corner lot. Jones parked on the side street, walked to a side entrance, and tried the door. It was locked. He walked around the corner and approached the front entrance. A large window fronted the building, but the lights were off in the lobby. He walked to the window, cupped his hands against the glass, and looked inside. He could make out a reception desk and four visitor chairs. Old calendars and glossy posters covered the walls. He tried the front door. It was locked. Jones trudged back to the cruiser.

"Captain, the place is deserted. No one's been around in a long while."

"Hmm. Okay. You can return to patrol duty."

"Will do, Captain." But the line was already dead.

Earlier that day, Chief Harrington had postponed calling CEO Tyler in the hope that his Reliant team would report a breakthrough at the morning's meeting. They had been burning $10,000 a day and had yet to find a trace of the Jennings crew. He walked to the conference room.

Captain Harris was already present. Ashley Hurd and Paul Collins filed in shortly after. They stopped by the counter, filled mugs with coffee, grabbed a pastry each, and sat down.

Harrington opened the meeting. "Good day everyone." He paused, then said, "Louise is missing?" He turned to Popeye.

"She's chasing a very promising lead. She'll join us as soon as she can," Popeye said.

"Okay, let's get started." Harrison paused, looked at them one at a time, then said, "I badly need to hear some progress today. Our client is understandably anxious to see the Jennings gang arrested." He gave Popeye an inquiring look.

Popeye nodded. "We know they're still in St. Louis." He looked over at Ashley.

Ashley, with excitement in her voice, said, "One of Louise's search engines has flagged a conflict with the address of a new numbered company in St. Louis and that of an existing plumbing company in Dutchtown."

"The business directory could be out of date," Harrington said.

"I contacted the plumbing company. They are in bankruptcy proceedings, and they've never heard of this new numbered company. It could be the Jennings gang's new front. I alerted the FBI, and they asked the St. Louis police to send an officer to investigate the address, but the place looks empty."

"It's a dead end, then?" asked Harrington.

"No," Ashley answered, still excited. "The search engines flagged the purchase of a cargo van in St. Louis yesterday using the numbered company's credit card. I sent photos of the gang to the car dealership, and their sales agent identified Tom Cole as the purchaser, somewhat disguised, but it was him. Cole drove away with the van this morning."

"Well done, Ashley," the Chief said. "Do the purchase papers give an address?"

"The bogus one."

"Damn. Where do we go from here?"

"Louise is analyzing all the purchases made from the same credit card."

At that moment, Louise rushed in and sat down at the table, looking elated. Everyone turned expectantly to her.

"I'm on to something," she announced. "Did Ashley tell you I've been analyzing all the transactions done with that numbered company's credit card?"

Everyone nodded a yes, and Louise continued. "I saw camping gear, gas masks, rental of a forklift, a trailer . . . and the most intriguing one—bulletproof panels from the Armorcore company in Texas."

"Bulletproof panels? Why would they need those?" Harrington asked.

"No idea. The panels were delivered this morning at an address on North Broadway in St. Louis. I've passed on this information to the FBI and they're sending three St. Louis police cruisers and two SWAT teams to that address as we speak."

"That's great news. Now, let's just hope they're at that address," Harrington said.

"I've sent photos of them to the dispatcher at Armorcore, and he's forwarded the photos to the delivery driver. I should hear back any minute."

Everyone was nodding their heads and clasping their hands.

"I've more to report," Louise said. "I've detected a lot of activity on the Internet concerning Michael Tyler. The search was amateurish and poorly focused, so I suspect it was carried out by one of Gerta Jennings' teammates."

"That confirms that Tyler is their next target," Harrington said. "I need to report this to Tyler."

Louise's iPhone pinged. She looked at the screen. "It's Armorcore. I need to take this." She rose and walked quickly into the hallway.

"Louise Jackson speaking."

"Ms. Jackson, this is Ken Ryan at Armorcore. I'm calling about those photographs you sent us earlier?"

"Yes, Mr. Ryan. Did your driver have a look at them?"

"Yes, he did, and he recognized two of the people in the photos. Do you need their names?"

"Yes, please."

"Let me read my notes here. One is Larry Schmidt. The other is Malcolm Jennings. Does that help you?"

"Yes, it does. And your driver delivered those panels to 2835 North Broadway in St. Louis, Missouri, right?"

"Yes, he did."

"Thank you, Mr. Ryan. You've been a great help. The FBI will be contacting you as well, I'm sure."

"Glad to be of service, Ms. Jackson." The dispatcher paused, then said, "I checked your firm out after your call earlier today. Thank you for helping the FBI in combating crime. Good luck." Ryan ended the call.

Louise returned to the conference room. All the faces stared at her in anticipation. She let out a deep breath and said, "We've got them!"

CHAPTER 22

THE STAKEOUT

The end of Jones' shift was finally approaching, and he looked forward to returning home to his wife, Lynette. She would be serving him fried chicken breasts tonight. His favorite. His mouth watered at the thought.

The crackle of his radio interrupted Jones's daydream. "This is Captain Ambrose, Jones. I need you to drive over to North Broadway and Wright St., pronto."

Jones took a moment to digest the instructions, then said, "But, Captain, my shift is over in ten minutes."

"So is mine and that of the four other patrol officers who are hauling ass to that address right now. This is an emergency, Jones!"

"An emergency?"

"Those fugitives from Pershing Place are hiding in a warehouse at the corner of Wright Street and North Broadway. We need to seal the area until SWAT gets there. So hurry!"

"Okay, Captain."

"Now listen, Jones. You'll drive to the Days Inn parking lot on the corner of North 9th and Wright. Call me when you get there. And Jones, no siren, no roof lights."

"Understood, Captain. I'm on my way." *Why do I accept all these dangerous assignments?* Jones berated himself. *I need to learn to say no.*

He called Lynette. "Hi honey. I'm sorry, but I have to work late today."

"Oh. Something's come up?"

"Yes. The Captain needs me on a critical surveillance assignment. Not sure how long it'll take. I'll call when I know more."

"Okay, hon. Keep me posted. I'll keep your chicken warm."

"Love you." He blew a kiss and hung up.

He ached to tell Lynette how dangerous the assignment was, but that would only make matters worse. She would fuss over him, which he enjoyed, but then she'd pressure him to quit and go work for her father in the printing shop. He didn't look forward to having that conversation again.

When Jones reached the Days Inn, he parked as instructed and called Captain Ambrose. "Captain, this is Jones. I'm in the Days Inn parking lot. What should I do now?"

"Finally. Did you walk there?" Ambrose sighed, then said. "Never mind. You see a fence that looks onto the back of the corner warehouse? Go look over the fence and tell me what you see."

Noooo . . . Jones thought. *I'm going to get my head shot off.* He sat, shaking, for a minute, then plucked up his courage, climbed out of the car, and trudged toward the corrugated metal fence, keeping his head low. *There's no way I'm poking my head over that fence,* he thought to himself. He looked for holes in the rusty metal panels, found some, kneeled, and peeked through. He saw an empty backlot and a warehouse wall with a roll-up door and a personnel door. He heard drilling sounds.

A tall, slim man came out of the personnel door, lit a cigarette, and looked around, then leaned back against the wall.

Jones brought up the fugitives' photos on his iPhone. They were hard to focus on because of his shaking hand, but he recognized Larry Schmidt. He looked through the hole again. The man threw his cigarette butt on the ground, squished it with his foot, and returned inside. In a crouching position, Jones ran back to his cruiser, squeezed himself behind the wheel, and called his captain. "This is Jones. I saw one of the fugitives in the back lot. It was Larry Schmidt. Oh, and I heard drilling from inside the warehouse. There has to be at least two of them in there."

"Make that three," Ambrose said. "I saw one posted at the office window when I drove by." Ambrose was silent for a moment, then said, "Position your cruiser in the middle of Wright Street and block off 9th. Two of us are blocking North Broadway in the north and south directions. We have them boxed in like rats. Now we wait for SWAT to arrive. Got that?"

"Yes, Captain."

Jones positioned his cruiser as instructed, then waited. He struggled to control his shaking. He stared at the shotgun sitting upright in its rack. *Would I be safer with that weapon if a firefight breaks out?* he wondered. *I'll crouch behind the car like they do in the movies. That'll be the safest.* Jones climbed out, crouched behind the car, unholstered his Glock, and chambered a round.

CHAPTER 23

THE FBI CAN TASTE VICTORY

Special Agent O'Keefe raced into Special Agent in Charge Hale's office shouting, "We've got them!"

Hale raised her head from the documents on her desk. "Finally some good news. Tell me about it."

"We have the Jennings gang cornered in a warehouse in St. Louis. On North Broadway in the Old North District," O'Keefe said excitedly.

"Is the entire gang in there?"

"At least three of them are. The St. Louis police have the place sealed off with three patrol cruisers, and two SWAT teams and a helicopter are on the way."

"That's great news," Hale said, rubbing her hands together excitedly. "How did you find out about the place?"

O'Keefe hesitated, then said, "Reliant did, from bulletproof panels the gang had delivered to that address."

Hale pursed her lips, looked out her floor to ceiling windows, and cursed, "Damn that Reliant group." She turned to face O'Keefe again. "Why are they always one step ahead of us?"

O'Keefe lowered his gaze. "It's that cyber expert, Louise Jackson. Our IT lads are baffled by the capabilities of Jackson's search engines and software."

Hale gazed into the distance, raised a hand to her lips, and said, "Keep that under your hat. I'll report to the Director that we're about to capture most of the Jennings gang today, and I'll skate around who discovered the hideout."

O'Keefe thought, *good luck with that*. Then he said, "I'm monitoring the operation. I expect some fireworks." He turned and raced out of the office.

CHAPTER 24

SWAT STORMS THE WAREHOUSE

The office intercom buzzed with a message to all SWAT officers to report to the briefing room immediately. Alfredo rose from his desk, rushed to the locker room, put on his SWAT gear, grabbed his rifle bag, and made his way to the briefing room. He was nervous. His supervisor had put him on probation and told him the only reason he wasn't fired was the shortage of trained sharpshooters since the latest wave of the pandemic.

The FBI Special Agent who had conducted the briefing on the failed Pershing Place raid stood at the head of auditorium. "Welcome back everyone," he announced. "We have a second opportunity to arrest members of the Jennings gang." He aimed his pointer at a satellite view of Old North St. Louis District. "The St. Louis police have confirmed that at least three of the fugitives are inside a warehouse at 2836 North Broadway." The agent pointed at the building. "Police cruisers are blocking all escape routes." He pointed at the three intersections on the screen. "SWAT team number one will take up position in front of these roll-up doors. Team number two will park their carrier in the Days Inn parking lot opposite the warehouse back lot and cover the back roll-up door and the personnel door." He aimed his pointer at those locations "Team one's sniper will take a position on the roof of the building across the street." He pointed at a building; "Team two's sniper will position himself on the roof of the hotel."

Alfredo prayed he would be positioned on the Days Inn roof. His money was on the fugitives making a run for it through the back lot. He would be able pick them off like plastic ducks in a shooting gallery and erase the blemish on his record of the Pershing Place screw up. He reached for his St. Sebastian medal and kissed it.

The FBI agent surveyed the assembly. "Questions?"

"Are there any civilians in the warehouse?" someone asked. Alfredo squirmed in his seat. He felt like everyone's eyes were staring at him.

The special agent said, "The thermal imaging shows three warm bodies inside the warehouse. We believe they are three fugitives. The St. Louis police will prevent any civilians from entering the warehouse in the meantime." He brought up the photos of the Jennings gang on the screen. "Remember. These men are Marine veterans and heavily armed. Expect strong resistance."

The agent surveyed the audience. No further questions came. "Let's go get them, guys!"

The SWAT members filed out of the room and jogged to their assigned BearCats. The captain of team one waved Alfredo over. "You're with me."

Noooo, Alfredo groaned inwardly. Dispirited, he followed the team captain into the personnel carrier.

The BearCat pulled up in front of the warehouse's roll-up doors, and the team jumped out and took cover behind the vehicle. The captain looked at Dale, the most experienced sniper in the group, and pointed at the building across the street. Dale nodded and took off, followed by his spotter.

The captain turned to Alfredo and a teammate called Marco and pointed at the warehouse roof. "You two will drop teargas canisters down the roof access panel." He turned to Alfredo. "Then you'll cover the back lot."

Marco grabbed an extension ladder from the carrier, ran to the wall of the warehouse, and leaned the ladder against it. He rushed back to the BearCat, grabbed a crowbar, a block of wood, some small blocks of plastic explosives, and ran back to the ladder.

Alfredo stood, mouth agape, as if frozen in place. The captain poked him sharply in the chest. "Agent Russo. I gave you an order."

Alfredo started, as if awakened from a bad dream. He reached for his sniper rifle, slipped the strap over his shoulder, picked up three canisters of teargas, and ran to Marco's side.

Once on the roof, Alfredo walked to the edge and peered at the back lot. The angle was all wrong. His tripod would be useless. He would have to stand by the edge and shoot down at the fugitives. *This'll be a turkey shoot.* He grimaced at the idea.

Marco had been prying at the roof access panel with a crowbar, but the panel wouldn't budge. He placed plastic explosives around the underside of the lip of the panel.

A shotgun blast echoed from the street below, followed by the shattering of glass. Team one had fired tear gas canisters through the warehouse windows.

A loud scraping sound caught Alfredo's attention. It came from the far end of the roof. A piece of roof tilted up and a head, covered with a gas mask, appeared through the opening. The masked apparition lobbed two hand grenades in Alfredo's direction. They rolled to about five feet from him. Alfredo lunged forward, grabbed one grenade, and threw it over the edge of the roof, but when he grabbed the second he fumbled it. It dropped at his feet. He reached to grab it again. The device exploded.

Earlier that afternoon, Steve had been watching the street from the front office window and fighting drowsiness. The constant whine from the drilling, as Larry and Malcolm assembled the fiberglass panels, wasn't helping.

The sun's reflection on the windows made it hard for Steve to see the street clearly. He stepped out the entrance door for some fresh air and a better look around and spotted the police cruiser blocking North Broadway at the Wright Street intersection. "Damn," he swore. He turned around, looked south, and saw another cruiser blocking North Broadway at St. Louis Avenue. He raced back into the warehouse and shouted, "The police are here!"

Malcolm and Larry had just finished assembling the last panel on the turtle. Malcolm waved Steve over. "Help Larry finish up here." Then he ran to the front office and returned a moment later. "The police have all the streets blocked. SWAT teams can't be far behind. All we can do is get the turtle in place fast and make a run for it."

Running to the overhead hoist, Steve raised the turtle. Larry drove the van underneath it. Steve lowered the shell until it rested on the roof of the van. The vehicle's suspension creaked loudly as the van's body sank lower to the ground, but the tires and the suspension held. Steve unhooked the lifting chains.

The roar of a large diesel engine resonated from the street. Malcolm ran to the closest window. "SWAT are here!" he shouted.

The blasts of shotguns and shattering of glass panes followed. Canisters rolled onto the floor from above, gray smoke hissing from them. Malcolm ran to the lunchroom and returned with gas masks. The men fitted the masks onto their faces.

Steve raced up to the roof using the access ladder, raised the small panel he had cut into the roof earlier, and peeked through the opening. When he saw two SWAT officers, he retrieved two hand grenades from his jacket, removed the safety clip on one, pulled the pin, and lobbed it onto the roof. He armed and lobbed the second grenade before slipping down the ladder.

A grenade exploded in the backlot, followed closely by an explosion on the roof. A cloud of dust and rust rained down on the men.

Steve ran through the smoke and reached the turtle. He opened a hinged panel that covered the passenger door and climbed into the bench seat.

Malcolm was at the rear roll-up door. He pressed the door switch, ran to the van, climbed in, and pulled the armored panel closed. It latched into place.

The men removed their gas masks. Larry looked out from a slot he had cut into the armored panel that covered the windshield and floored the accelerator. The engine roared, and the van lumbered into the back lot.

SWAT officers, who had lined up behind the back fence, peppered the turtle with bullets from their automatic weapons as Larry veered right and headed for the fence facing Wright Street. A bullet slipped through the slot in the front panel, pierced the windshield, and burrowed into the bench seat, missing Steve by an inch, but some bullet fragments nicked Larry's neck and shoulder.

"Are you hurt?" Malcolm asked as he saw beads of blood forming on his comrade's neck.

"Yes, but I don't think I'll stop and tend to that now," Larry spat jokingly between gritted teeth.

When the van struck the precut panel in the fence, the plastic ties broke and the panel flattened against the ground. The van ran over the panel and lurched into Wright Street. The tires were in shreds by now, and the bare rims sent sparks flying into the air.

The SWAT officers and the policemen rushed to reposition themselves along Wright Street and opened fire at the turtle again from there.

Larry had cut slots in the panels on both sides of the turtle. The men lowered their windows, slipped the barrels of their pistols through the slots and returned fire, pinning the SWAT and police officers behind their vehicles. But one officer advanced, protected behind a ballistic shield, and threw a grenade underneath the van. The grenade overshot and exploded on the far side of the vehicle, spraying shrapnel in the direction of the officers on that side.

The turtle climbed over the curb on the far side of Wright Street and punched through the precut panel in that fence. Larry stopped the van halfway through the opening, and the three men exited through the passenger door.

Steve shouted to his teammates, "Run guys! I'm blowing C-4."

A detonation cracked through the air at ear-splitting volume as a ball of fire shot twenty feet into the air. Fiberglass panels and ripped metal pieces flew in all directions. A cloud of black smoke hung over the vehicle and the fence line.

The men backed toward their escape vehicle, firing shots at the fence line. Malcolm reached the vehicle first and climbed behind the wheel, Larry slipped into the front passenger seat while Steve jumped onto the bench seat. Malcolm floored the accelerator and steered the van toward a parking lot adjacent to the abandoned lot. He barreled through the parking lot and exited onto Palm Street, shot down that street, reached Branch Street, kept the pedal to the floor, and thundered in the direction of the underpass at I-70.

As they reached the halfway in the underpass, Larry shouted, "Stop!"

Malcolm slammed on the brakes and turned to Larry. "Why?"

"We have a plan."

Larry and Steve jumped out and ran back to the entrance to the underpass. A large forklift and a 53-foot semitrailer sat on the corner lot. Larry climbed aboard the forklift, started the engine, maneuvered the forks underneath the semitrailer, lifted it, and backed up into the underpass. He lowered the semi crosswise on the roadway, blocking traffic in both directions.

As Larry was dismounting the forklift, the growl of a BearCat and the screech of heavy brakes reverberated against the concrete walls of the underpass. Steve threw three smoke grenades underneath the semi. The underpass filled with white smoke. Steve and Larry ran back to the van. Malcolm floored the accelerator pedal, and the vehicle burst out the far side of the underpass into open city streets.

They had barely covered two city blocks when the *wop wop* of a helicopter filled the air.

CHAPTER 25

THE ESCAPE

Malcolm turned to Larry. "Let Gerta know what's happening." Larry placed the call and turned the speaker on. "It's Larry. A SWAT team has stormed the warehouse. We're on the run in the escape van."

"Is everyone okay?" Gerta asked.

"We're all fine. We're heading for the garage at Barnes Hospital."

"Okay. Tom has parked the new van the in the Children's Hospital parking garage."

Gerta was silent for a moment. "Is that a helicopter I hear in the background?"

"Yes. There's one whirling overhead."

"Do you have a police scanner in the car?" Gerta asked.

"No, I forgot about that," Larry said, embarrassed.

"I have the app on my phone. I'll keep you informed. Stay on the line."

The *wop wop* of the helicopter grew louder, as their van crossed St. Louis Ave. Malcolm looked left and saw a BearCat barreling in his direction about a block away.

Gerta's voice came on the line. "There's a BearCat heading up St. Louis to intercept you."

"I just saw it. He's tailing us now," Malcolm said.

"There's another BearCat in play. This second one has instructions to intercept you on Cass Avenue."

Malcolm looked in his rearview mirror. The BearCat accelerated and bumped the van. *They'll be firing at us any minute now,* Malcolm thought. *We have to lose them somehow.*

He made a sharp left onto Howard Street, but the BearCat kept up with him. He made a sharp right onto 197th. The BearCat caught up this time and bumped the van again. Malcolm looked up in his rearview mirror and saw the black helmet of an officer appear on the top of the BearCat. *They're setting up an automatic weapon!*

Through gaps between buildings, he saw the second BearCat barreling up Cass. Swiftly, he mentally calculated the relative speeds of the BearCat and his own vehicle and hatched a desperate plan. He kept the pedal to the floor.

As Malcolm hurtled the van through the intersection at Cass Avenue, the BearCat coming up Cass clipped the rear end of the van and sent it whirling across the intersection. This was followed by a deafening sound of crushed metal as the two armored vehicles rammed each other.

Malcolm's van crashed, grille first, against a lamppost. The airbags deployed and deflated instantly. Steam belched out from the radiator.

He turned to his companions. "Everyone okay?"

"Couldn't be better," Steve answered.

"I'm good," Larry said, "but our van isn't." He pointed at the front hood damage and the radiator leak.

"What happened?" Gerta asked over the speaker.

"We shook off the BearCats," Malcolm answered. "But our van won't make it far." He considered the situation and made a snap decision. "Change of plan. We're heading for the speakeasy on Olive St. Get Tom to send his maps of the caves to my phone."

Gerta was quiet for a moment, then said, "Will do. Then I'll have Tom drive the van to the Lemp Brewery and wait for you there."

"Good." Malcolm backed up the van and steered along side streets in the direction of Olive Street. Steam hissed from the radiator and the engine began to knock. At the corner of Olive and Tenth, he lumbered into a parking lot. The men jumped out. Steve ran to the back of the van, retrieved the gun bag, and handed it to Larry. He grabbed six grenades and stuffed them into his pockets.

"Bring the bag with the caving gear," Malcolm said. Steve found the bag and pulled it out of the van.

Malcolm's phone dinged. Tom's maps had arrived. He looked around to get his bearings, then ran down the service alley that led to the rear of the speakeasy. Steve and Larry followed.

A deafening roar filled the air. The police helicopter whirled above the alley, hovered overhead for a moment, picked up altitude, and left.

Malcolm found the rear entrance. The label on a solid black steel door read 'The Speakeasy Bar & Grill.' He pointed to a camera mounted over the door. Larry and Steve hugged the wall, out of sight. Malcolm pressed the call button. A half-minute later a voice squawked back, "Yes?"

"Federal Express delivery."

The door opened. Malcolm rushed inside and bumped into a tall middle-aged man dressed in black. The man held his ground. Malcolm took a step back and asked, "Are you the manager?"

"Yes, but you're not Federal Express," the man replied in a steely voice. "And the bar is closed. We don't open until 9 p.m. No exceptions."

The roar of a BearCat engine echoed down the alley. Larry and Steve rushed inside, and Larry closed the door behind him and set the lock. "One of the BearCats is still operational," he said.

The men and their duffel bags crowded the manager back into the hallway. Malcolm raised his pistol to the man's chest. "Is there anyone else in here?"

The manager stared at the pistol, swallowed hard, then said, "The staff doesn't arrive until seven. There's no money in the tills."

Malcolm stared at the man, "We need access to the underground caves."

The manager stared at him, eyebrows raised. "Nobody's been down those caves for decades. I don't even know if the door will open. Why do you want to go in there anyway?"

"Take us there."

The man looked at the pistol and nodded. He turned, led the way to the basement, and stopped at a large, dark cedar door wet with condensation. The door was wide enough to roll beer barrels through. A large brass skeleton key hung from a hook on the doorframe. The manager picked it up, examined it, then inserted it in the keyhole. He tried turning the key counterclockwise, but the lock didn't budge. He tried clockwise but met with the same result. He turned to Malcolm and shook his head.

Malcolm waved him aside. He kicked the door close to the latch as hard as he could three times, then turned the key while pulling and pushing on the handle. The door creaked and opened to reveal a dark tunnel. A wave of cold, humid air flowed out the opening. Malcolm flicked a switch by the doorframe, and a series of bare light bulbs illuminated the tunnel.

"I'll be damned," the manager said.

"Is there a storage room on this level?" Malcolm asked.

"Yes," the manager answered. "Why?"

"Take me to it."

The man led Malcolm down the hallway and stopped in front of a door. Malcolm jerked his head toward the door. The manager hesitated, glanced at Malcolm's pistol again, selected another key, and opened the door onto a large room packed with cases of beer and boxes of liquor.

Malcolm extended his free hand. "The keys and your cellphone." The man handed them over, and Malcolm jerked his head to indicate the room. When the man entered the room, Malcolm slammed the door closed and locked it. He returned to the tunnel entrance, where Larry and Steve had retrieved rubber boots, jackets, gloves, hats, and flashlights from Tom's duffle bag and laid them out on the ground. They put on the caving gear, grabbed their duffel bags, and entered the tunnel. Malcolm locked the door behind them.

The team followed a level concrete floor for about five hundred feet until the lighting fixtures ended and the tunnel went dark. They turned on their flashlights and faced a large cavern that must have been the lagering room of a brewery. The cavern had a lot of exits.

Malcolm took out his cellphone and brought up Tom's maps. He enlarged the image on the screen with his fingers, but it was still difficult to read. "I'm not clear about which way to go, and my fingers are freezing already."

Loud banging resonated from the tunnel. There was silence, then a small explosion followed.

"Fuck! SWAT must have blown the door open," Steve said.

"We can't stay here. We have to take our chances." Malcolm looked around at the different exits, then pointed at one. "I *think* it's that way."

Steve ran back into the tunnel, retrieved a smoke grenade from his pocket, armed it, and threw it down the tunnel. It exploded, and white smoke belched out of the opening.

Malcolm stopped at the entrance to a tunnel that was half full of sand and mud. Larry and Steve stood beside him.

"Shit," Steve said. "This is where we get to experience how moles live."

Larry turned to Malcolm. "I hope you're right about this."

The sound of men shuffling and running sounded from the cave behind them. Malcolm stared at the tunnel. "We either reenact Custer's Last Stand or we crawl through that tunnel."

"I favor the skedaddle maneuver," Steve said. Larry nodded.

Malcolm led the way. He climbed up a slope of sand and mud and crawled into the tunnel on hands and knees, holding his flashlight in one hand, pointing forward. Larry and Steve followed, dragging the duffel bags behind them.

The men reached the end of the mud tunnel and emerged into a huge, abandoned lager room. This one had three exits. Malcolm pulled out his cellphone. It was wet. "Damn. My phone got soaked," he groaned. The screen refused to light up. He tried powering the phone on and off without success.

Steve found some cloths in his duffel bag and he wiped the phone dry. It still wouldn't light up. He looked up at Malcolm. "We're fucked."

The men sat down, despondent, shivering. "We can't wait for the phone to dry out," Malcolm said. We'll have to take our chances with choosing an exit before the flashlights die out."

The men stood up and looked at the three possible exits. Suddenly they heard a dog bark, then the beam from a flashlight appeared from one of the exits. The light beam moved closer and the sound of the barks grew louder.

"There you are!" came the welcome voice of Tom as he passed his flashlight over his three dirty, shivering comrades. Lucky was jumping around and yapping excitedly.

When Tom had learned of the change of plan, he had called Fred Fischer at the Lemp Brewery Business Park at once.

"Fischer here."

"Hi, Mr. Fischer. This is Tom Devin. I need to go down to the Lemp Cave again."

"Oh. Another wager?" he chuckled. "When do you want to go down? Will you be by yourself again?"

"I need to go down right now, and this time I'll bring my dog."

"Whoa! This is short notice. My shift is over and I'm on Miller time. Call me tomorrow."

"It can't wait till tomorrow. It must be right now. I can compensate you for the trouble. How about $2,000 like last time?"

Fischer was silent for a moment, then said, "Be at the Fermenting Department door in a half hour and bring $3,000." He hung up.

Malcolm. Larry, and Steve hugged Tom in turn. Tom took a step back and stared at the men. "Did I look this miserable when *I* came out of the caves?"

In no mood for jokes, Malcolm said, "Let's just get the hell out of here. You lead the way."

Half an hour later, the men reached the stairs to the brewery subbasement. Tom banged hard on the locked door. Nobody answered. He looked at his cellphone. He had reception. He dialed Fischer's number.

Ten minutes later, Fischer opened the door, staring in surprise as the group filed out. "Jesus. Where did you guys come from?"

Tom answered for the team. "My friends entered at Uhrig's Cave."

Fischer gave Tom a puzzled look. "You're a lot cleaner than last time, but I still want my equipment washed before you leave."

"Sure. But I'm not walking under the shower this time."

The men cleaned themselves up with rags that Fischer provided. Tom washed Lucky's paws, then led the men to his van.

When they finally climbed to the second floor and filed into the printing office, Gerta and Danielle greeted them with hugs. The women served hot cup-a-soup to the men and a dog biscuit to Lucky.

The SWAT team had retreated from the tunnel when Steve had lobbed smoke grenades at them, retrieved gas masks from the BearCats, and returned to the chase. They advanced cautiously through the white smoke, expecting to be met with gunfire or, worse, frag grenades. When they got to the cavern, they followed the fugitives' tracks and eventually reached the tunnel entrance half-filled with sand and mud, where they stopped and stared at the imprints of hands and knees leading up into the dark opening.

Their team captain arrived. "What are you guys waiting for?"

One officer stepped forward. "Captain. These guys have automatic weapons and grenades. It would be suicide to crawl down this rat hole on hands and knees."

The captain looked at the rest of his team. All stood erect, facing forward, their faces expressionless. He got the message. "All right. Let's regroup at our vehicles." He pointed at two men. "Stan and Luigi, you stay behind and stand guard."

The SWAT team filed out of the cave, heads hung low.

Captain Ambrose's cruiser skidded to a stop in front of the Fermenting Department entrance door at the old Lemp Brewery. He and a patrol officer raced to the door and tried the handle. It was locked. He struck the door three times with his fist. Nobody came. He returned to the cruiser and called the number he had been given for the lead hand at the business park.

"Fischer here."

"This is Captain Ambrose with the St. Louis Police Department. I understand you're in charge of escorting visitors though the Lemp Cavern?"

"Yes. I lead groups to the entrance to the cave in the brewery's subbasement, but I don't escort them underground. They have to hire a professional guide for that. Do you need access to the cavern?"

"No. I need to know if a group of men exited the caves earlier today."

"As a matter of fact, yes. Four men climbed out around 6 p.m. One of them I knew. I let him down the caves yesterday, but the other three, I never saw before. They said they entered through Uhrig's Cave, but I don't think that was true."

"Oh. Why do you say that?"

"They were covered in mud from head to toe. That route is not that dirty."

"I'm sending you some photos over the phone. Could you look at them and call me back immediately?"

"Sure. But what's this about? Some crazy illegal wager?"

"A wager? Why do you say that?"

CHAPTER 26

THE NIGHT AT THE PRINTING OFFICE

Malcolm and his men slogged up the steps to the second floor of Gerta's printing office, Tom with a duffle bag full of clean uniforms. Lucky was first at the door and barked their arrival.

"Thank God you're all safe," Gerta said as she opened the door. She placed a hand on Malcolm's arm. "The news said two police officers were killed?"

Malcolm lowered his gaze and remained silent. Steve stepped forward. "They weren't coming for a social visit."

Gerta noticed the blood on Larry's shirt. "You're hurt?"

"Bullet fragments. They nicked my shoulder."

Gerta turned to Danielle. "Bring me the first aid kit." She guided Larry to the washroom. "Let's go clean those wounds."

Tom had laid the clean uniforms on a table. "I've brought dry clothes for everybody." He put some tables and chairs together while Danielle brought out bread, cold cuts, condiments, and juice.

"I feel civilized again," a cleaned-up Malcolm said. He sat, pensive, waiting until everyone had assembled at the table, then said, "The police will have set up roadblocks on every road out of St. Louis. We'd best spend the night here." Everyone stared back waiting for more instructions. Malcolm looked at Gerta. "How are we for identity papers?"

"I'm finished except for printing them. Danielle and Tom will help me with that." She turned to Danielle, who nodded back.

Malcolm stared into the distance for a moment, then said, "We'll leave early tomorrow and try to blend in with the morning traffic."

Larry raised his hand. "We need to cross the Mississippi to reach New York City. The cops will have roadblocks on all the bridges, guaranteed."

Malcolm considered this, then said, "We'll drive south and cross at Nashville. That's a ten hour drive from here. We should be all right."

They all looked at each other and nodded in agreement. Larry spoke next. "I suggest we leave the Jeep behind. It's more conspicuous than the vans."

Malcolm gave the matter some thought. "Okay." He looked up at the group. "Any other suggestions?"

"When will we reach New York City?" Larry asked.

Malcolm turned to Steve. "Can you put together an itinerary?" Steve nodded.

Larry stood up. "I'll go transfer everything from the Jeep into the vans." He signaled for Steve to follow him.

"Good idea," Malcolm said. "Make sure the insides of the two vans look like an electrical contractor's vehicle," he called after them. "And divide the weapons equally. If we lose one van, we'll still be able to complete the job."

Remembering the van abandoned at the Detroit border, Danielle elbowed Steve, who reddened.

"We need to label those vans," Gerta said. She looked up at Tom and Danielle. "I'll need your help to print labels."

Malcolm sat, pensive, then looked up at Gerta. "How do you figure the FBI located the warehouse?"

"It had to have been a transaction that contained the warehouse's address," Gerta replied. She furrowed her brows. "The delivery of the armored panels?"

"Right. But that would have been a long shot, wouldn't it? Hundreds of thousands of transactions to sift through, looking for key words."

"Louise Jackson, at Reliant, has the search engines to do that," Gerta said.

"In that case, our business number, credit cards, and vehicle registrations must be blown too."

Gerta nodded. "I need to produce new ones before we leave tomorrow." She turned to Danielle and Tom. "We'll be burning the midnight oil."

"Anything the rest of us can do to help?" Malcolm asked.

"Label the vans. Trace escape routes to Nashville. Prepare an itinerary to get us to New York City." Gerta said. She rose, walked over to Malcolm. "I'm glad we're all safe. My prayers have been answered so far." She kissed him.

CHAPTER 27

THE FBI REGROUPS

O'Keefe sat facing Hale for his second dressing down in less than a week.

"Agent O'Keefe, help me explain to the Director, how it is that after two full SWAT teams cornered three fugitives in a warehouse, two of our officers are dead, four are injured, and the criminals got away scot-free. I think I can keep a lid on our two BearCats ramming each other." Hale waited, but no answer came.

"Jesus Christ!" Hale snapped. "Who was attacking whom?"

O'Keefe squirmed in his chair. "Those three fugitives were heavily armed veteran Marines. They launched smoke and frag grenades at our officers." O'Keefe hesitated, then added, "The St. Louis field office ran the operation."

Hale glared at him. "Oh. Right. That's how I'll explain it. Our St. Louis field office botched the operation, while you and I were observing things from afar."

O'Keefe admired Hale's mastery of the art of sarcasm. He wisely refrained from commenting.

Hale pursed her lips, then said, "How is it, again, that Reliant discovered the hideout before we did?"

"Their search engines are better than ours."

"Impressive," Hale sneered. "That explains why a private detective agency has outperformed us. I'll be sure to tell the Director."

O'Keefe had no good answer to that, so he wisely kept his mouth shut.

"Do we have *any* idea where the Jennings are now?" Hale demanded.

"They were last seen at the Lemp Brewery Business Park two hours after the raid. A park attendant helped the three guys from the warehouse, plus the kid, Tom Cole, exit from the Lemp cavern. They left in a white Chevy cargo van."

"And . . . ?"

"The St. Louis police have set up roadblocks on all the major highways leaving the city, but they don't have the manpower to cover every street and side road." Seeing Hale's frustration, he added, "We have two choppers in the air, and we've alerted all the regional police departments. But there's been no sign of them so far."

"So the Jennings may still be hiding in St. Louis?"

"Most likely. We have the local news networks broadcasting their photos. They'll have to get on the move soon or risk being seen. That's when our highway surveillance will catch them."

Hale crossed her fingers, brought her hands to her chin, and sat deep in thought.

"There's more," O'Keefe said.

"Oh?"

"Reliant are convinced that the Jennings are targeting their client, Michael Tyler, another CEO, for their next assassination. Someone has downloaded building plans of Tyler's mansion in Long Island and his office tower in New York City. Reliant believes the Jennings will attack Tyler within a week or two. They've shared their findings with our New York City field office."

"Damn Reliant. One step ahead of us again."

Hale leaned back in her chair and swivelled toward the floor to ceiling windows. "Tyler will be bragging to the Director that his pet detective agency is better at protecting him than the FBI. That doesn't bode well for you and me."

O'Keefe correctly deduced that remaining silent was still the best policy.

Hale turned toward him again. "How do we get ahead of Reliant for a change?"

"I'll fly to the New York field office and coordinate the manhunt from there. I'll have our team set up a trap to catch them."

"Good!" Hale stared hard at O'Keefe. "We *need* to capture those fugitives. *Both* of us. Understood?"

"Message received." O'Keefe hesitated, then said, "If I fly to New York on the executive jet, it'll be faster."

Hale stared back blankly at him.

"Just a thought." O'Keefe rose, red-faced, and left.

CHAPTER 28

THE DRIVE TO NASHVILLE

Malcolm was first to rise. It was 5:30 a.m. He had slept on makeshift bedding: pieces of clothing and cushions spread on the floor. So had everyone else. He showered and washed with the supplies Gerta had purchased, marveling at Gerta's planning skills. *How did I ever convince this woman to team up with me?*

He cleared a section of the floor and performed his stretching and muscle-building exercises. Besides keeping him fit, the daily routine helped him cut back on painkillers and stay mentally sharp.

Steve had been keeping watch from the building lobby. The others rose at 6 a.m. and took turns in the two washrooms.

Gerta and Danielle made coffee and placed mugs and pastries on the table. After everyone had stuffed their belongings into duffle bags and piled them by the door, the team assembled around the table.

"Gerta, Danielle, Tom, and I," Malcolm announced, "will ride in one van. Steve and Larry will ride in the other." He turned to Gerta. "You have the new IDs for us?"

Gerta handed a package to each teammate. "These are your new identity documents and a bio to match." She waited until everyone had leafed through the documents, then added, "We work for a fiber optics contractor out of Kansas City, name and address in your handouts. If questioned, we are reporting to a job site in Nashville. That name and address are included as well."

Danielle turned to Steve. "Remember. This time we are electronic technicians, not plumbers." Danielle was teasing Steve about having mixed up their professions when crossing the border in Detroit a week earlier, forcing him and Danielle to escape on foot through Detroit side streets. That Malcolm had managed to pick them up later hadn't made it less scary.

"Will I ever live that down?" Steve asked.

"Never," Larry said as he threw a friendly punch to Steve's shoulder.

Danielle stood up. "I'll bring Tom his documents." Tom had relieved Steve on watch duty.

Malcolm turned to Larry. "Have you prepared a route for us?"

Larry nodded, then opened a road map on the table. "I suggest we split up and follow these roads out of the city." He ran his finger along the proposed routes.

Malcolm studied the map. "I agree." He looked up at his team. "Let's get a move on."

They picked up their duffle bags and satchels and exited the office. Tom ran back for his belongings and picked up Lucky's supplies.

The team members climbed into their assigned vans, whose labels now read 'Advanced Fiber Optics.'

At Chippewa Street, Malcolm turned north, and Steve south to cross the River Des Peres Channel and the Meramec River over separate bridges. They met no roadblocks. *The police forces are thin on the ground,* Malcolm thought. *We have the pandemic to thank for that.*

Malcolm's van emerged from the St. Louis suburbs and followed Highway 6 south. As it approached the city of Barnhart, the traffic grew heavy, then stopped.

"Shit!" Gerta said. "Roadblock ahead."

"I'll turn around," Malcolm said.

"No, don't," Gerta said as she put a hand on his arm. She studied the GPS screen. "There are no side roads for miles. If we turn around now, we'll just draw attention to ourselves." She pointed a finger skyward. The distant *wop wop* of a helicopter reached their ears. "Keep going. I've got a plan."

"What plan?"

"I'll explain in a minute." She called Larry as Malcolm listened anxiously. "There's a roadblock on Highway 6, a few miles north of Barnhart, and we can't avoid it . . . No . . . Yes . . . Let's follow our plan." Gerta hung up and turned to Malcolm. "They're far behind us. They can divert to Highway 21 without drawing attention to themselves."

"Good. But what's *our* plan?"

"In a minute. I need to do this first." Gerta reached for the satchel with the signal jammer and tucked it under her knees. She opened it and made sure she could slip a hand inside and reach the switch easily. She then returned to her cellphone and punched frantically at the keys.

Malcolm looked in the rearview mirror. Tom and Danielle stared back, anxious. Beads of sweat covered Tom's forehead. Lucky sat between the two, and no doubt sensing the anxiety in the air, he reached over and licked Tom's cheek.

Malcolm locked eyes with Tom. "You're carrying? You have a spare magazine in your jacket?" Tom nodded. Malcolm looked at Danielle. She nodded back.

As they approached the roadblock, Gerta switched the jammer on and off at regular intervals. As they reached the roadblock, a large police officer, in a blue uniform, grey felt hat, and a black ballistic vest waved them to stop. He leaned in the open window and looked across at Gerta, then back at Tom and Danielle. "I need everyone's ID and the vehicle registration and insurance certificates."

Malcolm passed over the documents, and the officer passed them to a slim companion with a computer tablet who compared each document with a display of photographs on his tablet.

"Shit. Not again," the slim cop muttered. He switched the tablet on and off, then swore again and turned to his partner. "I've lost the signal *again*."

The large officer cursed. "We haven't got time for this," he groaned, then turned to Malcolm. "Where are you folks from?"

"Kansas City," Malcolm answered. This matched the documents he had given the officer.

"Where are you headed?"

"Nashville."

"What's your business in Nashville?"

"Installing fiber optic cabling and equipment at Denso Manufacturing."

The officer tipped his head toward the back of the van. "Please unlock the rear doors." Malcolm obliged. The officer walked to the back of the van, opened one rear door, and looked inside. He closed the door and returned to Malcolm's window. "Who are you reporting to at Denso?" Malcolm handed over a Denso business card.

The officer passed the card over to his sidekick. "Can you call this number?"

"Not if the signal is down." The slim officer pulled out his cellphone. "Oh. It's working." He dialed the number and put the phone on speaker for his teammate to hear. Larry's voice came on. "Denso Manufacturing. How may I direct your call?" The slim officer read from the business card. "Engineering Manager Danny Lamont, please."

"One moment, please," Larry said. After an interval he said, "Mr. Lamont is out at the moment. Would you like to leave a message on his voicemail?"

The slim officer looked up at his colleague. The large officer studied the long vehicle lineup, then shook his head. He handed the documents back to Malcolm. "Drive safely."

Malcolm drove on, checking the rearview mirror. Tom and Danielle were letting out a deep breath. Turning to Gerta, he said, "That was quite the performance. And it involved more planning than just prayers."

Gerta had found a Kleenex and was wiping her forehead. She looked up at Malcolm and smiled. "Delayed reaction."

Malcolm let a moment pass, then asked, "The officer was using his tablet to compare the photos on our documents with the photos on the FBI Most Wanted Fugitives website, wasn't he? That's why you were blocking the cell signal?"

"That's what I was counting on, but I couldn't be sure."

Malcolm mulled this over, then said, "Okay. And what about Larry answering the call to Denso Manufacturing?"

"The phone number on the fake Denso business card rings my cell phone. I call-forwarded the number to Larry's phone as we approached the roadblock."

"But how did Larry know to answer the call?"

"We rehearsed it last night."

"Have I been demoted to a 'need-to-know' basis?" Malcolm asked. He reached over and kissed Gerta on the cheek. "You are amazing!"

Gerta smiled and said, "Let's call Larry and compliment him on his performance." She put her phone on speaker as everyone cheered Larry for his switchboard answering skills.

After the excitement had abated, Danielle leaned back in her seat and said, "I think I've had enough excitement for one day." She rested one hand on Tom's knee. Lucky licked her hand.

"That goes for me too," Tom said. He reached for a Kleenex and wiped his forehead.

It was noon when the two vans crossed the Mississippi river and entered the state of Tennessee. Nashville was another four hours away. Steve had booked three rooms at the Days Inn on the outskirts of the city. They stopped at the Flying J Travel Center in Fairview and filled the vans with gas. Steve suggested they stop for dinner at a Dennys before checking into the hotel.

"It's too risky," Malcolm said. "We'll order takeout from the hotel room." Steve made a pouty face. Malcolm added, with a mischievous smile, "You can order whatever you like. Cost is no issue."

Steve raised his head, pursed his lips, then said, "Alright, but I'm ordering from Denny's."

When the vans parked at the Days Inn Malcolm nodded to Danielle. She walked to the office to check the group in and returned with keys to three rooms. Steve and Larry picked one room, Tom and Danielle another, and Malcolm and Gerta chose the one with a suite.

"Once you've settled in, let's meet in my room. We'll order takeout and eat together," Malcolm said.

Everyone carried their overnight bags to their respective rooms, then assembled in Malcolm and Gerta's suite. Larry had carried in a duffel bag with weapons.

Danielle took everyone's order from Denny's website, and placed the order with Uber Eats. She met the delivery man at the door, accepted the bags of warm food, tipped him, and closed the door. Steve walked over and took the bags to a coffee table. He placed the containers carefully on the coffee table; grilled chicken, garlic butter, chicken skillet, slow cooked pot roast, and country-fried steak. He raised his head. "There'll be leftovers for tomorrow's long drive."

Tom kept guard by the window and ate standing up. He shared his food with Lucky, who stood by his side.

Malcolm addressed the group, "It should be clear sailing all the way to New York City." He gave Gerta's hand a light squeeze. "Thank you for getting us safely through that roadblock." Then he turned to Larry. "And thank you for the superb handling of that call."

Steve raised his hand. "No need to thank *me*, but I prepared an escape plan in case things went sideways at the roadblock."

Malcolm turned to Steve. "Did your plan involve running the roadblock, blocking our escape by setting our van on fire, and cutting through the fields to be picked up by you and Larry?" Malcolm asked with a smile.

"That joke is getting old," Steve said. He sat down, pouting. Larry wrapped an arm around Steve's shoulders and gave him a squeeze.

"I just thank heaven we avoided a bloodbath," Gerta said.

"Whoa," Malcolm said as he faced Gerta, "You must think we're a bunch of violent criminals."

"Well, aren't we?" Gerta said. There was a pause before everyone burst out laughing. Lucky let out a yap.

Once the laughter stopped, Gerta announced, "Danielle and I will bunk together tonight and work on our research." Danielle sent Tom a sad face.

"Good plan," said Malcolm

"Where will we be staying in New York?" Larry asked.

Steve perked up. "I've booked three suites at the Candlewood in Secaucus, New Jersey."

"Why New Jersey? It would be more fun in Manhattan," Larry said.

"Maybe, but the hotel in Secaucus gives us a lot more escape routes if we have to make a run for it," Steve replied.

"Good thinking, Steve," Malcolm said. He turned to Gerta. "You've had a look at the hotel facilities?"

"Yes," Gerta said. "The suites come with a kitchen counter and a living room. We can work and take our meals in privacy. The Wi-Fi should be adequate. It's a good choice."

"Well done, Steve," Malcolm said.

Once they finished eating, the men returned to their rooms. Malcolm looked at Gerta and said, "I hope our luck holds."

CHAPTER 29

THE BLUEBIRD CAFÉ

Steve looked up the evening attractions in Nashville. To his disappointment, the Grand Ole Opry was closed on weekdays, and this was a Monday. Steve would have preferred jazz, but Nashville being the mecca of country music, when in Rome . . .

From the list of local nightclubs, the Bluebird Café caught his interest.

"Isn't it too risky showing your face in public?" Larry asked.

"I don't think so. I'll wear my cap and eyeglasses, and with my three-day stubble, nobody'll recognize me in a nightclub with low lighting. But if I get caught, I promise not to give away your location, even under torture." Steve's face lit up with a mischievous smile.

Larry shook his head. "You like living dangerously, don't you?"

"Do you know of a more exciting way to live?"

Steve walked over to Malcolm's room. Larry followed close behind. Malcolm was sitting in an armchair studying a document, while Gerta and Danielle sat at their laptops. Steve told Malcolm his plans for the evening.

"You like tempting fate, don't you," Malcolm said with narrowed eyebrows.

"I don't like it," Larry said. "If he gets spotted, it'll jeopardize our whole project."

"If I'm caught, I can be trusted to keep my mouth shut," Steve protested.

"The police could follow you here without your knowledge," Larry said.

"I can tell when someone is tailing me."

Malcolm was silent. Finally, he said, "You've proven yourself to me in the past, Steve. I trust you." He tapped Steve on the shoulder. "Enjoy yourself."

As Steve walked to the door, Malcolm called after him, "Remember, we're leaving at 0600 tomorrow morning."

Larry followed Steve but turned at the door to look back at Malcolm. "I don't like this," he said.

After the two men had left, Gerta turned to Malcolm and gave him a questioning look.

Malcolm bit his lip. "Steve has good instincts, and he can handle himself. I trust him to never compromise the team." Gerta just nodded and returned to her laptop.

Steve headed downtown and soon located the Bluebird Café. Its unpretentious facade stood at the end of a strip mall. Steve drove past the strip mall for three long blocks, then parked at a Walgreens, and walked back to the Bluebird.

Steve felt a buzz of excitement as he approached the iconic venue. He had read that Garth Brooks and Taylor Swift had made their debut here. He adjusted his cap and eyeglasses and walked in.

The café was almost empty. The dark polished wood tables and chairs shone despite the low lighting. He walked by a large picture frame filled with autographed photos of artists whose names he recognized. He continued to the end of the room and reached the bar. A hallway stood to the left of the bar. A red fire exit fixture hung from the ceiling and an arrow sign read 'Restrooms.' Steve walked to the end of the hallway, past the washroom doors, and faced a red fire exit door. *It must exit to the rear of the strip mall,* he decided. Steve turned around and sat at a table near the bar.

A server approached and placed a basket of tortilla chips and a bowl of salsa on the table. "Good evening. What can I get you?"

Steve looked up at the server. "Can you recommend a local beer?"

When she hesitated, he read from a card on the table. "How about a Blackstone Nut Brown Ale?"

"Sure. Anything to eat with that?"

"No. Not just yet. When will the show start?"

"This is Open Mic Night. Local artists will take turns presenting their latest tunes." She jerked her head in the direction of a small stand with a mic and a speaker in the corner of the room. "They'll start any time now." She smiled and left to get Steve's order.

During the next fifteen minutes, the café filled up with music lovers and the aromas of beer and wine. A young, nervous-looking man stepped to the mic and began singing his latest creation.

Steve noticed a man at a nearby table taking furtive glances in his direction. The man looked out of place in his dark blue jacket, gray V-neck sweater, and white shirt and tie. *He must have come straight from the office,* Steve thought. Suddenly the man rose and left the café.

Fernando Lopez, Special Agent in Charge of the FBI field office in Nashville, was relaxing at his home in the suburbs when his cell phone rang.

"Is this Special Agent Lopez? "

"Yes. Who's calling please?"

"This is Detective Brian Kelly with the Nashville Police Department. You may remember me from a job interview three months ago when I was applying to join the Bureau."

"Oh, yes, I remember you. What can I do for you, Detective?"

"I apologize for calling you at home, but I believe this is an emergency."

"What sort of emergency?"

"It's about the memo the St. Louis Field Office sent around asking all departments to be on the lookout for a gang of six fugitives, serial killers. The memo came with photos of the criminals."

"Yes, I read the special alert," Lopez said.

"I've just seen one of those fugitives at the Bluebird Café tonight."

"Are you positive?"

"He's somewhat disguised, with eyeglasses and stubble, but it's the one called Steve Adams, I'm positive."

Lopez asked, "Why did you call me first with this, Detective?"

Kelly hesitated, then said, "Well, to be honest, I don't trust my superiors to report the arrest fairly. They'll take the credit for themselves, and my name won't even be mentioned in the reports. I wanted you to know that I was behind the arrest of this criminal."

"Why me?"

"Because, during my interview, you mentioned I lacked experience in solving crimes and arresting criminals."

Lopez breathed out heavily. "Detective Kelly, get off this line and call this in now!"

"Will do, Special Agent Lopez. Again, I'm sorry to have disturbed you . . . "

But Kelly was speaking into a dead line. "Shit, shit, double fucking shit!" Kelly cursed aloud. That did not go at all the way he had planned.

Immediately after Kelly reported his sighting to the Nashville West district, his commander, Michelle Lokey, came on the line. "Good work, Detective Kelly. I'll dispatch two patrol cruisers immediately to make the arrest, and I'll inform the FBI liaison"

"In the meantime, what do I do?" asked Kelly.

"Go back to the Bluebird and do not let the fugitive out of your sight. When the officers arrive, you'll coordinate the arrest." Commander Lokey paused, then added, "And make sure no bystanders get hurt."

"Understood," Kelly said. He considered for a moment, then said, "But shouldn't we tail the fugitive instead? He'll lead us to—"

The line was dead.

Steve was enjoying himself. The local talent had some original and lively music, the beer was flavourful, and the salsa was smoky and tangy.

The man in the office attire had returned and was sitting at a nearby table. He looked jittery, and kept stealing furtive looks in Steve's direction. *This is not good,* Steve thought. He rose slowly, stared intently at the restroom sign, then proceeded down the hallway. When he reached the fire door, he pushed the panic bar hard and exited the building. An alarm blasted through the café.

Kelly rose and raced down the hallway. He burst out of the exit door and came face-to-face with Steve. He unholstered his Glock and pointed it at Steve's chest. "You're under arrest," he said, but his hand was shaking so badly that he accidentally pulled the trigger. The weapon clicked. Kelly stared wide-eyed at his pistol.

"You forgot to chamber a round," Steve said. He had unholstered his own pistol and was pointing it at Kelly's chest. He pulled the trigger.

The autopsy would reveal that the bullet tore through the right ventricle of Kelly's heart and embedded itself in his spinal cord. Detective Kelly had died instantly.

At that moment, a police cruiser, sirens blaring and lights flashing, turned into the back alley. The vehicle screeched to a halt. The glare from the cruiser's headlights blinded Steve. He turned and ran down the alley. Two officers jumped out of the cruiser. One ran to attend to the fallen detective, and the other gave chase on foot.

Steve sensed that the police officer was gaining on him. He stopped and turned around. The officer stopped too, about thirty yards back, raised his weapon, and fired. And missed. Steve raised his pistol in a two-hand grip, extended and locked his arms, lined the sight with the target's chest, breathed out, and pulled the trigger. The officer wavered and fell to the ground.

A second patrol cruiser was bolting down the alley now, sirens wailing. Steve took off, cutting through an abandoned lot and zigzagging between trees and shrubs. His chest was on fire, but he didn't let up the pace until the sound of the siren grew dim.

Steve took shelter behind a warehouse. He caught his breath, then pulled out his phone and brought up a street map. He studied the map, then called Malcolm.

"Steve? Are you all right?"

"Some dude recognized me in the café and called the cops. I got away, but I'm hiding behind a warehouse."

"Are you hurt?"

"I'm fine, but I can't get back to my van without being seen. Can you send someone to pick me up?"

"I'll send Larry right away. Where are you?"

"Tell him to drive to the Allen Arena, to the passenger drop-off circle. I'll watch out for him."

"He'll be there shortly."

Steve walked at a normal pace to the Allen Arena, following side streets, keeping an eye out for police cars. He recognized Larry's van, idling in the passenger drop-off circle. He walked over and climbed in.

"In a bit of trouble, are we?" Larry said. "Someone recognize you?"

Steve answered with a sheepish grin. "What were the odds?" He consulted the map on his phone. "My van's in the parking lot at Walgreens. Drop me off at the pharmacy entrance. I'll meet you back at the hotel."

Larry stared at Steve. "Malcolm has us packing. We're leaving for New York *now*."

"Uh ho. I'm in deep shit, aren't I?" Steve hung his head and faked contrition.

"Yeah, I think you could say that."

Steve walked into the Walgreen's, pretending to be a customer, then walked out to his van. When he drove into the Days Inn's parking lot, the crew had already packed and were ready to leave. Malcolm took him aside. "What happened at the Bluebird?"

Steve fidgeted as he answered. "Someone recognized me. A police officer in civvies. He had a weapon and tried to arrest me. It did not end well . . . for him." Steve bit his lip.

"Had he called for backup?"

"Yes. Two police cruisers showed up, but I got away through backlots. I'm sure I lost them."

"Good. We'll chalk this up to bad luck." Malcolm turned and looked toward the hotel entrance. "Get your things. We need to leave fast."

Once the vans were loaded and ready, Malcolm addressed the group, "We'll drive nonstop to New York City. It's a twenty-hour drive. We'll switch drivers every two hours. I'll lead the way."

They climbed aboard, and the caravan headed for Secaucus, New Jersey.

CHAPTER 30

FBI NEW YORK

Agent O'Keefe flew Emirates from O'Hare to JFK. Screw the Fly American directive, he said to himself. His secretary promised to be discreet when she made the booking but balked at making it a first-class seat. It didn't matter in the end. When the Emirates ground attendant saw O'Keefe's FBI credentials, she upgraded his ticket to first-class.

O'Keefe beamed when the flight attendant brought him a newspaper and a flute of champagne. The uniform of the cabin crew sent his hormones racing. The entire two-hour flight to JFK was a delight.

A departmental limo driver met O'Keefe at arrivals. The limo drove across the Brooklyn Bridge, sparred with traffic through Midtown Manhattan, and delivered O'Keefe to the FBI building at Federal Plaza. O'Keefe walked through the security check and took the elevator to the 23rd floor. At reception, he asked for Special Agent in Charge Matt Callaghan.

"Aiden. Long time no see." Callaghan shook his hand and led him down the hallway.

"Keeping well?" Callaghan asked as they walked.

"Not bad, thanks, could be better."

Callaghan stopped and faced O'Keefe. "Anything to do with Agent Hale stealing your promotion?"

"No, no, nothing to do with that . . . injustice. Well, not directly."

"If it's any consolation, I still believe you were the better candidate."

"Thanks," O'Keefe said. "It's about those damn serial killers who are still on the lam after three months. The Director is breathing down Hale's neck, who is breathing down mine. And to make matters worse, that private detective agency CEO Michael Tyler hired is always one step ahead of us, and Tyler needles the Director with that."

"They're sharp, no doubt about it. Their IT specialist, Louise Jackson, just sent us the details of some recent dark web activity concerning Tyler. She believes the Jennings are behind it." Callaghan looked up at O'Keefe. "What does your IT team say about it?"

"They're baffled by Jackson's ability to penetrate those dark web sites and chat rooms, but they agree with her findings." O'Keefe let a moment pass, then added, "That's why I'm here. We need to set up a trap to capture the Jennings gang."

"I've assigned Special Agent Jacqueline Cochran as our point person. She'll coordinate the local police departments."

"When can I meet her?"

"How about right now?" Callaghan picked up his phone and, after a short back-and-forth, hung up. "She's on her way."

Moments later, a black woman in gray pants and a navy-blue blazer over a crisp white shirt tapped on the doorframe of Callaghan's office. She was tall, about five ten.

"Agent Cochran." Callaghan waved her in. He made the introductions, then added, "Agent O'Keefe will join you at tomorrow's meeting. Can he ride with you?"

"Absolutely." Cochran turned to O'Keefe. "Glad to have you overseeing this operation, Agent O'Keefe."

"Where is the meeting and who'll be attending?" O'Keefe asked.

"At Mr. Tyler's residence in Sands Point, Long Island, at 9 a.m. Nassau County police will send a detective, and Tyler's security chief will attend. I've also invited Reliant to join us."

"Reliant? Was that necessary?"

"I think so. They produced the intelligence we're working from. More to the point, Tyler wants them there."

O'Keefe nodded reluctantly, then asked, "Isn't Tyler attending?"

"He will. Via Zoom." Cochran continued. "And tomorrow afternoon, we're meeting with the security chief of Tyler's building on 5th Avenue in Manhattan. NYPD is sending a detective, Reliant will attend as well."

O'Keefe rubbed his chin pensively. Jacqueline let a moment pass, then asked, "Can I drop you off at your hotel? We can talk more on the way."

"That would be great. Thanks."

"Where are you staying?"

"The Homewood Suites on 37th Street."

"Excellent location."

As Cochran dropped off O'Keefe at his hotel, she said, "It's an hour's drive to Tyler's residence. I'll pick you up at 7:45 tomorrow morning."

"I'll be ready." O'Keefe said.

CHAPTER 31

RELIANT DRIVES TO NEW YORK CITY

Chief Harrington preferred delivering his daily report to Tyler by email to avoid the man's abusive language, but the situation demanded immediate action. The Jennings gang would be attacking soon, and Reliant urgently needed to review Tyler's security arrangements. He braced himself and placed the call.

Tyler picked up, skipped the salutations, and broke into a rant. "These bloody serial killers are still on the lam. Who do I need to hire to catch these murderers? The friggin' army?"

Harrington answered calmly. "We're making good progress, Mr. Tyler. We discovered their hideout in St. Louis, and based on our intel, the FBI's SWAT teams nearly captured them. We're hard on their trail, and their luck will run out soon."

Tyler cleared his throat. "I give you credit for locating them on my dime, mind you, but you're still one step behind them."

Harrington ignored the backhanded compliment and moved to the subject he wanted to discuss. "We're seeing a lot of web research about you. We think it's the gang. They've even downloaded plans of your residence and your office building. We believe they'll attack soon."

"Damn. The bastards are after me for sure. What's your next move?"

"We've alerted the FBI, but we need to review your security arrangements urgently. We're just waiting on your security chief, Philip Fiorelli, to confirm a date and time."

Tyler cursed, then said, "I'll put a boot to Fiorelli's ass. How soon can you be here?"

"We can drive over tomorrow and carry out the review the next day."

"Good. Be here tomorrow. I'll have Fiorelli contact you shortly." Tyler ended the conversation.

Harrington summoned Popeye. "Get your team to New York City tomorrow and be ready to carry out a review of Fiorelli's preparedness the day after. We're not waiting for his call."

"Great. I'll get the team ready to roll tomorrow morning." Popeye nodded and left.

Popeye summoned everyone to the conference room and had the cafeteria deliver coffee and pastries. He arrived first and grabbed a coffee but skipped the pastries.

Popeye had just turned forty-six. He kept his six-foot frame fit by daily workouts, but his weight was creeping up. He knew he should reduce the size of his meal portions in keeping with his age, but for this, he needed the support of his wife, Sheila. Since the death of his colleague, Pierre Chamberlain, at the hands of the gang, Sheila had been coddling him, serving him his favorite treats: butter pecan pies, lemon cake, and French vanilla ice cream.

Ashley walked in, poured herself a coffee, chose a pastry, and sat. Popeye admired her fine figure despite her forty-five years. She kept fit through high energy sports: racquetball, squash, tennis. Ashley obviously enjoyed her single life, but that didn't stop her from flirting.

"Ha! I've caught you staring at me again," Ashley said. "Tsk, tsk. Have you told Sheila about the big crush you have on me?"

"Hmm . . . I think it's too early to tell Sheila. Truth be told, I make eyes at you because I believe it helps you perform your best."

"Well, that *is* true." Ashley said with a mischievous smile. She changed the subject. "I'm so disappointed the Jennings and their gang escaped from the raid in St. Louis. All of Louise's work came to nothing." Ashley sipped some coffee. "And they killed two SWAT agents. It's like brothers killing brothers."

The irony was not lost on Popeye. He, Ashley, and Louise had been recruited from the Marine Intelligence Corps, and they were now chasing Marine vets.

Louise walked in with a laptop under her arm. She grabbed a coffee and a pastry and sat down.

The recruit, Paul Collins, walked in, looking alert and excited. He nodded at Popeye before taking his seat.

Popeye opened the meeting by informing everyone that they were driving to New York City the next morning for the review of Tyler's security. Popeye then turned to Louise. "Any new developments?"

"One of the Jennings gang, Steve Adams, was spotted in Nashville last night at a nightclub, the Bluebird Café. The Nashville police confronted him, but he killed a local detective and escaped on foot. Ashley has been following up."

Ashley picked up where Louise had stopped. "The gang booked rooms at a Nashville Days Inn. The receptionist recognized some of them from photographs. They left in a hurry, before midnight, in two white vans."

"I am now ninety-nine percent certain that they're heading to New York to kill Tyler," Louise said.

"Why not a hundred percent?" Popeye asked.

"It's bad form to claim total certainty about anything," Louise said with a playful grin.

"When do you think they'll strike?" Popeye asked.

"If they drive non-stop, they'll reach New York City tonight. They'll need a few days to case Tyler's house and office building and plan their attack. My guess is they'll strike Saturday at the earliest."

"That gives us a few days to set up a trap. Where do you think they'll corner Tyler?" Popeye asked.

"If they stay true to their modus operandi, they'll target Tyler at his residence. They'll force his passcodes out of him, clean out his foreign accounts, then kill him."

Popeye rubbed his chin. "Tyler is their last target as far as we know. I expect they'll split up and disappear with new identities after this. This may be our last chance to catch them." Popeye raised his head and looked at his team. "But they're rushed now and making mistakes. That plays in our favor." Everyone nodded their heads.

Louise raised a hand. "With Chief Harrington's okay, I've kept the FBI's New York City field office informed of everything we know."

Popeye issued instructions. "We'll make New York our temporary headquarters. Louise, you'll pick accommodation for the team for five days. Ashley, you'll prepare an armored Suburban with weapons and supplies. Paul, you'll do a checklist of things to review with Tyler's security team." Everyone nodded and left to attend to their tasks.

The next day, Ashley sat proudly at the wheel of their Suburban and steered the vehicle along Interstate 80 toward New York City. Popeye sat shotgun, bent over his tablet. Louise and Paul occupied the bench seat.

It was late September. Red and yellow foliage covered the countryside as the Suburban crossed Ohio and Pennsylvania. Flocks of Canada geese flew and honked overhead.

"Let's stop for lunch in Youngstown," Ashley announced.

Everyone looked up.

"Are you thinking of a special place?" Popeye asked.

"An Italian restaurant would suit me," Ashley said.

Popeye surveyed the team with his eyes. Everyone shrugged their shoulders. "Italian it is then," he said.

Louise tapped keys on her laptop. After a minute she said, "How about a place called Station Square? It gets five stars on Yelp, and it's got American and vegetarian too."

Everyone nodded agreement. "Station Square it is," Popeye ruled.

Popeye led the team into the restaurant and picked a table. Once everyone was served, Ashley turned to Louise. "What kind of rooms have you booked?"

"Two suites at the Homewood Suites in Midtown Manhattan. One for the girls and one for the men. Each comes with two queens, a kitchenette, two worktables, and a living room. Oh, and there's an exercise room in the hotel."

Ashley nodded and smiled at that. Louise leaned close and, pretending to whisper but making sure Popeye could hear, asked, "Were you hoping to room with Popeye?"

Ashley whispered back, "Popeye isn't ready for an extramarital relationship yet."

"Wise decision," Louise said. "Cavorting with a superior invites legal trouble."

"And he has a good marriage with Sheila," Ashley said.

Popeye listened good-humouredly to the discussion.

Ashley drove the Suburban expertly through the Lincoln Tunnel, down the busy Manhattan streets, and stopped at the front entrance to the Homewood Suites in Midtown. A porter pulled a hotel cart to the van and loaded it with the team's luggage while Louise went to check in at the reception desk. Ashley handed the key fob to the parking valet. The porter pulled the luggage cart to the elevators.

After everyone had settled in, Popeye summoned the team to his suite. "We meet Tyler's security chief, Philip Fiorelli, tomorrow morning at nine," he announced.

Louise consulted her iPhone. "Tyler's residence is on Shepherds Lane at Sands Point, Long Island. It's an hour's drive from here."

Popeye made a mental calculation, then said, "We'll leave at seven. That'll give us an hour to look over the premises and the approaches and the exits to the property before we talk to Fiorelli." Everyone nodded and Popeye continued. "We're also meeting with Tyler's building security chief in the afternoon, around 2 p.m."

Louise raised a hand. "I've posted satellite views of Tyler's residence, and street views of the office building, on the project website." The others opened their laptops and began to study the information Louise had posted.

A half hour later, Ashley asked, "How about dinner in town followed by a Broadway show?"

"I suggest dinner only," Popeye said with a chuckle. "We need to prepare carefully for tomorrow's meetings."

"I need time to complete my checklists," Paul said.

"And I want to keep checking for online activity related to the gang," Louise said.

Ashley looked at Popeye. "Will there be time for you to read your crime novels?" she asked with fake concern.

"I only read them when I can't fall asleep," Popeye answered with a smile. "Thanks for your concern, Ashley."

Undeterred, Ashley addressed the group. "Let's get a move on. We need a good dinner to build up our energy if we're going to catch those criminals."

CHAPTER 32

THE JENNINGS GANG REACHES NEW YORK CITY

Gerta guided Malcolm to a parking lot in an industrial part of Nashville. Malcolm parked in a sheltered area while Larry and Steve installed new plates on the two vans before the caravan returned to Highway 31E and headed east.

The sun rose at 7 a.m. over West Virginia. Colorful September foliage filled the landscape all the way to the horizon. Malcolm sat at the wheel, while Gerta worked on her tablet, and Tom, Lucky, and Danielle slept on the bench seat.

"Let's stop for breakfast," Gerta said. She searched the Internet. "What about the Omelet Shop? I like the sound of that. It's in Parkersburg, up ahead a few miles. They've got a takeout window."

"Sounds good," Malcolm said. He looked at Danielle in the rearview mirror. "Are you awake, honey?"

Danielle stirred and opened her eyes. "Yes dad?"

"Can you sit at the wheel and order? You've got the best disguise." Danielle nodded and reached for the bag with her glasses and hat.

Gerta phoned Steve to let him know where they were stopping.

"Yummy. Sounds good," Steve said over the speaker. "But will the omelets be as good as the ones Tom makes?"

"There's no way they can possibly beat *my* pancakes," Tom boasted. Everyone laughed.

They were at a picnic table in a city park, enjoying their meal, when Steve asked, "We'll be at the hotel in Secaucus in about twelve hours. Then what's the plan?"

"We'll be too tired for doing anything but sleep once we've checked in," Malcolm said. Tomorrow will be the big day."

The others stopped eating and waited for more details. "We'll case the locations, then negotiate with the security chiefs. We'll do Tyler's residence in the morning, his office building in the afternoon. Then we can decide on how and where to corner him." Everyone nodded.

Gerta turned to Larry and Steve. "I've loaded satellite views, road maps, and construction plans on my tablet. You guys should take my tablet and study the documents during the ride today. We'll do the same in our van and compare notes later."

Malcolm placed a hand on Gerta's arm. "Good thinking, honey."

They drove into Candlewood Suites Secaucus around nine that evening. Gerta called Steve and put the phone on speaker. "Danielle will book us in and get the room keys, and Tom will bring over the luggage carts. Everyone wears baseball caps and glasses."

"Gotcha," Steve answered.

Malcolm, Gerta, and Danielle settled into a two-bedroom suite, while Larry, Steve, Tom, and Lucky shared the other two suites. Everyone showered and rushed to bed without stopping to admire the amenities of their temporary headquarters.

Disturbing dreams haunted Malcolm's sleep. In one dream, he was lowering his brother Eddie's body from the underside of the bridge over the Euphrates River. Eddie's body was caked with dried blood, dirt, and black ash, but his eyes opened and he stared at Malcolm. "Thanks for avenging me, bro. Did it bring you some peace?"

"No, but I've settled the score the best way I could." Malcolm replied.

Eddie placed a hand on Malcolm's shoulder. "That's all I can ask for."

Malcolm woke up dripping in sweat. It was past midnight. He rose quietly, walked to the washroom, and splashed water on his face. His hip throbbed with pain. He took a Percocet and stared into the mirror. *If only there were a pill that could relieve the anger and sorrow in our hearts.*

CHAPTER 33

THE FBI MEET FIORELLI

Sands Point, Long Island, stands at the end of a small peninsula that juts out into Hempstead Bay. Popeye and his team rode up Shepherds Lane toward Tyler's property. They followed the lane for half a mile, then turned onto a narrower lane that led through trees and shrubs. They drove past a stable before reaching a guardhouse. A liftgate blocked the entrance to the parking lot of Tyler's mansion.

Popeye stopped at the liftgate and introduced himself to the guard. Security chief Fiorelli came out to greet them. "You're a bit early for the meeting, but that's good. Come on in. We'll chat over some coffee."

"Thanks," Popeye said, "but if it's okay with you, we'd prefer to explore the property on our own before the meeting. Paul," he added, pointing to Agent Collins, "can stay behind and start to review your security arrangements with you."

"Oh. Okay." Fiorelli signaled for the guard to raise the liftgate. "You can park near the mansion. See you back here at nine." Fiorelli and Paul walked into the guardhouse.

Popeye parked the Suburban in front of the residence. The team climbed out and stood there for a moment admiring Tyler's mansion. Cream-colored stone and stucco covered the two-story structure. Green shrubs and flower beds embellished the front facade. A curved wall beside the building's entrance attested to a designer's touch. The mansion sat on seven acres of park-like waterfront lawns. It oozed wealth and luxury.

"This place must be worth ten million dollars easy, even in this post-pandemic market," Ashley said.

Popeye led his team to the back of the residence, where they found a swimming pool surrounded by a stone patio. Floor to ceiling windows and French doors covered the rear of the house.

They turned and admired the blue gray water of Hempstead Bay. The city of New Rochelle was visible across the water some six miles away.

"If I were the Jennings, I'd come by boat," Ashley said.

"I agree," Malcolm said. "Escaping by boat would be much less risky than by car. The only road out is Shepherds Lane, easy to block with a couple of cruisers."

Louise opened her tablet, and after a moment, she said, "I see at least fifteen marinas bordering on Hampstead Bay, and they're all within easy reach." She looked up at Popeye. "I'll monitor the boat rentals. It's a long shot, but it could pay off." Popeye nodded.

The team walked back toward the guardhouse. As they approached the parking lot, they saw a man and a woman wearing blue FBI jackets looking intently at their Suburban.

Popeye reached the woman first. "Good morning. I'm Captain John Morris, Reliant Detective Agency."

"Good morning, Captain Morris. I'm Special Agent Jacqueline Cochran, FBI New York City field office." She turned to her companion. "And this is Special Agent Aiden O'Keefe from the Chicago field office." Popeye introduced his team, and everyone shook hands.

"Chicago?" Popeye asked O'Keefe. "That's where the gang hails from."

"Yes. The Chicago field office is coordinating the manhunt," O'Keefe said. He turned to Louise. "So you're the famous Louise Jackson. Our IT team would love to get a look under the hood of your search engines. They suspect research level software that relies heavily on some very advanced AI."

"I'm sorry, but it's proprietary," Louise said. "Without those search engines, we'd be out of business overnight."

At that moment, a police cruiser with Nassau County police patches on the front doors drove up to the liftgate. Two men climbed out. The FBI and Reliant teams walked over and introduced themselves, and everyone entered the guardhouse.

Fiorelli greeted the Nassau County officers. "Chief Meadows, Chief Palmer. It's good to see you both. Keeping well?"

"Couldn't be better," Chief Meadows said. "And you, Phil?"

"Just great, thank you." He signaled for everyone to sit around a large meeting table.

"Help yourself to coffee and pastries," Fiorelli said, pointing to a side table covered with baked goods, a large coffee pot, mugs, cream, and sugar. "Courtesy of my favorite pastry shop in Port Washington."

Fiorelli brought his laptop to the table. "Let me bring Mr. Tyler into the meeting." He opened his Zoom app, and Tyler appeared on the screen.

Without waiting for introductions, Tyler opened with, "Good morning, everyone. Wow. There's enough of youse guys to *maybe* capture those serial killers for a change." The joke fell flat.

After Fiorelli had introduced everyone, Tyler spoke again, "My detectives, Captain Morris and his team, they say the Jennings gang will attack any day now. Does the FBI agree?"

Jacqueline answered, "Yes. The FBI agrees with Reliant's overall assessment of the situation, and we're grateful to them for uncovering the criminals' plans." O'Keefe stiffened when he heard this.

"So how *exactly* do you guys intend to protect me?" Tyler asked with an edge to his voice.

"The gang's previous two assassinations were carried out at the victims' private homes," Jacqueline said, "but your office is also a possible target, so we'll set up close surveillance at both locations." Jacqueline surveyed the faces of the Nassau County officers. They nodded back. Jacqueline then turned to Fiorelli. "And we'll have two SWAT teams on high alert near both locations too."

Fiorelli leaned forward. "We're not trained, nor equipped, to tackle criminals with military training and weapons," he blurted out. "We can protect Mr. Tyler, Mrs. Tyler, and the housekeeper during an attack on the mansion, but we can't take on those criminals and try to arrest them."

Popeye looked at Paul for confirmation, Paul nodded his head in agreement.

"When do you think they'll attack? "Jacqueline turned to Louise, who replied, "Based on the Internet activity we have observed, we expect the attack within the next few days." The others looked at each other with raised eyebrows.

Popeye picked up from Louise. "We believe this is our last chance to capture the entire team in one place, that Mr. Tyler is the last target on their list. Afterwards, we expect them to split up and disappear with new identities." A tense silence settled over the conference table.

Tyler's voice piped out from the laptop screen. "I hope your SWAT teams are more competent than those in St. Louis." O'Keefe stiffened, silent and red-faced.

Chief Meadows looked up at Popeye. "I doubt the Jennings will strike here. Poor escape routes."

"If they attack here, they'll likely land on the beach in a Zodiac." Popeye said, then turned to Jacqueline. "I suggest you alert all the local marinas and send them photos of the fugitives. The gang will need to rent a Zodiac locally."

Jacqueline nodded. "We'll have one SWAT marine unit stationed here." She turned to the Nassau police officers. "Can you have your forces in place by tomorrow morning?" Chief Meadows nodded.

Fiorelli raised his hand. "My team will focus on keeping Mr. and Mrs. Tyler and their housekeeper out of harm's way."

Jacqueline rose. "We need to get going. We're meeting with the security chief at Mr. Tyler's office building today at two. The NYPD will be attending." She turned to Popeye. "You're joining us?" Popeye nodded.

Tyler piped in, "I'll be there."

Sitting at his large mahogany desk, Tyler turned the laptop off and stared at Sherry, his secretary. She sat across his desk, notepad in hand, with a look of apprehension in her eyes.

Tyler leaned forward, "Sherry, I want you to know how pleased I am with the candidates you've been sending me for your replacement. The last one was particularly well qualified and . . . cooperative." Sherry swallowed hard and remained silent. Tyler continued. "I'll be working late tomorrow night, until nine, maybe later. Could you book an interview for seven?"

Sherry straightened, relief showing on her face. "Of course, Mr. Tyler. I'll call the agency. It shouldn't be a problem. Will you need me to stay behind?"

"Yes, please."

As Sherry rose to leave, Tyler said, "Oh, Sherry. I've spoken to my friend Gabriel at Magnum Retail. He's looking forward to interviewing you. I've put in a good word for you." Tyler smiled at her and added, "And don't worry. Gabby will not be asking for *special* services. I've cleared that with him." Tyler pursed his lips. "Just thought I'd ease your mind."

Sherry nodded and left.

CHAPTER 34

THE JENNINGS MEET WITH FIORELLI

Malcolm was the first to rise. He put on sweatpants and a T-shirt, moved the coffee table aside in the living room, and started on his stretching and muscle-building exercises.

Danielle walked out of her bedroom dressed in jogging attire, waved at her father, and slipped quietly out of the suite.

Gerta was the next to rise. She emerged from the bedroom wearing jeans and a white button-down shirt, with discreet makeup on her face, her red hair blow-dried, brushed, and tied in a ponytail. She slipped into the kitchenette and made a pot of coffee.

An hour later, the team had gathered at the table, enjoying the breakfast that Danielle had ordered from room service.

"What's the plan for today?" Steve asked.

Malcolm put down his mug. "You, Danielle, and Tom will go shopping. Larry made a list of items we need." He turned to Gerta and Larry. "We're going to visit with security chief Fiorelli at Tyler's house, and then security chief Gomez at Tyler's office building." He looked at Gerta expectantly.

Gerta spoke. "I called Fiorelli, impersonating an AT&T tech offering to upgrade the modem at his guardhouse, run some connectivity tests, and review his Internet contract with him. He has a meeting all morning, but he can see us after lunch. I said we'd be there at one."

"Great. And Gomez?"

"He's working the evening shift this week. He can meet with us any time after five today."

Danielle approached her parents and said, "I admire your courage." Malcolm returned a look of surprise. "I mean, it takes pluck to accost these men and demand their cooperation," she explained.

Malcolm looked affectionately at Danielle. "Without the research you and your mother did on these guys' backgrounds, we'd have no leverage to work with. You did good work."

Gerta placed a hand on Malcolm's shoulder. "Thanks to the back door I left behind while programming for NSA, I was able to go back into their data banks and look through Fiorelli's and Gomez's phone and email communications and their Internet search history. We found some good stuff."

Danielle beamed. "I really enjoyed the detective work. Thanks for teaching me, Mom." Gerta placed a hand on her daughter's arm and rubbed it gently. Danielle added, "But what if neither of the security chiefs cooperates?"

Malcolm bit his lip before answering. "We'd need a new plan."

Once breakfast was finished. Steve, Tom, and Danielle left to do their assigned shopping. Lucky followed close behind his master.

Larry steered the van north onto Shepherds Lane. A wrought iron fence bordered the road, and the foliage glowed with the full autumn colors of red, yellow, and tan.

"This lane is even narrower than it looks on the satellite view," Malcolm said.

They drove past a stable. Then Larry stopped on the side of the road. The guardhouse was visible through the foliage. "The coast is clear," Malcolm said. "We're on."

Gerta flipped the Wi-Fi switch on her signal jammer as Larry drove up to the guardhouse. Dressed in blue technician work uniforms and carrying tool bags, Larry and Malcolm walked to the entrance. Gerta followed, carrying the signal jammer in one satchel and her laptop in another. Malcolm knocked, and Fiorelli opened the door.

"Good morning!" Malcolm said. "We're with AT&T. They sent us to replace your modem and run connectivity tests on your Wi-Fi."

Fiorelli stared at them, wide-eyed. "That's good timing. Our Wi-Fi just failed a minute ago." He stepped outside, looked at the logo on the van, which read 'Advanced Fiber Optics,' then pointed at the open doorway. "Come on in."

Once inside, Malcolm said, "We'll check your router first."

"That's in my office," Fiorelli said. He led the way. Malcolm and Gerta took seats in front of Fiorelli's desk. Larry closed the office door and remained standing. Gerta slipped a hand in her satchel and flicked the switch that blocked cell phone signals.

Fiorelli stared at Malcolm and Gerta with a puzzled look. He sat at his desk and pointed to the router on the side table. "The router is . . ." His body stiffened and his face turned pale. He grabbed the edge of the desk with both hands and stared, mouth agape, first at Malcolm, then at Gerta. "I'll be damned!"

Malcolm spoke. "Relax, Mr. Fiorelli. We're just here to discuss a business proposition with you."

Fiorelli released his grip on the desk and leaned back. He chuckled nervously. "You guys gave me quite a shock. The FBI were here barely an hour ago to warn me about you, but never in my wildest dreams . . ." He blinked and swallowed. "They said you plan to rob and kill Mr. Tyler. You guys have quite the reputation." He let out another nervous chuckle.

Malcolm let a moment pass, then said, "Here's our proposal. You look the other way while we deal with Tyler, and we cut you in on the take, say, ten percent? We'll transfer your share to any account of your choosing."

Fiorelli straightened. "You can't be serious. I'll be charged as an accomplice and spend the rest of my life on the run." He pursed his lips, furrowed his brow, and asked, "Ten percent of how much?"

"The fifty million in the accounts of Tyler's shell company in the British Virgin Islands."

Fiorelli's face remained blank. He said, "So I get five million and live in hiding for the rest of my life? It's not worth it."

Malcolm was silent for a moment, then said, "What about twenty percent then? And we'll give you half a million up front so you can prepare your disappearance."

Fiorelli frowned. "I'm curious. What makes you think you can buy me off?"

Malcolm leaned forward. "Because you're already a criminal."

Fiorelli sat back. "What the fuck are you talking about?"

Malcolm fixed Fiorelli with a cool stare. "We know you stole two Warhols—a Marilyn and a Double Elvis—from Tyler's house and replaced them with fakes." Fiorelli looked stunned. Malcolm continued. "We also know who the black-market dealer who bought them from you is, and how much he paid for them. Two million, wasn't it?"

Fiorelli stared, his mouth agape, but after a moment, he regained his composure and said, "You guys are bluffing." He paused and stared intently at Malcolm. "You can't prove any of this."

Malcolm turned to Gerta and nodded. Gerta took out her laptop, opened a file, and turned the laptop around for Fiorelli to see. She flipped through copies of emails and banking transactions relating to the stolen paintings.

Fiorelli sat bug-eyed. He clenched his jaw, narrowed his eyes, and spoke. "If you guys are so damn smart, you know I'm connected. You don't want to fuck with the Family."

Malcolm only replied, in a calm voice, "Do we have a deal?"

Fiorelli pursed his lips. He looked up at Larry standing by the door before returning his gaze to Malcolm. "How would it work? When would I get the rest of the money?"

Gerta answered. "We'll transfer the half million to your account right now. The rest you'll get when we get the passwords to Tyler's shell company accounts."

After a moment, Fiorelli said. "Let's say I agree with this scheme. How do I get my two guards to look the other way while you rob and murder Tyler?"

"Simple," said Malcolm. "By scheduling Pasquale and LaRosa for that shift, and you cut them in from your share." He smiled. "Just like you did with the art theft."

Fiorelli stared back at him with a shocked look. After another silence, he asked, "When do you plan to do this?"

"The sooner the better, but Tyler has to be at home, and alone."

Fiorelli bit his lip, then said, "Let me check the logbook." He rose and walked to the office door. Larry opened the door and followed him. They returned a minute later, Fiorelli holding a large notebook. He sat down, looked up at Malcolm, and asked, "At what time?"

"Between eight in the evening and midnight."

Fiorelli studied the log. "Tomorrow night Tyler will be home, and Mrs. Tyler will be at her book club. I can send the housekeeper out on some errand."

Malcolm turned to Gerta and Larry. They both nodded back. "Tomorrow night it is," he said.

"How will you guys do this?"

"We'll land on the beach with a Zodiac and enter the house through the back patio. We'll leave the same way."

Fiorelli thought for a moment. "That should work. Outboard motors are a familiar sound around here, but what about gunfire?"

"We'll use a silencer."

Fiorelli rubbed his chin, looking pensive.

Gerta asked, "Will you need new identity papers?"

Fiorelli looked up. "No. We'll *discover* Tyler's body after you leave, call the police, and say we saw and heard nothing. As long as you use silencers, and Tyler doesn't scream or anything, they'll have no reason to suspect us."

Malcolm fixed Fiorelli with a searching look but remained silent. Fiorelli finally said, "Okay. I want the half million now." He wrote an account number on a paper note and handed it to Gerta.

Malcolm nodded at Gerta, who reached into her satchel and unblocked the Wi-Fi. She pulled her laptop over and went to work. Fiorelli opened his own laptop and logged into his offshore account.

Gerta looked up. "Is your laptop secure?"

"It should be. I had a tech guy set it up for me."

"Can I check for you?"

Fiorelli hesitated, then said, "Okay." He pushed his laptop over to Gerta. She tapped intently at the keyboard for a few moments, then returned it to him. "Yes. Your connections are secure."

When the half million dollars appeared in his account, Fiorelli smiled.

Back in the van heading toward New York City, Larry turned to Malcolm. "I don't trust that mobster." Malcolm stared ahead with narrowed eyes. "Neither do I."

CHAPTER 35

FIORELLI HATCHES A PLAN

As Fiorelli watched the Jennings driving away, he whispered to himself, "I'll be damned." He opened a drawer on his desk, retrieved the business cards from the morning's meeting, and called the number on one of the cards.

"Special Agent Jacqueline Cochran here."

"Agent Cochran, this is Fiorelli. I've just met your boys!"

Jacqueline paused, startled, then said, "Security chief Fiorelli? Hi. Why are you at my sons' school?"

"What? No, no. not *your* boys. The Jennings gang. The serial killers!"

"When? Where?"

"A minute ago! In my office at Sands Point."

"The Jennings gang? In your office?"

"Three of them. Two men and a woman. They called earlier, impersonating AT&T technicians, but I recognized them when they got here."

"What on earth did they want with you? What did they say?"

"They offered to cut me in on the extortion of Mr. Tyler. I and the guards just need to look the other way while they rob and kill him in his house."

"Wow! And what did you say?"

"I pretended to go along with them. We're setting a trap, aren't we?"

"Yes, that's right." Jacqueline paused, then said, "Did they say when they plan to attack?"

"They certainly did," Fiorelli said. "Tomorrow night, 8 p.m. They're going to land on the beach in a Zodiac and sneak into the house through the back patio doors. My security guards will be at the front of the house at that time and pretend not to hear."

"Have you told anybody else about this?"

"No, you're my first call, but I'm calling Mr. Tyler next."

Jacqueline was silent for a moment, then said, "I'll set up a Zoom meeting with everybody to organize an ambush." She paused, then added, "Well done, Chief Fiorelli," and hung up.

Fiorelli dialed Tyler's direct line. His boss sounded winded. "This better be important, Fiorelli," he wheezed. "My direct line is for emergencies only, as you well know."

"This *is* an emergency, Mr. Tyler." Fiorelli hesitated for a moment. "You sound winded, Mr. Tyler. Is everything all right?"

"Everything's fine. Hang on a minute."

Tyler put the receiver down, but Fiorelli could hear the conversation. "That was great, sweetheart. Sherry will let you know my decision. You can clean up in my washroom." Tyler returned to the phone. "What is this about?"

"You won't believe this, Mr. Tyler." Fiorelli paused for effect. "The serial killers were in my office five minutes ago."

"Christ. That *is* unbelievable." Tyler paused. "So you arrested them?"

"Huh? No, but I called the FBI as soon as they left."

"Are you telling me you let those bastards walk away and did nothing to stop them? What the hell am I paying you guys for?"

"It wasn't like that, Mr. Tyler. I was alone with them. They were armed, and my guards were doing the rounds. Those killers would have put a bullet through my head before I could have even drawn my pistol."

Tyler breathed heavily, then said, "Okay. But what did they want with *you*?"

"They offered to bribe me. The guards and I are to look the other way while they attack you in your house. I played along. Now we're setting up an ambush."

Tyler was silent for a moment, then asked, "What are the FBI doing?"

"Their agent, Jacqueline Cochran, she's calling a Zoom meeting with everybody to plan the ambush."

"Did those killers say when they going to attack?"

"Tomorrow night at eight."

"Jesus Christ! When is that Zoom meeting?"

"Cochran will be calling you any minute now."

"Good. Now get off the line. No, wait. What did the Jennings say, exactly?"

Fiorelli summarized the conversation, leaving out the paintings, then added, "I've thought of something."

"What?"

"Is this line totally private?"

"Yes. Come on. Spit it out. Don't make me play twenty questions."

"Some time back, you asked me if I could arrange a hit for you and make it look like an accident."

"Stop right there! This is a friggin phone line. Jesus!" Tyler slammed his phone down.

The rebuke stung Fiorelli. *I should have discussed this face-to-face with him. But damn, this is too good an opportunity to miss.* He called his captain.

"Russo here," the voice said.

"Hi Sebastiano. It's Fiorelli."

"Felice! What's up? You in trouble again?" Russo chuckled.

"Not exactly, but I need your help."

"Oh? What kind of help?"

"You remember the job we carried out last year? Tyler's paintings?"

"Yes. That was a sweet job. We made good money from that one." Russo paused, then said, "Don't tell me. Tyler spotted the fakes?"

"No, no, but someone else did, and they're blackmailing me."

"Now, hold on. What kind of idiot would do that? Don't they know you're connected?"

"Yes, they do, but they don't care. It's those serial killers, the Jennings gang."

"No kidding! Those Rambos who killed the two SWAT officers in St. Louis last week?"

"Yup. The same. They were in my office ten minutes ago."

"What did they say?"

"They want to rob and murder Tyler in his house, and unless I look the other way while they're doing it, they'll tell the police about the paintings."

Russo was silent for a moment. "How could they possibly know about that job? Who snitched?"

"I don't know. But they have all the details—who bought the paintings, who supplied the fakes. Fuck, they even know how much money we sold them for."

"What proof do they have?"

"Copies of emails and recordings of phone calls. They showed them to me."

"Now hold on, Felice. That was your job to manage. Someone in your team snitched for sure." He adopted a fatherly tone. "You can tell me the truth, Felice. Better if you fess up now than I find out later. Did they put a gun to your head?" Russo waited for a moment, then added, "As your captain, I'll have to set an example, but I won't kill you, I promise."

"No, no. It was nothing like that." Fiorelli was panting now. "The Jennings have this woman, some computer wizard. She figured everything out somehow."

"But why would they bother doing all that research? How much money do they want?"

"They're after Tyler's money."

"Does Tyler have that much money?"

"They mentioned millions in hidden overseas funds. Once they force his passwords out of him, that computer woman must know how to transfer the money and hide it someplace."

Russo was silent for a moment, then said, "What do you need?"

"Two hitmen. For tomorrow night."

"Why hitmen?"

"I want them to take out the Jennings gang when they show up to rob Tyler."

"What about the soldiers you've got already. Pasquale and LaRosa? I can get you some assault rifles."

"Ha! Those two jokers would try to outrun a bullet. No, no. For this job, I need two sharpshooters that can pick off a target from five hundred yards away in the dark."

"Whoa! That kind of talent doesn't grow on trees. How many targets are we talking about?"

"I'm guessing three or four."

Russo was silent for a moment, then said, "Okay Felice. I'll see what I can do, but this is going on your tab. And remember, those guys charge by the hit."

"Oh, and one more thing, Sebastiano," Fiorelli said. "It's critical that the hitmen use the same type of rifle and cartridges that the SWAT sharpshooters use. A firefight is sure to break out between SWAT, the police officers, and the Jennings gang when the gang lands on the beach. Your hits have to look like SWAT fired the shots."

"I'll make sure they carry the same weapons," Russo assured him.

"Thanks Sebastiano. I'll wait for your call." But Russo had hung up already.

CHAPTER 36

THE HITMEN

The next time Fiorelli's phone rang, it was Russo. "Hi Felice. I've lined up two men for tomorrow night. When do you want them?"

"Have them report here at nine tonight. I'll go over the details with them then." Fiorelli paused, then added, "How much?"

"They charge twenty thousand dollars per hit, fifty percent up front, the rest when the job is done. I told them there would be three, maybe four targets. That's what you said."

"There could be more. Depends."

"What does that mean, *depends*?"

"Jennings didn't say how many of them will be coming, and I can't very well call them and ask."

Russo sighed heavily. "This is coming out of your account. Are you sure the job is worth it?"

"Hey. I'm protecting you as well. If they share their information with the cops, your name will come up too. Think of the lawyers' fees alone just to beat that rap." Russo was silent. Fiorelli added, "I'm working on a side job with Tyler. If it pans out, it'll be big enough to clear my account."

"In the meantime, the interest accumulates."

Fiorelli cursed under his breath, then said, "I need the men here at nine tonight."

"Count on it." Russo hung up.

Fiorelli rose, walked to the window, and stared at the brilliant autumn foliage and the twilight settling over Hempstead Bay. The breeze had died.

The evening was serene. But nature's bounty left him unmoved. "Shit, shit, shit!" he cursed.

The two hitmen drove up to the guardhouse in a black Lincoln Town Car. Both were in their mid-forties, five foot ten in height, and wore black leather jackets over black turtleneck sweaters and black pants.

Fiorelli showed them to his office. He sat behind his desk. "What do I call you gentlemen?"

"Call me Number One," the man on the right said.

"Which makes me Number Two," the other one said, unsmiling.

Fiorelli looked at them with raised eyebrows, but he only nodded and placed a satellite map of the property on the desk. After retrieving photos of the Jennings gang from his desk drawer, he placed these beside the map and looked up at the hitmen. They listened intently as Fiorelli explained the gang's plan to land on the beach and enter the residence through the rear patio doors. Fiorelli pointed at where the law enforcement forces would be lying in wait.

The hitmen leaned over the satellite view of the property and the local roads. Fiorelli stressed that all the Jennings gang members had to be killed as soon as they set foot on the beach.

"We're talking three or four of them, right?" Number One asked.

"Yes, though there could be more." The hitman frowned and looked at his partner. "But the prime target is that woman," Fiorelli added. He pointed to the photograph of Gerta. The hitmen studied the photo, then nodded, bent over the documents, muttered to each other and pointed at different locations.

Fiorelli interrupted them. "I hope Russo told you to bring the same type of rifle and cartridges that the SWAT sharpshooters use. That's absolutely critical."

The hitmen glanced at each other, smiled, nodded at Fiorelli, and resumed their quiet study of the map and photos. When they were done, the three men walked outside and strolled through the property. Outdoor lights illuminated the immediate grounds, but the parkland remained in darkness.

"The moon will be out at nine thirty tomorrow night," Number One said. "That'll make it hard for us to hide." He turned to Fiorelli. "But we'll figure it out."

Fiorelli hesitated, then said, "There's an extra hit I want to discuss with you."

The hitmen moved closer. "And what hit is that?" Number Two asked.

Tyler instructed his driver to drop him off at the entrance to the guardhouse instead of the main house as was customary. Fiorelli, who had been on the lookout for his employer, opened the guardhouse door for Tyler. The CEO walked past a guard smoking a cigarette by the liftgate, and entered the guardhouse. He barged into Fiorelli's office and slammed the door behind him. Scowling at Fiorelli, he demanded, "What's this bright idea you wanted to discuss over the goddam phone?"

Fiorelli straightened in his chair and opened his arms. "I'm sorry, boss, but you said your line was secure."

Tyler, red-faced, replied, "No telephone line is *completely* secure."

Fiorelli swallowed and said, "I came across a unique opportunity, and I didn't want you to miss out on it."

Tyler squared his jaw and said, "And what is this *opportunity*? It better be good."

CHAPTER 37

THE AMBUSH (PART I)

The sun was low in the sky when Popeye and Ashley drove up the laneway to Tyler's house. It was 6 p.m. They passed a Nassau County patrol cruiser parked by the stables and continued to the guardhouse.

Fiorelli was standing outside. "Glad to see you folks," he said with his best smile. "The Nassau police are setting up already. There's only two of youse guys?"

"We'll be observing only. This is an FBI operation now. That was agreed at yesterday's meeting, if you remember."

Moments later, Cochran and O'Keefe drove up in a white Dodge Charger. They parked behind Reliant's Suburban, climbed out, and joined Popeye, Ashley, and Fiorelli. "Agent Jackson isn't joining us?" Jaqueline asked.

"No, Louise and Agent Collins are monitoring Internet and phone activities from our hotel suite. They'll be passing on anything relevant they find."

Jacqueline nodded. "Thank Louise for alerting us about the gang renting a Zodiac this morning."

"You are very welcome, though I'm sure your team would have caught on soon enough."

"Still. We talked with the shop manager at North Shore Marina in New Rochelle, and he confirmed, again, having recognized Tom Cole and Danielle Jennings from photographs despite their disguise. They drove away in a white Chevy cargo van, pulling the trailer with the Zodiac."

Jacqueline paused, then added, "But we don't know where they went from there. Any idea?"

Popeye shook his head. "If they used the same credit card again, Louise and Collins will pick up their trail."

"I appreciate the help," Jacqueline said, "but I have to confess my reservations about this new law giving private contractors surveillance and arrest powers equal to ours."

An awkward silence followed until, to everyone's relief, it was interrupted by a police cruiser that drove in and parked by the stables. Nassau County Chief Casey Meadows emerged heavily from the vehicle, lumbered over, shook everyone's hand, and then announced, "I'll go check on my officers." He left and made his way toward the beach.

The growling of a Lenco BearCat resounded in the laneway. The vehicle parked by the stables and six officers in full combat gear jumped out. The SWAT captain directed his officers to different locations amidst the trees and shrubs.

The roar of an outboard motor announced the arrival of a huge black Zodiac on the beach. A captain and another SWAT officer jumped onto the sand, while two other officers remained in the craft. The two SWAT captains met and held an intense discussion, waving their arms and pointing in different directions. When the discussion concluded, the captain and officer from the Zodiac climbed back into the craft, which backed up, turned, and disappeared down the shoreline.

Popeye and Ashley entered the guardhouse and set up their gear around a table. Fiorelli followed them and then continued on to his office.

Dusk was descending on the nearby Sands Point Preserve when the two hitmen drove in at the wheel of a black Lincoln. It was 7 p.m. After passing the empty park guardhouse, the Lincoln turned right into a service lane that led to the Falaise Museum. The car stopped in front of steel gates that blocked the lane. Hitman Number Two climbed out, retrieved a bolt cutter from the trunk, and cut the chain that held the gates shut. The Lincoln rode through.

At the museum, Number Two climbed out of the car again. This time, he retrieved a weapons case from the trunk, tapped the car's rear fender, and proceeded on foot through the parkland.

The sun had set, but a half-moon illuminated his path through the trees. He reached the beachfront and followed it until he was in site of Tyler's residence. He located a grouping of bushes and trees that provided cover while still giving him a view of the beach and the patio behind the house.

He opened the weapons case and lifted out a Remington 700B sniper rifle, a box of .308 cartridges, a night vision scope, and a silencer. He fitted the night vision scope to the rifle and screwed the silencer on the end of the barrel. He rested the weapon on a tree branch at chest height, then swung it slowly from left to right, sighting the beach, then the patio. Satisfied with his setup, he laid the weapon down and waited.

After dropping off his companion, Hitman Number One drove back to Middle Neck Road past the turnoff to Tyler's and continued to the next lane, where he turned left and drove north toward the water. The road ended at a turnaround a short distance from the beach. He could see Tyler's house in the distance.

He parked the Lincoln and climbed out. The turnaround was deserted. He retrieved a rifle case from the trunk and walked toward the beach. Trees and shrubs grew thin there, but he found a sheltered position with a clear view of Tyler's beachfront and rear patio. The lights were on in the house, and he could see clearly through the wall-to-ceiling windows. His scope adjusted automatically to light intensity and would prevent any glare from the house lights from blinding him. He set up his equipment, then called Number Two.

"You in position?"

"Yes. You?"

"Yes."

"Confirming again. When the targets disembark on the beach, I'll pick off the woman first, then the others, starting water side. You pick them off starting beach side."

"Understood."

"When it's done, I'll pick you up where I dropped you off."

They signed off.

At 7:30 p.m., Popeye and Ashley left the guardhouse and walked to within sight of the beach. Popeye looked at his watch. "The gang will be on the water by now if they mean to land on the beach at 8 p.m. as they told Fiorelli."

At that moment, the rumble from a large outboard motor sounded from the other side of Hempstead Bay.

"Sounds like they're on time," Ashley said.

A few minutes later, they made out the outline of a large black Zodiac on the horizon, and fifteen minutes later, the craft approached the beach at running speed and climbed onto the sand before juddering to a stop. Seconds later, the SWAT Zodiac thundered out of the darkness, aiming a powerful spotlight at the intruder, and landed alongside the Jennings gang's craft.

Simultaneously, officers emerged from the nearby bushes, brandishing assault rifles, and surrounded the rogue Zodiac.

Shielding his eyes from the glare of the spotlight, a man stood, frozen, aboard the Zodiac and shouted, "Don't shoot! I'm not armed."

A SWAT captain approached. "Climb out and keep your hands folded behind your head," he shouted.

A man in his mid-twenties, dressed in a bulky black jacket and blue jeans, disembarked awkwardly, eyes squinting, hands clasped tightly behind his head. His sneakers sank in the wet sand. An officer yanked him around and tied his hands behind his back.

"Where are the others?" the SWAT captain asked.

The man returned a puzzled look. "What others?"

Popeye had approached by now and followed the conversation. He cursed under his breath, "Shit!" and signaled to Ashley to follow him. The two raced to their Suburban.

CHAPTER 38

THE JENNINGS MEET WITH GOMEZ

The day before, after the meeting with Fiorelli, Malcolm, Gerta, and Larry drove back to Manhattan and parked the van in the underground parking on 59th Street, one block east of Tyler's building. Malcolm got out first and signaled for his companions to follow him. Dressed in blue technician uniforms, with Gerta carrying her laptop in a satchel, the team entered the building at number 719 on Fifth Avenue. They walked past a security guard and stopped. A throng of people was coming and going through the atrium, entering and exiting the high-end boutiques and the bank of elevators like ants in an anthill.

Malcolm located the security office at the far back of the atrium. A brass sign on the door read Chief of Security F. Gomez. He looked through the floor to ceiling glass partition. A man sat behind a large, dark brown, L-shaped desk, holding a document in his hands. A laptop rested on a shelf to his right. A high bookcase covered the wall behind him.

Malcolm knocked on the doorframe. The man looked up and waved him in.

"Can I help you?" Gomez asked.

Malcolm offered a hand to shake. "We're from Downing Fiber Optics. We're here to work on the communications system?"

"Yes. Right." Gomez rose, shook hands, and introduced himself. "Frank Gomez. Security chief." He extended a hand toward the chairs across from his desk. Malcolm and Gerta sat down. Larry closed the office door behind him and remained standing.

Gomez sat behind his desk. "Can I see your work order?"

"We're here to discuss a proposal with you, Mr. Gomez," Malcolm said.

"A proposal? But you just said . . ." Gomez stared quizzically at Malcolm and Gerta in turn. Then his face turned pale. "*Dios Mio*! You're the killers the FBI were talking about." He glanced at the atrium through the floor-to-ceiling glass wall, but no guards were within earshot. He looked at the phone on his desk, uncertain what to do next.

Malcolm leaned forward and spoke calmly, "Then you already know what we're here to talk about."

Gomez stared at Malcolm, looking stunned. He glanced again at his phone and swallowed hard. "What do you want from me?"

"We need a master key card that will open all the doors and operate the service elevators in this building."

"You can't be serious," Gomez said. He glanced out at the atrium again. "My guards are outside. You'll never get away if you fire a weapon in here."

"We have a more convincing argument," Malcolm said. Gomez raised his eyebrows.

Gerta leaned forward. "Mr. Francisco Gomez Estrada, we know your real identity. You are an illegal immigrant with fake papers." She paused to let that sink in, then continued. "Unless you help us, we'll inform the Immigration and Naturalization Service of your true identity and you'll be deported back to Mexico, where we also know you face some very serious criminal charges."

Gomez stared at her open-mouthed as beads of sweat formed on his forehead. "You guys have me confused with someone else. I have a green card. I'm here under the DACA program. In fact, I'll be naturalized in just a few months' from now."

Gerta shook her head. "We know about your fake birth certificate and fake high school diploma. We know your criminal record in Mexico."

Gomez jittered in his seat, chewed his lip, then said, "You're bluffing. You can't prove any of this. I'm alerting my security guards." Gomez reached for his desk phone and lifted the receiver. Malcolm and Gerta remained seated. They were smiling now. Gomez stopped in mid-motion. He stared at Gerta. "What proof have you got?"

Gerta placed her laptop on Gomez's desk, brought up a file, and turned the screen around for him to see. She scrolled through copies of Gomez's real identity documents and a copy of his criminal record in Mexico.

Gomez's jaw trembled. "How did you get this information?"

Gerta leaned forward. "We know about your wife back in Mexico, that she's caring for your elderly parents. We know that you send money to her on a regular basis. We admire you for that. We'd like to help you."

Gomez looked at her, wide-eyed, disbelieving.

Malcolm leaned forward as well and said, "The FBI must have already told you that our target is Michael Tyler. His head office is on the thirty-fifth floor, am I right?" Gomez nodded. "The man has over fifty million in overseas accounts. We will cut you in for twenty percent in exchange for the master key card."

"We'll deposit your share in an account of your choosing," Gerta added.

Gomez stared at Gerta and Malcolm but remained silent.

"You'll need money upfront to plan your exit," Gerta said. "We'll transfer five hundred thousand to your account right now. If you don't have a secure account, we'll open one for you."

Gomez looked pale but alert. "How do I know if you'll come through with the rest of the money?"

"You can join us during the robbery and see for yourself how much the take is," Malcolm said.

"I don't want to be around when you rob the man. The FBI said you plan to kill him as well." Gomez paused, then asked, "Even if I agree to take the money, where would I go? The States and Mexico have an extradition treaty."

Gerta reached into her satchel and retrieved a passport, a social security card, driver's license, and a credit card. She handed them to Gomez. "I prepared a new identity for you."

Gomez examined the documents. He looked up at Malcolm. "You said half a million now?"

Malcolm nodded. "And nine and a half million later."

Gomez stroked his chin. "When do you want to do this?"

"Tomorrow evening between eight and ten."

"How do you know Tyler will be in his office?"

"We keep tabs on the man. If there's a change, we'll call you."

Gerta looked at Gomez. "Shall I transfer your advance now?"

Gomez hesitated. "Will it leave a trace?"

"Not if your computer transactions are secure," Gerta said. "Let me see your laptop."

"That's okay. I've had a tech guy set that up for me already." Gomez reached into his wallet, retrieved a card, and handed it to Gerta, "This is the account."

Gerta initiated the transfer of funds while Gomez watched his account on his laptop. When the deposit appeared on his screen, Gomez exclaimed, "*No mames!*"

He reached into a drawer in his desk, pulled out a key card, and handed it to Malcolm. Malcolm passed it back to Larry, who left the office with the card.

"Is that all you need from me?" Gomez asked.

"Not quite," Malcolm replied. "You need to fill out a work permit to give us access to the communication room tomorrow evening. And leave word with the guards on that shift that we'll be working there." Gomez nodded. Malcolm added, "You said the FBI were here earlier?"

Gomez nodded. "And so were the NYPD and some detective agency."

"What surveillance are they putting in place?"

"Two NYPD cruisers will be posted outside, one across from the entrance and one across from the underground garage exit, starting tonight. They're putting two Emergency Service Units on high alert. That's our SWAT teams." Gomez paused, then added, "I'm supposed to hold information sessions with all my security guards, starting with this evening's shift, and distribute photos of you guys."

Malcolm and Gerta stared at each other, then Malcolm turned to Gomez. "No information session and no photos to the guards on tomorrow night's shift."

Gomez nodded. "I can do that."

"Don't tell anyone," Gerta said, "not even your wife, about this or your travel plans. The FBI will be monitoring your calls, your emails, and your Internet activity. We'll communicate with you on this phone." She handed Gomez a burner.

Larry entered the office, returned the key card to Malcolm, and nodded. Gerta put her laptop back in her satchel and stood up. Malcolm shook hands with Gomez and headed for the door with Gerta and Larry close behind.

Back in their suite, Malcolm and Larry studied the drawings and satellite views of Tyler's office building, while Gerta sat at the other worktable and worked on her laptop.

Danielle came in with their dinner orders. She said to her dad, "Steve and Tom will eat and work in their suite. Steve said he doesn't want to disturb the grownups." Malcolm and Larry smiled.

Danielle sat down at the worktable next to her mother. Malcolm straightened and walked over to Gerta and Danielle. He kissed them both on the top of their heads, then headed for the door, signaling Larry to follow him. "Bring the food. Let's go eat with the lads."

In the other suite, Steve and Tom had gathered chairs around a coffee table to form a conference area. Malcolm and Larry walked in and sat beside them.

"How did the preparations go today?" Malcolm asked.

"The young ones did most of the work," Steve said, winking at Tom. "I just supervised."

Tom beamed as he said, "Danielle and I located a twenty-foot Zodiac at a marina in New Rochelle. It comes with a 120hp motor and a trailer. We reserved it over the phone. We'll pick it up tomorrow morning and drive it to a community dock."

"Good work," Malcolm said.

Steve looked at Malcolm and said, "We should take the Zodiac out for a spin around the bay. To make sure everything works well."

Malcolm smiled. "I'm okay with that long as you can stick to our schedule." He punched Steve lightly on the shoulder.

Larry smiled. "Everything is falling into place."

CHAPTER 39

RELIANT RACES TO TYLER'S OFFICE

Popeye jumped behind the wheel, turned the vehicle around, and floored the accelerator. He barreled down Shepherds Lane, heading back toward the city.

Ashley called Louise and put her on speaker.

"We've been duped," Popeye said. "The Jennings gang will be attacking Tyler at his office."

There was a shocked silence at the other end of the line. Then Louise said, "That explains the latest information we've just discovered."

"What information?" Popeye asked.

"Security chief Gomez has disappeared."

"What do you mean, disappeared?"

"He hasn't reported for duty tonight. Building management doesn't know where he is and can't reach him. He hasn't used his phone, his laptop, or his credit cards since noon. They sent some people to his apartment, but there was no one there, and he's not in any local hospital. Paul and I have checked all flights, trains, and buses out of the city. There's no trace of him. He's gone dark."

Popeye turned to Ashley. "Call Tyler right away."

After several attempts, Ashley gave up. "His lines are dead, both the switchboard and his private line. They must have been jammed."

"Call Jacqueline and put your phone on speaker." When Jacqueline picked up, Popeye informed her about Gomez's disappearance and Tyler's phone lines being jammed.

"I'll alert the NYPD SWAT teams right away."

"We won't be there for another half hour," Popeye said.

O'Keefe shook his head and cursed under his breath. "Let's hope SWAT gets there on time."

CHAPTER 40

JAMAL

Earlier that afternoon, Tom, Lucky, and Steve had driven to the Mott Haven neighborhood in the Bronx. Tom parked in the alley behind the bakery as he had been instructed. The man they were to meet, Jamal, was already waiting by the back door. Tom picked up a bulging brown envelope, held Lucky back as he closed the vehicle door, and, with Steve following right behind him, handed the envelope to Jamal. Jamal opened it, leafed through the pile of bills inside it, nodded, turned, and tapped on the door behind him. A large man in a flat-topped baker's hat and apron opened the door, looked fixedly at Jamal, took the envelope, and disappeared inside.

"It'll be a minute," Jamal said.

A minute passed and the door opened. The large man handed a brown bag to Jamal, who handed it on to Tom. Tom reached into the bag and pulled out a packet of white powder wrapped in clear plastic. He looked up at Jamal and nodded.

Steve locked eyes with Jamal. "Ready to do the job we talked about?"

"I'm ready," Jamal said. He followed Tom and Steve to the van and climbed in. Tom drove to the municipal dock in New Rochelle.

The men hooked the trailer with the Zodiac to the van, Tom backed the trailer down the public ramp into the water, and Steve and Jamal untied the Zodiac from the trailer and tied it to the dock. Steve fetched a duffel bag from the van and handed it to Jamal. "That's a marine GPS. The coordinates of Tyler's residence are programmed in. You know how to use this?"

"Yeah, sure," Jamal answered. "I use a similar one when I go fishing in the Sound with my uncle Tyrell."

The men climbed aboard the Zodiac. Lucky jumped in and began sniffing every inch of the vessel. Jamal took out the GPS and placed it on the console.

Steve looked Jamal in the eyes. "Remember. It's important you arrive at 8 p.m. precisely. A man called Fiorelli will be expecting you." Steve handed an envelope to Jamal. "This is the two thousand dollars we agreed on."

Jamal opened the envelope, counted the $100 bills, looked up, and nodded. "Don't worry. I'll be there on time."

He walked to the captain's seat, examined the controls, turned on the spotlight, and fired up the outboard motor. It rumbled smoothly to life. Jamal steered the Zodiac toward open water, waved at Steve, and gunned the engine. The Zodiac was soon just a dark dot on Hempstead Bay.

CHAPTER 41

THE AMBUSH (PART II)

The SWAT captain furrowed his brows, glared at Jamal, and untied his hand. "Show me some ID," he barked.

Jamal retrieved his wallet and handed over his driver's license The captain examined the document, then asked, "Why are you here, Mr. Harrison?"

"Delivery to a Mr. Fiorelli."

Two officers had already climbed aboard the Zodiac to search it. Now they returned with a duffel bag. They laid it on the beach in front of the captain.

Jamal said, "They paid me to deliver this package."

"Who paid you?"

"Uh . . . some guy about my age, and another, older guy."

"Names?"

"I heard the young one being called Tom, and he called the old guy Steve."

The captain brought up some photographs on his cellphone and showed them to Jamal.

"These two?" he asked, pointing at photos of Tom and Steve.

"Yup, that's them. What's going on anyway?"

"What's in the bag?' the captain asked.

"I don't know," Jamal answered, red-faced.

The captain stared at him. "You want us to believe you didn't know what you were delivering?"

"Uh . . . I assumed it was coke."

"If you didn't know these guys, what stopped you from taking off with the drugs?"

"I know who Mr. Fiorelli is. He's connected. We don't fuck with the mob."

"Open the bag."

Jamal leaned over to open the bag, but before he reached the zipper, the left side of his head exploded, sending brain matter and blood splattering over the sand and the nearby officers. An instant later, the muffled crack from a suppressed rifle resounded from the parkland. Jamal's body collapsed onto the bag and the sand.

Everyone ducked down and all eyes turned in the direction of the parkland where the shot had come from. The trees and bushes stood undisturbed. The captain jerked his head in the direction of the woods and two officers raced, crouching, toward the trees. Two others ran to their BearCat, and the two police officers rushed back to their cruiser.

The captain kneeled beside Jamal, inspected the injury, and shook his head. He signaled an officer to move the body aside and opened the duffel bag. There was a small bag of white powder inside with a sheet of paper tied to it. The captain aimed a flashlight at the note. It read, *Mr. Fiorelli, thank you for your help. M. J.*

At that moment, another crack from a suppressed rifle split the air. The shot came from a different area of the beach, but no one had been hit. All eyes turned in the direction the shot had come from. The captain signaled two officers to go investigate.

Someone shouted from the rear patio of the house. "Help! Someone's been shot!"

Jacqueline, followed by the captain and two officers, sped toward the house. As she approached the rear patio door, Jaqueline could clearly make out a bullet hole in one of the glass panes. She entered the house. A woman lay flat on the floor, facing up. A pool of blood had formed under her back. One of Fiorelli's security guards—Jaqueline had only met him briefly the day before but remembered his name, Pasquale—was kneeling beside the body, his face white with shock. An officer arrived with a first aid kit and kneeled beside the body, checking for signs of life. He looked up at Jaqueline and shook his head.

She leaned over the body. "Who is she?"

Pasquale answered sheepishly, "It's Mrs. Tyler."

CHAPTER 42

THE HITMEN ESCAPE

Hitman Number One returned his rifle to the carrying case and raced back to his car. He threw the case in the back seat of the Lincoln and jumped behind the wheel. The two police officers who were approaching at a run fired at the vehicle. Bullets pinged against the panels of the Lincoln and pierced holes through the windshield. Number One floored the accelerator and raced down Shorewood Drive, turned right on Middle Neck Road, and headed toward the Sands Point Preserve. In the distance, he made out the headlights of a BearCat and a patrol cruiser turn ahead of him and also head toward the Preserve. He turned off his headlights at once and followed at a distance. When they reached the park's guardhouse, both police vehicles turned sharply into the lane that led to the Falaise Museum.

Number One stopped at the guardhouse, unsure of what to do next. Just then, his phone buzzed. He fumbled in his pocket and picked up. The voice of Number Two, breathless, announced, "Change of plans. Pick me up at Castle Gould." Number One sped straight ahead in the direction of Castle Gould, about a hundred yards further on. As soon as he entered the castle's parking lot, Number Two appeared in the headlights, ran to the car, threw his case into the back seat, and climbed in. As the Lincoln raced away, gunfire resounded through the parkland, but it soon faded to nothing.

"The fuckers must have had a thermal scope," Number Two said. "There's no other way they could have followed me through the forest."

Number One turned to his companion. "You all right?"

"Yeah, I'm fine. You?"

"I'm fine too."

"Where the hell were the targets that Fiorelli talked about?" Number Two said as they sped out of the Preserve. "And the firefight?" His partner shook his head but remained silent. After a moment, Number Two said, "Hey, that was a great shot you made through the patio windows."

"Thanks." Number One glanced at him and grinned.

They turned right on Middle Neck Road and headed south on Cow Neck Road toward Port Washington. As they entered the village, a police cruiser closed in on them, patrol siren blaring and roof lights flashing.

Number One stopped the Lincoln in the middle of the road. The police cruiser screeched to a halt two car lengths behind. The siren went silent. Number One turned to his partner. "Brace yourself."

He put the Lincoln into reverse and floored the accelerator. Both men leaned back in their seats and pressed their heads against the headrests.

The police cruiser had no push bumper. The impact crushed the vehicle's front grille, buckled the hood and front side panels, and shattered the front windshield. Steam hissed from the radiator.

The two hitmen were pressed deep into their seats by the impact. The rebound sent both men airborne, like weightless astronauts, until they were caught by their seatbelts. Their chins struck their chest bones and strained their neck muscles. They grunted, crashed back into their seats, and lay still. The air bags had not deployed. Both windshields lay shattered. Number One groaned, regained his bearings, then turned to Number Two. "You all right?"

His companion gave his head a shake, loosened the muscles of his neck, then answered, "Right as rain." Both men broke out laughing.

They climbed out and walked over to the patrol cruiser. The driver's door stood open, and the driver lay flat, face up, on the asphalt. He groaned, but did not get up. The other officer lay half in the seat and half on the ground, unconscious. His seat belt was undone, and the air bag lay deflated. His head rested to one side, in an unnatural pose, and blood dripped from his forehead.

The men returned to the Lincoln and drove off. Pieces of the car's body dropped off and banged against the roadway. Number One steered the car into a side street and parked. "We need to dump this car. We're leaving a better trail than Hansel and Gretel."

They climbed out and stared at the wreck. "What do we do now?" Number Two asked.

"I know the owner of a body shop near here. He's in the Family. I'll call Russo and have him send someone to pick us up." He led the way through side streets toward the shop, talking to Russo as they went.

CHAPTER 43

THE RAID ON TYLER

The clock on the van's dashboard read 6:30 p.m. Steve sat at the wheel. Gerta sat beside him, Malcolm and Larry behind. Steve steered the van through the Lincoln Tunnel, emerged on the New York City side, then headed for Tyler's building. The traffic was heavy. Cars were honking at each other to no effect.

Gerta called Tyler's office and was told by his secretary that Mr. Tyler was in a conference call with Asian clients, and would she like to leave a message? Gerta said no and thanked her. "He's in the office," she told Malcolm.

Steve turned north on Fifth Ave and drove past the front entrance to Tyler's office tower. An NYPD cruiser stood parked across from the building entrance. Another cruiser idled on a side street across from the exit from the building's underground parking.

Steve turned right on Fifty-Seventh Street. Throngs of people filled the sidewalk. He turned into the service lane behind Tyler's building. It was empty. He parked next to a service entrance. Malcolm, Gerta, and Larry, in blue uniforms and hard hats, climbed out, grabbed satchels, cases, and duffel bags, and headed to the service entrance. Steve drove out of the lane and drove to a nearby parking garage.

Malcolm opened the service door with the master key card, and the group filed in.

"I'll wait for Steve," Gerta said. Malcolm and Larry went on ahead, located the telecommunications room, entered, and laid down their bags and cases. They looked around, getting their bearings. The equipment layout matched their drawings perfectly.

"You get started on the telecommunications panel, and I'll go report to the office," Malcolm said.

He made his way to the atrium and located the security office. A guard sat at a console facing a wall of closed-circuit TV monitors. He waved Malcolm in. "You must be Downing Fiber Optics. I saw you come in through the service entrance. Chief Gomez told me you'd be coming. I have your work order right here."

"Yeah, hi. I'm Art Downing," Malcolm replied, handing the man a business card.

The guard consulted the work order. "You're upgrading the building's phone and Internet service?"

"Yes. We're ready to get started."

"Have your men taken the safety orientation training?" the guard asked. Malcolm handed him the fake certificates Gerta had prepared.

"Good. I'll get you to sign our logbook and you're good to go." He pushed a logbook toward Malcolm. "Where will you guys be?"

"The telecommunications room first, then we'll run tests in the instrument cabinets on all the floors."

"You're not touching my TV monitors, are you?"

"We'll have to turn off the phone and Internet service for a short while, but I'll give you advance warning."

The guard nodded, then said, "How long will you guys be?"

"We'll be done by midnight."

"Good. Give me a holler if you need anything." Malcolm nodded and left.

When he returned to the telecommunications room, Steve and Gerta had arrived. Larry was kneeling inside a cabinet, pulling at wires. He turned and smiled at Malcolm. "I've disconnected the modules for the fortieth floor. That cuts off their desk phones and computers."

"Good. Let's go visit our friend," Malcolm said. Gerta grabbed the satchels containing her laptop and the signal jammer, Larry picked up the duffle bag with the weapons, and the three followed Malcolm to the service elevator.

The security guard's cell phone rang. "Security office," he answered.

"Hi! This is Sherry with Retail Conglomerate on the Fortieth floor. Our desk phones and all our computers just went down. What happened?"

"Oh, yeah. A crew is upgrading the building's telecommunication systems. They were supposed to warn me before cutting anybody off. I'm very sorry about that."

"We need communications reestablished right away. Our CEO is working on an important project with overseas clients. Can you delay the work until after ten?"

"Let me talk to the work crew. I'll get back to you shortly."

"Much appreciated. Thank you."

The guard walked to the telecommunications room but found it empty. He retrieved Malcolm's business card and dialed the number.

Gerta answered. "Downing Fiber Optics."

She listened to the guard's request, then said, "I'll pass your message on to the field supervisor. He'll get back to you shortly."

"Make sure you do. This is important."

The team stopped in front of the door to Retail Conglomerate's suite of offices. Gerta switched on the signal jammer, killing all Wi-Fi and cell phone communications in the vicinity. Malcolm led the way into reception.

Sherry rose behind her desk at the sight of the four uniformed technicians. "Thank God you're here," she said. "We've lost our phones and our Internet. We need those back right away."

Malcolm looked around the reception area and adjoining hallway. "Who else is in the offices?"

Sherry stiffened at the abruptness of the question. "Mr. Tyler is conducting a job interview in his office, but there's no one else here tonight."

Gerta headed down the hallway that led to a row of offices. Malcolm and Larry walked to a double door with a brass plaque announcing Tyler's name and title. Sherry rose and shouted after them. "Hold on. You can't walk in unannounced!"

Steve stepped briskly over, pushed Sherry back in her chair, and wrapped her arms behind the chair's back with plastic ties. "What the hell are you doing?" Sherry yelled as she struggled against him.

"I'm sorry, ma'am," Steve said as he covered her mouth with duct tape.

Malcolm and Larry barged into Tyler's office. They found a woman bent over a large mahogany desk with Tyler standing behind her, his hands gripping her waist. The woman was dressed in business attire, but the hem of her black, pin-striped blazer and shirt were pushed up, revealing white buttocks. Tyler, his white shirt unbuttoned, pants and underpants below his knees, genitals exposed, and forehead glistening with sweat, stared back wide-eyed.

He quickly overcame his shock and shouted angrily, "What the hell are you guys doing in my office? Get the fuck out of here right now!"

The woman straightened hastily, pulled up her underpants, and pushed down her skirt. Malcolm moved forward, took the woman's hand, and guided her to a visitor's chair. Larry strode around the desk and pushed Tyler down into his chair. He pressed a knife against the now terrified man's throat.

The executive sat, bug-eyed, frozen in place. He swallowed hard, then, regaining some confidence, said, "I recognize you guys. You're that band of killers, the Jennings gang."

Steve and Gerta entered Tyler's office. Gerta addressed Malcolm. "There's no one else here."

Steve walked over to the woman in the visitor's chair, placed a hand on her shoulder, and said, "If you can sit quietly, I won't have to tie you down." The woman looked up at him, wide-eyed, and remained silent.

Gerta walked over to Tyler's desk and placed her laptop on it. She reached into the satchel and switched off the Wi-Fi blocking. She locked eyes with Tyler and pointed at his laptop on the credenza beside him. "Switch on your laptop," she commanded.

Tyler stared back at Gerta, clenched his jaw, but obeyed. Larry kept the pressure on the blade.

"Open the bank accounts of your shell company in the British Virgin Islands," Gerta said.

"I've no access to those accounts," Tyler answered. "You need to talk to my accountants." He smirked.

Larry increased the pressure on the blade. A bead of blood leaked onto Tyler's neck. Sweat glistened on his forehead, but he remained silent.

"Looks like you need a different kind of convincing," Larry said. He grabbed Tyler's scrotum with one hand and pierced the skin with his knife.

"Ow! Stop! What the fuck!" Tyler howled. He tried to rise, but the pressure of the knife kept him glued to his seat. In a trembling voice, he said, "All right, all right, I'll try to access the accounts." He retrieved a notebook from his desk, found the page he needed, then tapped keys on his laptop. A bank account appeared on the screen. "You guys are in luck. There is one account I can open."

Gerta reached over and noted the account balance: $10 million. "Start a transfer, and I'll fill in the rest," she said. Tyler initiated a transfer of funds, and Gerta turned the laptop around and filled in the destination.

Tyler looked up at Malcolm, and said, "You guys are rich now. You'd better hightail it before security comes looking for you."

Gerta leaned forward and stared hard at Tyler. "There's another forty million in that shell company's accounts. We've seen all the transfers you've made for the last five years. Open the other accounts."

Tyler spat between gritted teeth, "The police have this building under surveillance. They'll soon figure out something is wrong and come for you. You'd better run with the ten million you've already got." Without waiting for an answer, Tyler grabbed Larry's hand, pushed the knife aside, then dove across the desk. He knocked Gerta over and tumbled onto the floor. He got up and hopped toward the door, holding up his pants with one hand, howling for help at the top of his lungs.

Steve ran forward and kneed Tyler in the groin. The executive dropped to his knees and moaned as he cupped his genitals with both hands. Larry walked over, grabbed Tyler by the collar, and dragged him back to his executive chair.

Tyler was sweating profusely and breathing heavily. Larry grabbed his scrotum again and sank the blade deeper than before.

"Aiieee!" Tyler howled, fear and pain in his voice. "Stop, for Christ's sake." Larry kept the pressure on the blade.

"All right," Tyler said breathlessly. He reached for his laptop, opened the other accounts, and initiated transfers for another $40 million.

Once the transfers were complete, Tyler leaned back in his chair, looked up at Malcolm, and said, "Now you've got all the money there is to steal.

I suggest you put some aside for when you guys are rotting in jail. You'll need it to buy crack to while away the hours of boredom."

Malcolm turned to Larry, "He's all yours."

Larry grabbed Tyler's penis, cut it off, and laid it on the desk. Tyler stared at it in horror, open-mouthed as if silently screaming. Larry retrieved a piece of string from his pocket and placed it on the desk. "You'd better tourniquet the stub until help arrives."

Tyler looked up at Larry, his mouth opening and closing like a guppy, but no sound came out.

"Let's get going," Malcolm said and headed toward the door. Gerta picked up the satchels with her equipment and followed him, Steve close behind. Larry picked up Tyler's penis, walked to the washroom, and flushed it down the toilet. Emerging with a smile on his face, he grabbed the bag of weapons and followed Steve.

CHAPTER 44

THE ESCAPE TO WAREHOUSE 19

Steve cracked opened the rear service door and peeked into the service lane. "Shit," he cursed. He turned to his teammates. "I can see police cruisers with lights flashing, and a BearCat, blocking access to Fifty-Sixth Street. We can't leave without being seen." Seeing the anxious look on his companions' faces, he added, "But I can clear a path for us." He reached into the weapons bag and retrieved six grenades. He kneeled and lined up three smoke grenades on the floor, then formed a second line with three frag grenades. He rose, propped the service door ajar with one foot, and armed and threw the grenades, one after the other, in the direction of the patrol vehicles. As soon as the first grenade detonated, Steve turned to his teammates. "Now!"

Gray smoke filled the lane as Steve tore down the alley toward Fifty-Seventh Street with his teammates close behind. They raced along the sidewalk, dodging between panicky pedestrians, then dove down a ramp leading to an underground garage.

Their van sat facing forward, in line with the exit ramp. Steve jumped behind the wheel. His teammates scrambled aboard helter-skelter. He floored the accelerator. The van bolted up the ramp, crashed through the liftgate, and hurtled onto Fifty-Seventh.

Steve steered eastward along the street, then turned south on Park Avenue. With one hand pressing firmly on the horn, he passed cars, delivery trucks, and limousines, at times on their left and at times on their right.

Police sirens blared behind him. He skewed right on Thirty-Ninth and sped westward toward the Lincoln Tunnel.

Ignoring the arrow that pointed toward the tunnel, Steve continued along Thirty-Ninth Street down to the Hudson River wharves. With a sharp crank of the steering wheel, he dove into an underground garage. The team jumped out, grabbed satchels, cases, duffel bags, and raced up the ramp onto the street.

They walked briskly toward the ferry terminal. Gerta pulled out tickets and handed one to each of her teammates. The troop squeezed through the turnstile and climbed aboard the ferry to Lincoln Harbor, New Jersey. Five minutes later, the ferry left the dock.

Everyone sat, tense and anxious, during the six-minute crossing. To break the strain, Malcolm turned to Larry and grinned. "I wasn't expecting you to Bobbitt the guy. Nice touch."

Larry smiled back and said, "It was Gerta's idea. She convinced me the best revenge would be to strike at his manhood as well as his money and his freedom."

"His freedom?" Malcolm asked.

"Gerta is reserving a surprise for Tyler."

The team disembarked at Lincoln Harbor and made their way to the street. To everyone's relief, another white Chevy cargo van was waiting there, Tom behind the wheel and Lucky on his lap. Danielle waved from the passenger seat.

Popeye and Ashley barreled through the Queens Midtown Tunnel, emerged in Midtown Manhattan, and sped toward Tyler's building. When they arrived, they confronted what looked like a war zone. Ambulances lined Fifty-Sixth Street and the building's service lane. First responders were attending to injured police officers, and acrid smoke hung in the air. A Lenco BearCat and two police cruisers stood by the building's entrance on Fifth Avenue.

Popeye squeezed the Suburban into a tight parking space, and he and Ashley disembarked and hurried toward the police tape. After looking at their credentials, and making a call, the officer in charge of access control let them cross the police cordon. Popeye turned to Ashley. "See what you can find out from the officers here. I'll check inside the building." Ashley nodded.

Popeye entered the atrium, approached the nearest police officer, and asked to speak to the NYPD detective in charge. The officer took Popeye's credentials and made a call. After a short back-and-forth, he hung up and escorted Popeye to the elevator. "He's on the fortieth floor."

The detective met Popeye at the elevator, introduced himself, then said, "Jacqueline Cochran said to let you in on the investigation. Welcome aboard."

Popeye thanked him, then asked, "How's my client?"

"Tyler? Not a happy camper. The perps chopped off his dick—"

"Jesus Christ!" Popeye gasped.

"—but he had the presence of mind to tourniquet what was left of it. The first responders rushed him to the ER." The detective bit his lip and shook his head.

"Any other victims?"

"Two women were in the office during the attack—Tyler's secretary and a job applicant. First responders are treating them for shock, but they weren't injured." The detective paused, then added, "I can't let you enter the suite until the forensic team completes their work. That will take a while."

Popeye called Ashley and Louise on a conference line. He summarized the situation at Tyler's suite, then commented, "Why didn't they kill Tyler like the others?"

"Can't say, but they cleaned out his shell company accounts in the British Virgin Islands," Louise said. "From what I can see, fifty million was transferred out."

"They're going to split up and disappear, now, I'm sure of that," Popeye said. "Any sign of where they went from here?"

"My search engines are filtering through all communications and transactions from the New York City area. Paul and I are reading everything they flag, but nothing so far."

"Can you follow what the FBI and the police are doing?"

"Yes. The police are setting up checkpoints on all the tunnels, bridges, and ferries leading out of the city. They're monitoring the cameras at subway, train, and bus stations, and the ferry terminals too."

"Do we have access to those cameras?"

"Yes." Louise answered. "And I'm running facial recognition software on the feeds. But that software generates a lot of false positives. Paul and I will get overwhelmed very quickly. And if they're wearing disguises, that will only make it harder."

"Ashley and I are coming over right now to lend a hand," Popeye said. He took the elevator down to the atrium and found Ashley.

"Did you learn anything helpful?" Popeye asked.

"Not much. After lobbing smoke and frag grenades down the service lane, the gang escaped in a white Chevy cargo van. A BearCat and two police cruisers gave chase, but I don't know anything more for now."

"Let's go help Louise and Paul check the camera feeds."

"Any progress on locating the Jennings?" Popeye asked as he rushed into their suite at the hotel.

"We've picked up their trail," Louise said. "They got on a ferry at the Hudson River wharves and crossed to the Jersey side."

Ashley looked at the camera footage. "There. I see them. At the Lincoln Ferry Terminal. They're wearing blue technicians' uniforms and eyeglasses, but I recognize Malcolm and Gerta Jennings. And there's Larry Schmidt and Steve Adams."

Louise checked the time stamp. "That was a half hour ago." She looked at the other cameras in the terminal. "Damn. I lose them when they leave the terminal."

"The must have had a vehicle waiting for them," Popeye said. "Tom Cole and Danielle Jennings must have picked them up." He pondered this for a moment, then said, "I better call Jacqueline Cochran with this."

Jacqueline confirmed that her team had seen the footage as well. "The Jersey police are setting up roadblocks on all major routes out of Jersey City," she told him.

Popeye hung up and sat, pensive. He shook his head and said, "We need a lucky break." He looked up at Louise. "Where would *you* go if you were them?"

"I'd fly out of the country as soon as I could."

"Me too," Popeye said. "Let's focus on the airports."

After leaving Lincoln Harbor, Tom steered the van through side streets, heading northwest. His destination was Warehouse 19 in Hawthorne, New Jersey. The proprietor of Warehouse 19, Gunter Klein, was a close friend of Gerta's Uncle Karl of Wagner Machinery in Chicago. Both Gunter and Karl had immigrated to Chicago after the war and worked as machinists there. Gunter had retired a few years earlier and moved to Hawthorne to help his son start a machine shop, but he and Karl had stayed in close touch.

This was the second time Gerta had called on Uncle Gunter. The team had stopped over, four months earlier, to relabel their vehicles after assassinating Jamie Stonely, their first target, in his luxury condo in Manhattan.

Gunter greeted Gerta with a hug and Malcolm with a handshake. "Is everyone safe? Were you followed?"

"We're all okay. I don't think we were followed," Gerta answered.

"Good." Gunter signaled to one of his men to guide Tom's van inside the warehouse. He pointed to four vehicles parked in an adjacent bay and announced, proudly, "Your *limos* are ready. Two Ford Fusions, one Honda Accord, and a Toyota Camry, all with new papers."

"That's great," Gerta said. "Was it hard to arrange?"

"Stolen cars with papers are a dime a dozen in Jersey City. Well, maybe more than a dime," Gunter said, smiling mischievously. "Fifteen thousand each." He looked at Gerta. "Thank you for transferring the money so promptly. And for adding a generous tip." He winked at her.

Gerta placed a hand on his arm and said, "We're indebted to you, Uncle Gunter."

Malcolm and his team transferred the weapons and supplies from the van to the cars. From the list he had prepared in New York, Larry indicated what weapons went into what car.

Gunter approached Malcolm and said, "Once your van is empty, I'll have my man drive it to a local recycler, a business partner of mine. He'll have it crushed and out to the steel mill by tomorrow morning."

"Much appreciated," Malcolm said, then signaled for the team to join him. They formed a circle and regarded each other solemnly. Lucky, sensing something was up, fidgeted and yipped. The time had come for the team to split up, forever.

CHAPTER 45

THE TEAM SPLITS UP

Malcolm's team stood in a circle, silent, looking at each other. A devilish smile rose on Steve's face as he said, "This marks the end of a beautiful friendship." Gerta walked over and gave him a hug. Malcolm followed suit. Steve gazed affectionately at his two leaders. "I'll never forget you two and the good times we've had. Come and visit me in Casablanca."

Gerta put a hand on Steve's arm. "Let us know how you're doing."

"Will do," Steve said. He turned to his other teammates and hugged each one in turn, then patted Lucky on the head, climbed aboard the white Ford Fusion, smiled, waved, and drove off.

Larry was next to do the rounds, dispensing hugs. He stopped in front of Malcolm and Gerta. "I will miss you, my friends. I'll send you my address in San Francisco. Come and visit sometime." He climbed in the blue Ford Fusion and drove off.

Danielle and Tom stood facing Malcolm and Gerta. "We'll send you daily updates on our progress," Danielle promised.

Gerta hugged her daughter and held her for a long time. She then turned to Tom and hugged him. "You take good care of our girl."

"I will," Tom said. His eyes were teary. He turned to Malcolm, and the men hugged. Lucky placed his front paws on Tom's thigh and barked.

Malcolm fixed a solemn look on Danielle and Tom and said, "You take care of each other. We'll come visit you in Vancouver once you've settled down."

Danielle and Tom climbed into the white Honda Accord. Lucky jumped in the rear seat. They waved and drove off.

Gerta, teary-eyed, huddled against Malcolm.

Malcolm hugged her and said, "They'll be all right. They're smart and resourceful."

"Do you have to be so darn wise all the time?" Gerta said, and jabbed Malcolm lightly in in the ribs.

They walked over to Gunter. He had stood back during the parting scene, but his eyes betrayed his emotion.

"I can't thank you enough for what you did for us, Uncle Gunter," Gerta said. "How can I possibly repay you?"

Gunter gave Gerta a hug. "Enjoy life to the fullest and keep safe, that's how."

Malcolm shook Gunter's hand. The men nodded at each other. The couple climbed into the black Toyota Camry, waved goodbye, and drove off.

It was 11 p.m. A quarter moon sat low on the horizon. The Camry sailed smoothly along country roads. Malcolm turned to Gerta. "To Seattle and a new life."

CHAPTER 46

THE FBI CLOSES IN ON STEVE

The clock on Louise's laptop read 2 a.m. when she shouted "Gotcha!" Popeye, Ashley, and Paul leaned back from their own laptops, bleary-eyed, and stared at her. Louise turned toward them. "I know where *one* of them is going."

"Which one? Where?" her teammates asked in unison.

"Steve Adams. He's booked on a direct flight to Dubai, on Emirates out of JFK, leaving today."

Popeye furrowed his brows. "How do you know it's him? Surely, he hasn't booked under his real name."

Louise beamed. "No, he hasn't, but my facial recognition software spotted him among the passport photos of everyone booked on all outgoing international flights. He's traveling under the name Stephen Daniels." Louise's teammates clapped in admiration.

"Well done, Louise," Popeye said. "I'm calling Jacqueline Cochran with this information. I'll patch you in."

Jacqueline thanked Popeye and Louise for the lead. "I'll have surveillance set at the JFK terminal, both inside and out. If any of the Jennings gang shows up to see Adams off, we'll arrest them too." Jacqueline was silent for a moment, then added, "This is one break we really needed. The gang has evaded all our roadblocks and our highway cameras since they were last seen leaving the Lincoln Harbor ferry terminal in Jersey."

"We believe they'll be splitting up," Popeye said. "Adams leaving the country confirms that."

"I agree," Jacqueline said. "We're watching *all* international flights."

"They'll need cars," Popeye said.

Jacqueline was silent for a moment, then said, "We'll look at all recent vehicle thefts, vehicle rentals, and sales in the area. We may get lucky."

"We have instructions to keep looking for every member of the Jennings gang until further notice," Popeye said. "Anything we find, we'll share with you."

After exchanging more encouraging words, Popeye ended the call.

Jacqueline and O'Keefe paced nervously around Terminal 4 at JFK. The NYPD had assigned four cruisers to lie in wait, out of site of the drop-off to the terminal. An Emergency Service Unit, their name for SWAT, stood ready on standby. Undercover officers were stationed in the departure lounge of Emirates EK204 to Dubai. The flight's ground and air crew had been briefed and shown photos of passenger 'Stephen Daniels,' and the FBI's tech team had set up facial recognition software on all the terminal's cameras.

O'Keefe called Special Agent in Charge Hale in Chicago, barely able to restrain his excitement. "Everything is in place. Steve Adams will be reporting for the flight to Dubai any minute now. As soon as he shows his face, we'll capture him."

"Finally," Hale said. "We're one step ahead of those criminals for once." She paused, then asked, "Has Tyler's pet detective agency claimed credit yet for discovering Adams's plans?"

"Not that I know of." O'Keefe hesitated, then added, "Why are you asking?"

"I've told the Director we'll be getting some excellent publicity for a change from this arrest." Hale was quiet for a moment, then added, "Make sure you and Jacqueline are in all the press release photos."

Before O'Keefe could answer, the loudspeakers announced the final boarding for EK204 from Gate 22.

"I need to run," O'Keefe said. "I'll call you back as soon as the arrest is made." He and Jacqueline raced toward the departure lounge.

There was still no sign of Steve Adams. The ground attendants were closing the boarding gate. Jacqueline rushed to the gate, brandished her FBI badge, and ran down the bridge toward the aircraft.

O'Keefe waited by the departure counter, wringing his hands. Jacqueline reappeared five minutes later. She shook her head. "Adams is not on the aircraft." She raised her cellphone, dialed the number for Louise at Reliant, and pressed the speaker tab.

"Hi, Louise? This is Jacqueline Cochran. I'm with Agent O'Keefe at JFK. The Emirate flight to Dubai has taken off, but Adams is not on board."

O'Keefe didn't wait for Louise's reply. He walked to the side and dialed Hale in Chicago. He felt nauseated.

CHAPTER 47

CASABLANCA

Steve leaned back into the business class seat on Royal Air Maroc's direct flight from Dulles Airport to Casablanca. The attendant brought over a glass of champagne, some munchies, and a copy of the Washington Post. Steve folded the paper on his knees and stared out the window. The engines roared, and the acceleration pushed Steve back in his seat. A feeling of elation overwhelmed him. He thanked Gerta, mentally, for having broken into the airport's camera system programming and fooling the facial recognition software.

Steve's plane landed at the Mohammed V airport in Casablanca seven hours later. It was 10:20 a.m. local time. He disembarked with his carry-on and lined up at passport control. The border agent granted him a 90-day tourist visa. Steve would apply for permanent residency before the visa expired.

He flagged a taxi, climbed into the rear seat of the white Mercedes, and instructed the driver to take him to the Four Seasons Hotel. This turned out to be a five-story structure of white concrete with large square windows. A porter, whose golden nametag read Moustafa, opened the taxi's door. "Bienvenue au Four Seasons, monsieur." He took Steve's traveling bag and led the way, over marble flooring, to the check-in counter.

After Steve had checked in, another porter carried his luggage to an elevator that took them up to a fourth-floor suite. Steve gave a generous tip, which produced the desired results—a radiant smile and a parting bow.

Steve explored his new abode. The apartment had a spacious living room with floor to ceiling windows and a balcony that overlooked the beach. He inspected the kitchen counter and smiled at the well-stocked minibar. After a shower, he crashed on a bed covered in soft, clean linen and didn't wake up again until five in the afternoon.

Steve sat on the side of the bed, and dug his toes into the plush beige carpet. Hunger gnawed at his stomach, but he resisted the temptation to call room service. He dressed, went down to the lobby, and had the concierge call a cab.

Another white Mercedes appeared almost instantly. "Rick's Café, s'il vous plaît," Steve instructed.

"Oui monsieur," the taxi driver said. Looking at Steve in the rearview mirror, he asked, "American?" Steve nodded. The driver continued. "Americans love to visit Rick's Café. Casablanca was a beautiful movie."

"Yes. It's a classic," Steve agreed.

"You came for the surfing tournament?"

"No. I don't surf. I've watched it on TV. When's the tournament?"

"Next week. People come from all over the world. It's famous."

"Thanks for the suggestion."

The drive to the café took five minutes. The driver stopped in front of a white building. Heavy wooden doors flanked by two palm trees marked the entrance. Large black letters, directly overhead, read 'Rick's Café.' Steve paid and tipped the driver, climbed out of the taxi, and entered the café.

A smartly dressed maître d' greeted him. "Welcome to Rick's Café, monsieur. Are you joining us for dinner, or would you prefer to sit at the bar?"

"The bar, please."

"This way, please." The maître d' led the way. At the bar, he turned and said, "This evening is jazz night."

"Great. I've come a long way for your jazz night,"

"It's a casual jam session, but the performers are world class." The maître d' bowed and left.

Steve beamed as he settled at the bar. The barman approached and asked, "Et pour monsieur?"

"Do you serve orange glamour cocktails?"

"Certainly, monsieur."

CHAPTER 48

SAN FRANCISCO

Larry steered the blue Ford Fusion in the direction of Scranton, Pennsylvania. His destination, San Francisco, lay 3,000 miles away. He planned on driving twelve hours a day, on secondary roads, to reach the Bay Area in five days.

He was excited by more than just the escape from New York City. Driving through the Great Plains and the West Coast mountain ranges would be a new experience for him. Only in movies had he viewed the famed Sierra Nevada.

The five days of driving went by quickly. His beard filled in nicely, and the yellow-tinted John Lennon eyeglasses felt natural by now. He felt optimistic and at peace.

At 51, Larry, was too young to want to retire. He would need to find work to fill the time. An introvert and a perfectionist by nature, he had been devoted to his mother and also to Malcolm, whose steady, competent leadership he admired immensely. Malcolm and Gerta had cared for him as well as mentored him. He felt trepidatious about having to function without their support. He would need to make trustworthy friends in San Francisco to fill that gap.

Larry had given his future a lot of thought. He intended to buy a small business in San Francisco, a café and music shop, in the Haight-Ashbury neighborhood. Next, he would look for a charming antique house in need of renovating. These plans energized him now.

Five days later, after settling into his room at the Kabuki Hotel, he sent an encrypted email to Gerta which read, "Dear Gerta and Malcolm, I've arrived in San Francisco. All is well. Larry."

CHAPTER 49

WEBER CALLS HALE

The phone on Hale's desk buzzed. She glanced at it with apprehension, but she picked up. The office receptionist announced, "A call from Inspector Weber of the Waterloo Regional Police Service, Agent Hale." Hale furrowed her brows and searched her memory. A vague recollection came to her. Once connected, she said, "This is Special Agent in Charge, Arlene Hale. How can I help you, Inspector Weber?"

"Hello, Agent Hale. Thank you for taking my call. I'm calling to discuss the Jennings file. Do you have time now?"

Hale recalled a conversation between Chief Edwards of the Waterloo Regional Police Service, the Director and herself, where they had agreed to exchange information on the Jennings file. She answered "Yes, I do."

"I want to discuss Tom Cole, a member of the gang. I'm trying to convince the young man to return home and face the charges against him in Canada."

"Please refresh my memory. What is Tom Cole accused of up there?"

"Accessory to the murder of Carl Tillman, Tillman's wife, and a magazine reporter. And an earlier case, the murder of Douglas Ferguson, a member of the Jennings crew."

"Tom Cole killed a member of the Jennings gang in Canada?"

"Ferguson was under arrest at the time. For aggravated sexual assault against a close friend of Tom, a mother-figure to him."

"Sounds more like justice than murder," Hale said, shaking her head. "I suggest you give Cole a medal for that one."

"You have a point. There are extenuating circumstances, and that's the reason I want him back before he gets killed in another firefight."

"Have you filed an extradition request?"

"No. Cole is a dual citizen. Extraditing him would be a long, tedious process."

"I see. What do you need from us?"

"What is the case against Tom Cole, as the FBI sees it?"

Hale ran through the details in her mind, then said, "Cole was not present during any of the confrontations between our forces and the Jennings gang, but we could charge him with aiding and abetting. The gang killed two SWAT officers and injured six police officers during our last attempt to arrest them, so there's no love lost." Hale paused, then asked, "What are you suggesting?"

"If I convince Cole to return to Canada and turn himself in, I'm asking that the FBI not request his extradition back to the US."

Hale was silent for a moment, then said, "I'll have to discuss your proposal with the Director, but I'm going to recommend we accept it. I'll get back to you, Inspector Weber."

"Thank you, Agent Hale."

CHAPTER 50

SHARON

Two weeks had passed since Sharon Doyle's sexual assault. The medication and the behavior modification therapy that Dr. Whitfield had prescribed was working. The feelings of depression, self-guilt, and anxiety were diminishing in intensity. So was the fear of being alone.

After having completed the morning chores at the barn, Sharon and Robert sat at the kitchen table, savoring their strong coffee.

Sharon thought for a moment, then asked, "Do you ever plan to reopen your Airbnb?"

"Yes, eventually."

"You'll need to move back into your house for that." Sharon hesitated again before adding, "I could move into one of your bedrooms for a while, so I wouldn't be alone at night. And I'd help with the chores at your place."

"That would work well for me. But there's no rush."

"I'm ready when you are," Sharon said. "But I'm not proposing a romantic relationship, not yet. You understand that?'

"I do. I'm happy with your companionship. Watching you get better is reward enough." Robert smiled. Sharon reached over and kissed him on the cheek.

They heard a vehicle driving into the yard. Robert walked to the door and looked through the window. He saw an old red pickup. "It's Uncle Bill," Robert said as he opened the door.

Uncle Bill entered the kitchen, shook hands with Robert, and saluted Sharon. "I'm delivering a package," he said, handing a FedEx box to

Robert. "It's from St. Louis, addressed to me, but the two letters inside are addressed to you."

Robert retrieved two envelopes from inside the package. He opened one. "It's from Tom," he said.

Bill squared his shoulders. "I better leave you to read that letter in private. I'll be going. Let me know if there's anything I can do." He walked to the door.

"Please stay for coffee. I can read the letter later," Robert said.

Bill turned and said, "I'm holding you back from reading a letter from your son. I'll stay for coffee some other time." Robert nodded. Bill waved and let himself out.

"News from Tom? That's wonderful. You go ahead and read the letter," Sharon said.

Robert read the letter, then looked up at Sharon. "He and Danielle are well. He sends his love to both of us. He promised to stay in touch, but he didn't say where he was going next. "

"Thank God they're safe. It must be terrifying to be constantly running from the law."

Robert lowered the letter. "The young rascal brags about having helped the Jennings team avoid capture by leading them through a system of caves. I know I shouldn't, but I can't help feeling proud of him."

"I'm proud of him too," Sharon said. "He must be blind with love for Danielle to be taking all those risks." Sharon sat pensive for a moment, then said, "Danielle is a tough gal. They're a good match."

Robert placed a hand on hers. "You're tough as well. I admire your determination to recover from what you've been through. It can't be easy. Look at how strong you are already."

"I have your support to thank for it." Sharon looked at him tenderly. "Oh. What about that second letter?"

Robert opened the second letter. It was short, a single paragraph that read:

Mr. Cole, we need to delete all evidence linking Tom to Duke's murder. I will delete the digital copies of the video footage from the hospital cameras stored in hospital files, police files, and in cloud storage. The hard evidence, which is stored in the police evidence room, you will have to destroy. I have set up an account with one million in funds to help you with that. You can withdraw the funds from any ATM using the enclosed bank card. The PIN code is 2010. There is no daily limit, and withdrawals of any amount will not trigger a report with the Financial Crimes Enforcement Unit. Good Luck. GJ

"It's from Gerta Jennings," Robert said. "She's giving me access to funds to help with Tom's defense. She wants me to try and destroy any hard evidence the police have against him."

Sharon returned a puzzled look. "I don't understand. How could you possibly do that?" She furrowed her brows and added, "What evidence do the police have, anyway? They found no fingerprints, right?"

Robert lowered his gaze to his hands holding the letter. "I already knew about the camera footage placing Tom at the hospital at the time of Ferguson's murder, but the lawyer that Rick lined up for Tom's defence found out, while preparing a plea bargain, that police forensics found a hair follicle that places Tom in Ferguson's room. That's bad."

"That's terrible. But what can *you* do to make something like that disappear?"

Robert considered for a moment, then said, "Would it be okay with you if I consulted Patrick about this?"

Sharon returned a puzzled look. "What help can my son provide with any of this?"

Robert hesitated for a long moment before answering. "The distributor Patrick works for supplies and installs evidence lockers for police departments. He could advise me on how those lockers work and how I could get into one."

Sharon straightened in her seat. "Are you suggesting that Patrick help you commit a crime?" She paused, then added, through trembling lips, "Patrick and Tom were close friends, but I don't want my son in jail for helping a friend."

Robert bit his lip, wrung his hands together, looking down at them, then said, "I sure could use Patrick's know-how." He looked up at Sharon. "I wouldn't ask him to do anything he's not comfortable doing."

Sharon lowered her gaze. "You have me feeling bad about refusing to help Tom." She looked up at Robert. "I'm okay with you consulting with Patrick."

At that moment, they heard a car roll into the driveway. A door opened and closed. Robert walked to the front door, looked through the window, and said, "It's Inspector Weber."

CHAPTER 51

WEBER VISITS ROBERT

Robert opened the front door. "Good morning, Inspector Weber."

"Good morning, Mr. Cole." Weber walked in and followed Robert to the kitchen. "And good morning to you, Mrs. Doyle. How are you doing?"

"I'm doing well, thank you." Sharon rose and shook hands with the inspector. "Can I offer you some coffee or tea?"

"Coffee would be great, thank you."

The inspector sat and looked at Robert. "I'm glad to find you here. I wanted to talk to you about Tom." He gave Robert a searching look. "Have you heard from him lately?"

Robert hesitated before answering. "No. He hasn't called you? I suggested he do so when I last talked to him. That was a week ago."

"He hasn't called me." The inspector cupped his hands around the mug of coffee. He fixed Robert with another penetrating stare. "Forensics have found evidence that places Tom in Douglas Ferguson's hospital room on the day Ferguson was murdered." Robert was silent. Weber continued. "His situation could have a reasonable outcome if he came forward now. He would face trial, but the judge and the jury will feel sympathy for him, with Ferguson having brutally assaulted Mrs. Doyle, a mother figure to Tom. Your son could be out in seven years with good behavior."

Robert thought about this, then said, "What about Tillman's murder?"

"Forensics have found no evidence that places Tom in Tillman's house during the murders." Weber paused, then added, "If I remember, Tom told you his role was to watch the vehicles on the side road while the Jennings were doing what he thought was a debt collection?" Robert nodded.

"I believe him," Weber said. "If Tom agreed to testify against the Jennings during any future trial, he wouldn't be facing any further charges."

Robert pondered for a moment, then asked, "What about the FBI's case against Tom?"

"The FBI told us they have no evidence that places Tom at any of the crime scenes or the confrontations with police, so they've agreed not to request extradition if he surrenders and cooperates in Canada."

Robert met Weber's gaze. "I have no way of reaching Tom. All I can do is pass on your message to him when he contacts me next."

Weber nodded and rose to leave.

Robert walked with the inspector to the front porch. He watched the patrol cruiser disappear down the road, then returned to the kitchen.

"Do you think Tom will come home?" Sharon asked.

Robert lowered his gaze. "There's little chance of him ever coming back here."

"Why do you say that?"

"In his letter, Tom said that he and Danielle intend to settle somewhere safe and send me news regularly."

"I'm so relieved they're not hurt." Sharon leaned over the table and placed a hand on Robert's arm. "You're a good father, Robert. And a good companion."

Weber sat at his desk and let out a deep sigh and thought, *I just hope the kids don't get killed during a firefight when the FBI finally arrests the gang.*

Constable Kidnie entered the office and sat down across from his superior. "How did the visit with Cole go?"

"He said he doesn't know where his son is but that he'll recommend to Tom that he call me when they next speak. I believe him." Weber rubbed his hands together. "I hope the kid calls me."

"You care for that young man, don't you?"

Weber stared into the distance and said, "He reminds me of my son, Ben. Bright and full of life. Cut down so young."

Constable Kidnie lowered his head. "Yes. He was a sharp lad. Fell in with the wrong crowd."

Ben had been delivering drugs for a local dealer when he stumbled into a drug bust and was killed during the firefight that ensued.

"Yes. I blame myself for not spending more time with him, listening to him, helping him choose a career, make better friends."

Both men fell silent.

CHAPTER 52

TYLER'S COMEUPPANCE

The first responders rushed Tyler to Mount Sinai West Hospital and wheeled him to the pre-op holding area. A nurse and two attendants prepped him there. The surgeon arrived and introduced himself to Tyler as an anesthesiologist placed a breathing mask on him.

"I want my own doctor here," Tyler demanded. "Now!" He was unconscious before anyone could answer.

The surgical team cauterized and stitched the skin on the stub of Tyler's penis and bandaged it. An attendant wheeled him to the recovery room. No family members or friends were waiting for him.

He came to in a large, bright, private room. A nurse came to his side. "How are you feeling, Mr. Tyler?"

"Where's my personal doctor?"

"He's on his way, Mr. Tyler."

The surgeon walked into the room. He examined the bandages over Tyler's penile stub before saying, "The operation went well. You'll be able to urinate normally in a few days when we remove the catheter. Then you'll be ready to return home."

Tyler stared at the bandages and the catheter tube and wailed, "Where's my prick?" He looked up at the surgeon. "You have to find it and reattach it."

The surgeon looked at Tyler uncomfortably and said, "I'm sorry, Mr. Tyler, but the paramedics looked all over your office suite and couldn't fine your severed penis."

"Nooooo!" Tyler screamed. "This can't be happening. This is a nightmare!"

He was now hyperventilating and cupping the bandaged member with his hands. The surgeon instructed the nurse to administer a sedative immediately. The medication put Tyler to sleep, but he came to an hour later. It had been a fitful sleep. He sat up in bed. A nurse brought him breakfast on a tray, but he didn't touch it. His iPhone rang. The call display showed as Chief Harrington, Reliant. Skipping the usual courtesies, Tyler barked, "What the hell were your boys doing while I was being attacked, robbed, and mutilated?" Without waiting for a reply, he continued with, "It's a miracle I wasn't lynched like they did Stonely." He paused, then added, in a quavering voice, "The bastards cut off my prick."

Harrington let Tyler's rant run its course, then said, "We apologize for not protecting you adequately, but in our defense, you agreed that arresting the Jennings gang would be an FBI operation. Our role was only to assist them."

"Yeah, the FBI set up a *brilliant* ambush, but at the wrong fucking place!" Tyler yelled into the receiver, then went quiet.

Harrington let a moment pass, then said, "Please accept our condolences for the loss of your wife." He paused, but when no reaction came, he asked, "Is this news to you? Have the police not informed you yet? If so, I apologize for the shock I have caused you."

"My security chief informed me about the terrible accident. A stray bullet, he said." Tyler went quiet for a moment, then asked, "Have you guys caught the Jennings gang yet?"

"No, but we are combing through all Internet and phone communications for any trace of them. The FBI have set up roadblocks, and they are monitoring all cameras at major transit points. We'll locate them soon."

Tyler breathed heavily into the phone and said, "In other words, you have no idea where these criminals are. Well, you can stop all your pointless research. You're fired!" Tyler savored his words. "And don't bother sending any more invoices. No results, no moolah." He hung up.

Tyler leaned back in his bed, and forgot his distress for a moment, enjoying the thought that Fiorelli had succeeded in knocking off his wife.

The fucker is sure to call me shortly to gloat, he thought to himself, but I hope the idiot won't mouth off over the phone.

His ruminations were interrupted by the arrival of Agents Cochran and O'Keefe. They each pulled up a chair and sat by Tyler's bed. Jacqueline spoke first. "How are you doing, Mr. Tyler?"

"Terrible, *thanks*. The bastards mutilated me. Where *were* you guys?" He glared at Jacqueline and asked, "Have you at least apprehended those criminals yet?"

"Not yet," Jacqueline replied. She watched Tyler carefully as she asked, "Have you been informed of the tragic death of Mrs. Tyler?"

"Yes. Reliant told me." Tyler faked a moment of grief, then switched to equally fake anger. "What the hell happened? My wife got killed on your watch. It had to be a stray bullet from one of your officers!"

"No, sir," Jacqueline said, continuing to watch his reactions. "A sharpshooter shot Mrs. Tyler as she was watching the developments through the patio windows. It was intentional."

"That makes no sense," Tyler said. "Why would a stranger target my wife? It had to be one of your men."

Jacqueline continued locking eyes with Tyler. "The bullet came from a hitman hired by your security chief. We believe you were complicit."

"What the hell are you saying? How dare you accuse me of planning the murder of my own wife! Where is your proof, young lady?" Tyler was red-faced and breathing hard now.

"It's Agent Cochran to you, sir," Jacqueline said. "We know all about the arrangements you made with Mr. Fiorelli, but so far we only have his side of the story. We'd like to know yours."

Tyler's stared back at her, eyes blazing, but remained silent.

Jacqueline continued. "We have arrested Mr. Fiorelli, and his lawyer is plea bargaining with my colleagues as we speak. In exchange for a lighter sentence, Mr. Fiorelli will testify that the two of you conspired to murder your wife for the life insurance payout."

Tyler was sweating profusely now. "I never agreed to any such thing. It's his word against mine."

"We have a recording of your conversation with Fiorelli in his office the evening before the murder."

"Impossible. You're bluffing."

"Gerta Jennings recorded your planning session from Fiorelli's laptop camera and microphone. She provided us with copies." Tyler stared back, mouth agape.

Jacqueline rose and said, "Michael Tyler, I am placing you under arrest for conspiracy to murder your wife. A police officer will be stationed outside your room until you are well enough to be transported to a jail cell. You will then be arraigned in front of a judge." She proceeded to recite Tyler his Miranda rights.

As he listened, Tyler gradually recovered his composure and when Jaqueline was finished, he spat out, "I'm not saying another word without the presence of my lawyer."

"An excellent decision, Mr. Tyler."

With that, Jaqueline and O'Keefe headed toward the door, but Jacqueline stopped, turned, and said, "By the way, Gerta Jennings informed us that Mr. Fiorelli stole two Warhol paintings from you, the Marilyn and the Double Elvis. The ones now on your living room wall are fakes." The two agents left the room.

CHAPTER 53

ESCAPE TO VANCOUVER

Danielle waved to her parents from the car window as Tom drove away from the warehouse. Tears filled her eyes. Tom turned to her. "I suggest we drive through the night. I'm too pumped up to sleep anyway. We can switch drivers every two hours, okay?"

"Yes. That's fine with me. I'll climb over to the rear seat if I need a nap." She turned to look at Lucky, who currently occupied the rear seat. Lucky stretched forward and licked her cheek.

They drove along secondary highways, stopping at roadside diners for breakfast and lunch, and ended the day's journey at a motel in Cedar Rapids, Iowa.

As they sat at a restaurant table for a late dinner, Tom said, "I don't think we need to drive this hard anymore. We can reach Seattle in three days of easy driving from here. Is that all right with you?"

"Suits me fine," Danielle said.

Over the following days, Tom and Danielle crossed flat plains, badlands, and eventually reached the Rockies. They gazed at the mountains wide-eyed, stunned by the majesty of the snowy peaks. On reaching the Pacific coast, the young couple settled into the Sound Hotel in downtown Seattle. From their hotel room, Danielle called the contact her mother had given her: Leon, a marine tour operator and old friend of Gerta's. She had relied on him for help crossing the border in the past.

After the initial introductions, Leon said, "Gerta sent me all the details I need to take you and Tom into Canada. She even sent me a photo of your dog. I'll take you over with my tour boat. When can you folks be ready to cross?"

"The sooner the better. Tomorrow, if you can."

"Tomorrow works for me. I don't have any tours booked until the day after. Be on the dock at Shilshole Bay in front of the marina office at 6:30 a.m. Pack lightly. There's some walking involved, and a half hour floatplane ride, too. And dress warmly. It's a four-hour boat ride and the Sound is cold this time of year."

After ending the call, Danielle turned to Tom. "It's all arranged. We're taking a boat to Canada tomorrow morning. I'm so excited!"

Tom looked saddened by her news. "What's the rush in getting to Canada? I was hoping to take in the sites here first. The Beneath the Streets Underground History Tour for one."

"And I'd like to visit the Jimi Hendrix exhibits at the Museum of Pop Culture, but we're on the run from the FBI, young man." She looked sternly at Tom, but fondly. "Let's settle down safely in Vancouver first. Sightseeing can wait."

On their only evening in Seattle, Tom and Danielle went shopping for warm clothing at a local Dollarama, then ordered takeout at a seafood restaurant in Pike Place Market. As they dined in their hotel room, they discovered that Lucky loved seafood. Leaving a sad-looking dog in their room, they rounded off the evening in the hotel's bar and lounge.

At 6:30 a.m., Tom, Danielle, and Lucky stood on the dock in front of the marina office. A tall, rugged man in his mid-fifties, dressed like a sea captain, walked over and introduced himself. "Hi. I'm Leon. You must be Danielle and Tom?"

Danielle nodded. Leon stood for a moment, staring at them. "You guys look different than your photos on the FBI Most Wanted page. That's good." He gave Danielle a friendly smile. "I like your hair color. Suits you." Then he turned to Tom. "That close-cropped beard suits you well, too." Finally, he kneeled and petted Lucky. "*You* look exactly like the photo Gerta sent me." Laughing, he stood and jerked his head in the direction of the dock. "Let's get going."

Leon guided his three customers aboard a boat with a sign that read 'Salt Spring Island Tours.' "I also use the boat for sportfishing tours," he said. The fifty-foot vessel was fitted with four large outboard motors. The cabin housed a large galley and lounge.

Leon steered the craft through Puget Sound and into the Salish Sea toward its destination, Salt Spring Island. Once the boat was moored in Ganges Harbour, Leon turned to Tom and Danielle. "Welcome to Canada," he said with a broad smile "There is no Canadian Border Service on the island, but all tour operators are required to report at the marina." Leon pointed to it. "I'll walk up there, call Canadian Border Control, and declare two American passengers who have come to visit the island for the day. Border Control will decide whether to send an agent over or not. Sometimes they don't." Tom and Danielle stared anxiously back at him.

Leon raised a reassuring hand. "Don't worry. I'll deal with them if they send someone." Tom and Danielle did not look reassured. Leon pointed to the seaplane terminal at the far end of the dock. "You guys need to run down to the Harbour Air terminal. I've booked you on a flight to Vancouver's downtown harbor. Show them your Canadian passports and pick up your boarding passes. The plane leaves in one hour. Hurry up."

"What about Lucky?" Tom said.

"They rent pet carriers," Leon said. "Now go."

Tom and Danielle, traveling bags in hand, hurried toward the seaplane terminal. Lucky jogged along at Tom's feet.

Leon walked up to the marina office, called the Canadian Border Services Agency and informed them he had brought over two American tourists for the day. The agency's control operator instructed Leon to hold onto his visitors until an officer arrived.

Thirty minutes later, a CBSA boat moored at the dock and two strapping officers, dressed in dark blue uniforms, walked toward the office. They recognized Leon and approached him. "Where are your passengers?" The lead officer asked.

"They went to the restrooms a few minutes ago." Leon glanced in the direction of the washrooms, then looked back at the officers, and shrugged.

The officers walked briskly toward the restrooms. They returned shortly afterwards, shaking their heads. The lead officer stared at Leon. "You've lost them. You kept their passports, I hope?"

"Yes, I did." Leon handed over two US passports.

The lead officer opened the passports, retrieved his cellphone, and called his office. Within minutes, an alert went out to all ticket agents on the island, covering ferries, seaplanes, and boat rentals and tours. The alert contained the passport photos of a middle-aged couple with jet black hair and Latino complexions, going by the names Luis and Maria Fernandez.

The seaplane carrying Tom, Danielle, and Lucky landed at Vancouver Harbour some thirty minutes after leaving Salt Spring. The three disembarked and walked to the first taxi in the lineup. It dropped them off in front of a townhouse in Richmond, one of Vancouver's neighboring cities. Tom tipped the driver, and he and Danielle carried their traveling bags to the front door. Danielle consulted her phone, then pressed numbers onto the keypad that controlled the door. They walked into their new home.

The decor was modern, with bright pastel colors. Lucky raced ahead, sniffing every piece of furniture. Danielle entered the open concept kitchen, dining room, then living room. She sat on a couch and leaned back. "Whew! What a trip."

Tom sat next to her. He looked around, smiled, and said, "I like this place."

After exploring the bedrooms, bathrooms, and closets, Danielle texted her mother. "The townhouse is beautiful, Mom. Tom and I adore it. Love you. Danielle."

After resting on the couch for a few minutes, Danielle turned to Tom and said with a straight face, "Do you want to start looking for a hobby farm this afternoon, or would you rather we rest for a few days?" They broke out laughing and then kissed. Lucky jumped in between the two, licked their faces, and yipped.

CHAPTER 54

PATRICK

A cargo van with a label reading 'Business Storage Specialists' backed up to the loading dock at the Waterloo Regional Police Service headquarters at 200 Maple Grove Road in Cambridge, Ontario. Patrick, teammate Johnny, and team leader, Stephen, jumped out of the van and climbed the steps to the dock. Patrick opened the roll-up door of the cargo van, revealing two pallets with lockers wrapped in plastic film.

Stephen walked to the receiving counter and handed a waybill to the attending clerk. "We're delivering a bank of lockers. We're to install them in the evidence storage room."

The clerk read the waybill, looked up at the crates in the cargo van, then said, "Okay. Let me get an officer to escort you. Please wait here." He looked at the pallets again. "Will you need a forklift?"

"No. We'll use our pallet trucks," Stephen said.

A police officer arrived, checked the waybill, and signaled Stephen to follow him. Patrick and Johnny had already pulled the crates forward with their pallet jacks. They pulled the crates along as they followed Stephen and the police officer to the evidence room.

The police officer unlocked the room and opened it wide. He stood aside, supervising the operation.

As he walked into the room, Patrick searched for and located the surveillance camera that hung from the ceiling at the end of the room. He pulled his pallet jack forward and lowered the pallet directly below the camera. He then placed a box with hardware components on top of the lockers, blocking the camera's view of the room.

Johnny placed his pallet next to Patrick's, and the two men unwrapped the crates. They lifted the lockers off Johnny's pallet and placed them on the floor where they would be secured in place. The men then piled the plastic wrapping and strapping on the now empty pallet.

"I'll take this junk back to the van," Johnny said as he pulled the pallet truck out of the room. Johnny was some fifty feet away from the room when the men heard a loud thud, followed by a blood-curdling wail of pain and distress.

While the police officer raced over to check on Johnny, Patrick rushed to a counter in the corner of the room, opened a logbook, and ran his finger down the rows of entries. He was looking for the case number Robert Cole had given him. He located it and read the number of the corresponding locker. He raced to the bank of existing lockers, located the one he was looking for, pulled a key from his pocket, and opened it. Patrick then looked up at the doorway. Johnny's moaning was unrelenting. Patrick heard the police officer calling for assistance on his radio. Stephen, who had been keeping watch by the doorway, gave Patrick a thumbs up.

Patrick retrieved a plastic bag that contained a single strand of black hair and a manila envelope that held three hard discs. He closed the locker and locked it.

Patrick and Stephen walked over to Johnny and the police officer. Johnny sat on the floor, supporting his right elbow with one hand, and moaning softly. Two more officers had arrived. They helped Johnny stand up.

"We'll take him to the first aid station," one of the officers said. The two helped Johnny Walk away, moaning as he went.

The remaining police officer turned to Patrick and Stephen. "That was some fall. He slipped on a sheet of plastic wrapping and landed on his elbow." He fixed Stephen. "What do you guys want to do?"

"We'll join up with Johnny and drive him to Emerg. He'll need X-rays."

The officer nodded, then said, "Let us know when you can return to finish the installation. I'll go lock up."

Robert and Patrick sat on a bench facing the columbarium wall at the Kitchener Mount Hope Cemetery. Robert's late wife and Patrick's late father had both died during the first wave of the pandemic, and their ashes were interred in the wall.

Robert pulled three packets out of a bag and handed them to Patrick. "That's for a job well done. A hundred thousand dollars for each of you like we agreed."

"Thank you, Mr. Cole," Patrick said. "I still think it's too much, speaking for myself. I was glad to do it for Tom."

"You may need the money for legal expenses," Robert said. "They'll suspect you and your teammates of having destroyed the evidence against Tom, but they'll never be able to prove it."

"You're right, Mr. Cole. I'll save the money just in case."

Robert patted Patrick's arm and said, "I can't thank you enough." He paused, then added, "How's Johnny doing?"

Patrick shook his head. "The poor devil didn't fall properly. He actually fractured his elbow pretty badly. They've had to pin it back together. I don't understand. He's experienced. He hires out as a stunt man for film companies, but this time, he screwed up."

"I'm sorry to hear that. I'll bring you another packet for him as extra compensation."

"That's generous, Mr. Cole." Patrick grinned. "He'll appreciate it."

CHAPTER 55

OFFICER JONES

Officer Jason Jones surveyed the white walls of his hospital room. A pouch hanging from a stand dripped antibiotic and saline solution into his arm through plastic tubing. He assessed his situation. An attendant brought food and cold beverages four or more times a day. A nurse visited regularly, checked his vitals, adjusted the flow of painkillers, and made sure he felt comfortable. The television kept him entertained. *Life is good*, he said to himself.

Lynette, the love of his life, walked into the room and placed a plastic container on his side table. She approached the bed, leaned forward, kissed him on the forehead, fluffed his pillow, and whispered, "I brought you some chocolate brownies. They're still warm."

Jones beamed with joy. His stomach growled with anticipation as he reached for the container. He lifted the cover, chose a large chocolatey square, and brought it to his mouth. "Hmm, delicious," he mumbled. After four gulps, the brownie was gone, and Jones licked his fingers sensuously.

"How are you feeling, honey?" Lynette asked.

"I'm on the mend. Thanks to you and the hospital staff."

"The doctor said you'll be sprung tomorrow."

"So soon? I've suffered a life-threatening injury at the hands of dangerous criminals, and I'm still hooked to an IV line. They can't send me home like that," Jones protested.

"Honey. You got a bullet to the leg, not the heart. The doctor said he'll prescribe antibiotics and a nurse will visit daily to check on you. And I'll be there. The office has approved two weeks of compassionate leave for me."

Jones pursed his lips, then said, "I guess that could work. And I do miss your cooking."

Lynette beamed. "Have you signed those papers from the police department?"

"Yes. I've accepted the early retirement package. Captain Ambrose came yesterday, reviewed the papers with me, and took them back to the office."

"Those were generous terms. And my brother is looking forward to you working with him at the distribution warehouse."

"Okay. But that could be months away. That job will be physically demanding, and I mustn't compromise my recovery," Jones said.

"You'll be a supervisor, Jason. Others will do the heavy lifting."

"I hope you're right."

Lynette walked over, leaned in, and kissed him on the lips. "You'll do just fine, my big baby."

CHAPTER 56

MALCOLM AND GERTA

Malcolm woke up at 6 a.m. He and Gerta had spent the night in a motel on the outskirts of Pittsburgh. Having slept free of nightmares, Malcolm felt refreshed. He rose, walked to the window, parted the drapes, and surveyed the road outside. Everything looked peaceful. He cleared space on the carpeted floor and did his exercises.

Gerta woke, did her ablutions, and announced, "I'd like to stop in Toledo and visit my stepbrother, Jan. It's been years since I've seen him, and it's on the way. I was thinking lunch. Is that doable? "

"It won't be a problem if we don't dally."

They carried their traveling bags and the weapons bag to the Camry, climbed in, and headed for Toledo. The drive was smooth, and colorful foliage adorned the Pennsylvania countryside. They stopped for a quick breakfast at a road diner, and Gerta called Jan to set up lunch together.

Malcolm had been refreshing his memory of Jan. He asked, "Is Jan still married to . . . Elsa? Will she be joining us?"

Gerta hesitated, then said, "Yes, they're still married, but no, Elsa won't be there."

"Can't take the time away from work?"

Gerta bit her lip. "No. That's not it. Jan said she's afraid for her safety. The media is calling us cold-blooded murderers."

"Hmm . . . can't say I blame her. It's brave of Jan to sit down with us."

"I told him we've disguised our appearance. He felt better about that."

She gave Malcolm an appraising look. "I like those tortoiseshell eyeglasses, Professor Downing. And your stubble is filling out nicely. I see a reddish tinge. Do you have Viking genes by any chance?"

"That's a definite possibility. The Norsemen, as they were called back then, invaded and settled many parts of the British Isles. But I've never researched my ancestry."

Malcolm stared back at Gerta. "I like your red hair and those red eyeglasses. And that stubby ponytail makes you look years younger. It's lucky you're no longer of child-bearing age." Gerta jabbed him in the ribs and smiled.

Malcolm and Gerta arrived in Toledo shortly before noon. Jan had selected Grampy's on Huron Street for lunch. Gerta spotted her half-brother immediately and hurried to his booth. She smiled at him. "Hi Jan, it's good to see you. It's been too long."

Jan looked at her with a puzzled expression. Then his eyes widened. "Gerta!" He rose and hugged her. "Wow, I didn't recognize you at first." He took a step back and stared at her. "You look good, sister. What a treat to see you again. After reading the headlines, I gave up hope of ever seeing you again except in a . . ."

Gerta placed a hand on her half-brother's arm. "It's good of you to agree to have lunch with us. I'm sorry Elsa couldn't join us, but we understand. Please give her our best."

Jan bit his lip, nodded, then turned to Malcolm. "Hi Malcolm. Good to see you." The men shook hands. "Please sit down," Jan pointed to the bench seat across from him.

The three placed their order and then chatted. They chatted about old times and about the future. Their food arrived and they ate. An hour and a half had passed when Jan announced he had to get back to work. All three rose and hugged. Gerta dabbed her eyes with a napkin as Jan walked to the door, turned, waved, and left.

Malcolm and Gerta sat down and ordered a refill of coffee. A couple rose from their table and approached the booth, as if they had been waiting for an opening. "Hi Gerta," the woman said. "I didn't recognize you at first, but I knew that voice."

Gerta stared up, with furrowed brows, at the tall black woman. Then recognition brightened her face. "Louise Jackson? My God, I can't believe it's you. It's been years. Wow." She rose and hugged her visitor.

Malcolm straightened, lowered the zipper on his jacket, and slipped his right hand to his shoulder harness. He fixed Louise and then the tall, fit-looking man that stood by her side.

Gerta recognized Popeye from her research on the Reliant Detective Agency. "You must be Captain John Morris?" she said as she extended a hand to shake.

Popeye stepped forward and shook hands with her. "Please call me John. Glad to finally meet you, Ms. Jennings."

"Please call me Gerta." She took a step back to allow Malcolm to step out of the bench seat. "This is my husband, Malcolm." Louise and Popeye offered a hand to shake. Malcolm obliged.

"You must know about our agency," Popeye said.

"Yes, we know about your agency," Gerta said with a half-smile. She looked steadily at Louise. "Is this meeting a coincidence, or are you here to arrest us?"

Louise locked eyes with Gerta. "It's no coincidence. I remembered you having a half-brother in Toledo, and I've been keeping tabs on his incoming and outgoing calls and messages. I intercepted his text to you confirming today's lunch." She smiled and glanced at Popeye. "But no, we are *not* here to arrest you. Our client has terminated our contract." She turned to Popeye. "It was Captain Morris who insisted we meet with you today."

Gerta stared at Popeye with raised eyebrows. She pointed to the bench seat. "Please join us, then"

The two couples sat together. Louise and Popeye ordered coffee. After it arrived, she said, "You guys sure have given us a ride for our money. The decoy Zodiac at Tyler's residence, that was brilliant, but the false lead with Steve Adams supposedly flying Emirates to Dubai, that was inspired."

"The Zodiac decoy was Malcolm and Larry's idea," Gerta said. "But the false lead at JFK, that was mine. "

"Did Steve Adams even leave the country?" Louise asked.

"Yes, he did, but I won't tell you where he went." Gerta said. "I *will* confess that breaking into the airport's camera system and tampering with the face recognition program nearly defeated me. It's time for me to retire from this business."

Louise shook her head and smiled with admiration. "And providing the FBI with evidence implicating our client, Michael Tyler, and his security chief, Fiorelli, in a murder scheme, that was well done."

The two women smiled at each other.

Louise turned to Popeye. "The floor is yours, Captain Morris."

Popeye leaned forward and addressed Malcolm. "Now that our contract with Tyler is over, I wanted to contact you before you disappeared." Malcolm stared back, perplexed. Popeye continued. "It's about the operation in Fallujah where you led a patrol to recover the body of your brother, Edmund. First, I want to extend my condolences for the loss of your brother." Malcolm nodded. Popeye continued. "But I wanted to thank you in person for having recovered the bodies of Edmund's two teammates. One of those teammates was my stepbrother, Danny."

Malcolm stared, wide-eyed, then said, "I'm sorry to hear that."

Louise looked at Popeye in surprise and put a hand on his arm, "You never mentioned that before. I'm so sorry."

Popeye nodded back to her, then returned to Malcolm. "I and my family are grateful to you and your team for what you did. We were able to give Danny a proper funeral with full honors. It meant a lot to us." He paused, then added, "I know that Larry Schmidt and Steve Adams were part of the recovery operation. Please pass on my thanks to both."

Malcolm and Popeye looked at each other with moist eyes and fell silent. Gerta rested a hand on Malcolm's arm. Louise kept staring at Popeye, tenderness in her eyes.

Malcolm and Gerta reached Seattle three days later. They checked into a hotel with a fine view of the harbor and collapsed onto the couch. Gerta's cell phone dinged. A text had come in. She read it, then looked up at Malcolm. "It's from Danielle. They've arrived safely in Vancouver and love the townhouse I rented for them. Danielle said their next step will be to look for small farms for sale in the Fraser Valley." Gerta typed a return text, telling her they had arrived in Seattle. She turned to Malcolm, "I must thank Leon for getting the children to Canada safely."

"You've sent Leon his payment already? A hundred thousand, wasn't it?"

Gerta nodded. "He protested, said it was too much, but I sweet-talked him into accepting it. We'll need his help again in the future, so I told him to consider it a retainer." Malcolm smiled and nodded.

Gerta lay back on the couch, let out a deep sigh, then said, "I hope the children will be successful at farming."

"They're smart and resourceful," Malcolm said. "They'll do fine. Tom's a farm boy anyway. He knows about raising crops, and he can always ask his father for advice."

Gerta rested a hand on Malcolm's thigh. "And we're here to help as well if they need us. We'll visit them as soon as it's safe to do so."

"In the meantime," Malcolm said, "I'll be looking for a small electrical supply business to buy. Just to keep busy."

"And I'll be looking for a small house with a large garden."

Malcolm and Gerta enjoyed a seafood dinner in the hotel's dining room, then walked along the harbor in the cool evening air before returning to the hotel and enjoying a nightcap in the bar.

Malcolm had been quiet and pensive during their walk. Now he looked across the table at Gerta, "Do you think we'll ever adjust to a normal life again?"

Gerta laughed. "We better start looking for that electrical supply business first thing tomorrow. I don't want to see you bored."

She smiled, leaned over, and kissed him on the lips.